<u>Special Thanks</u>

Medallion took more than four years to write, including multiple rewrites. As life took its unpredictable twists and turns, I would have to put it aside for months at a time. Unfortunately for my family, just because I wasn't frantically typing away, it didn't mean they didn't have to hear about it all most every day. Amy, Bobby and Cierra, thank you for enduring your husband's / dads' relentless pursuit to write his first novel. I love you all!

Thanks and love to my wife Amy who would read and critique the one to four pages I had sweated over the night before. Impressing her as the first reader of every word I wrote was my goal, encouragement, and inspiration to keep writing. I once wrote an entire chapter in one sitting, thinking I was on a roll. She wasn't impressed with the less-than-spectacular direction I was taking the main character. I scrapped the entire chapter.

Katherine Masel believed in Medallion from the first time she read it. So much so, she financed the first professional editing. When I received the fifty-page critique, she spent dozens of hours going over every line, ensuring continuity, arguing over creative wording, debating sentence structure, and basically challenging the creative truth. Kathy, I am extremely grateful for your friendship, honesty and tenacity to make Medallion and really good read.

1

Thank you to my friends Peter Fraire and Bill Burton, principals of MitoffBurton Partners, the ad agency in El Paso, TX I was working for when I started writing. The agency and its employees inspired the ad agency and some of the characters in Medallion.

Thank you to Tom Finton, El Paso Inc. Publisher, for reading the raw manuscript and giving me my first and very encouraging critique. I was more than honored that you were impressed with Medallion.

Jerry and Lilly Knotts, owners of Artist Touch, in El Paso, TX are some of my biggest cheerleaders. Jerry designed a great cover that really grasps the essence of Medallion. I hope we see it printed in bookstores around the world.

Finally, but by far not the least important, thank you to all of my friends and strangers who have read one or more versions of Medallion. I wrote this story for your entertainment after all. Your honest feedback gave me the energy I needed to rewrite it until I was satisfied. One reader in California said, "It's like chocolate. It was really good and I wanted more."

TABLE OF CONTENTS

Chapter One

What are you doing here?" he asked. "Is this yours?"

Her hand was quick. The tip of her knife hit one of his ribs. His hands rose to the pain and the jolt of his fingers shifting the metal blade was all that she needed.

The knife sliced through Elliot's flesh and carved through a rib, puncturing his lung and severing his left ventricle. Just as fast as it went in, it came out. Elliot's eyes closed as he dropped to his knees with his hand over the wound. The blood ran along his hand. His eyes opened and there was no one. The punctured lung made his last breaths a struggle.

Elliot Jones collapsed against a planter. He tried plugging the hole in his chest with the index finger of his wounded hand, but his strength was fading. His blood pooled, melting the snow as it ran from the sidewalk to the curb.

The snowfall was unusual for El Paso. The city had a large Catholic population and they must have prayed for a white Christmas, thunderous requests, un-ignorable, even by God. That night, cotton ball sized flakes were falling when Elliot pushed the white button for the building's elevator, instantly illuminating to a pale yellow.

"Be careful walking to the lot tonight. The snow hasn't let up all day," Al Gonzales said, a security guard for the building.

While Elliot put on his black overcoat his hand got caught up in the material of the detachable lining. His wife had bought the coat for him the year before when he flew to Iowa in January for a new business presentation. He hadn't needed it before then, or again until that day. As he struggled briefly, he thought of that trip.

The win was the agency's largest since thirty years before when they landed the Goodway Grocery chain account. The person who had led that pitch was now the owner and president of the agency, William Price. It was well known that Elliot wanted that position someday. It was also well known that Price felt threatened by Elliot and had no intention of allowing him ownership.

Price knew that once Elliot became a partner, it wouldn't be long before Price needed to start thinking about retirement. He detested the thought and consequently, took it out on Elliot.

The elevator signaled its arrival. Elliot felt a hand on his shoulder. It startled him. He jerked and pulled away in self-defense.

Al said with a laugh, "Do you plan on staring at the elevator all night or are you going to get in?"

"I was lost in thought."

As the doors closed, Al reached and pushed the elevator's button. The doors slid open again. Elliot walked inside and pressed the lobby button.

Five Pinkerton security guards worked in the seventeen-story building. Roger and José, both of retirement age, had been there as long as anyone could remember. They rotated shifts at the security desk close to the entrance, Roger covering at night and José during the day. The oversized desk swallowed Roger's elderly frame as he sat there from 5:30 in the evening until to 3:00 the next morning. With a monitor for every floor illuminating his face, he was the eyes for the other guards as they made their rounds. One guard was responsible for the basement up to the fourth floor. Al roamed the fifth through tenth floors and two others secured floors from eleven to seventeen.

Elliot stood in a daze as the box lumber down. He momentarily wondered why Al was still there and not on another floor? But he was preoccupied as he closed his eyes and breathed deeply; fighting back the emotions the week had dealt him. He thought about his wife and the danger he put her in by a fate he had no control over.

He felt nauseous again as he had since the calls started on Monday. He pulled back his coat sleeve to see that it was 1:10 in the morning. He knew that if he was late for the meeting, the deal would be off and it could cost him his life.

When the elevator doors opened, he stepped out. He turned right and walked toward the exit. He

7

could see the security desk but Roger wasn't there. He hoped Roger would assign one of the other guards to walk him to the parking garage. Elliot pushed on the door, but it was locked. He knew there was only one glass door open to exit at night, but he wasn't thinking straight. He scanned the lobby but didn't see the old security guard. He went over to the unlocked door and walked out. The cold air rushed into his lungs.

"I can do this." He spoke in a whisper to himself and walked, shoulders hunched and hands in his pockets.

The garage where his BMW was parked was across from the agency's building on Kansas Street. When Elliot reached the curb, he barely looked up as he jaywalked, unconcerned about traffic at such an early hour.

He startled when someone bumped his left shoulder. They kept walking but Elliot stopped and stared. He wasn't looking where he was going and wondered if he bumped into them. It appeared to be a woman, and she, too, was covered by an overcoat. She was wearing athletic shoes.

Another late night professional, he thought.

"Ka-ching-le" was the sound when she dropped something. She kept walking. The object was shiny and glimmered silver under the streetlight.

Walking back to the curb he said, "Excuse me. You dropped something".

He picked up a silver medallion. Although it was the first time he'd seen one, he knew exactly what it was and what it represented. Elliot looked up. The woman was standing right in front of him.

"What are you doing here?" he asked. "Is this yours?"

She lunged at him with a metal blade and his hands rose up to the pain. He suddenly knew the answers to all of the questions he wanted to ask at the meeting. His thoughts turned to his wife. He wished he could tell her how sorry he was.

Chapter Two

The phone rang at 5:10 in the morning. Gene rolled over in his bed and fumbled for his glasses. Halfway through the fifth ring, he found the receiver and brought it to his cheek.

"Hello?" His voice was deep and groggy.

He heard his name repeated from a sobbing voice.

"Is this Lisa?" His head cleared. "What's wrong?"

He barely made out, "It's Elliot. It hurts so much. Gene, please, help me."

Blood rushed to Gene's face. Almost wide-awake, he grew frustrated and angry. Elliot must have gone too far this time. The last five nights had consisted of arguing between them. Gene had consoled Lisa many times that week. Even though his head told him not to get involved, his heart went out to her.

"Calm down, Lisa. What did he do?" He was already pulling on sweat pants.

"Gene, Listen." She spoke in a harsh tone. "He's dead. Elliott's dead."

Gene stood tall with one leg out of his sweats. "Oh my God, Lisa. What's happened? Where are you?"

Elliot was always criticized for driving too fast. Images of a horrible car accident were flooding Gene's mind.

"They showed me his body. It's him. Come get me."

"Where are you?"

"I'm at the morgue." She sounded confused. "The police brought me,"

"Hand the phone to someone who works there."

"Hurry. Please."

Gene heard voices in the background.

"This is Detective Stanton."

"I'm Gene Martine, Lisa's friend and Elliot Jones' boss." As he mouthed the words, he realized that if Elliot were dead, it would be stupid to say he was his boss. "Can you tell me what's happened?"

Detective Stanton cleared his throat. "What did you say your last name is?"

"Martine. What the hell is going on?" He furrowed his eye brows and rubbed his temple.

"Mr. Martine, are you available to come down here? It would be better if I talked with you in person and asked you a few questions."

Gene said, "Detective, is Elliot dead? What's happened?"

Stanton's voice remained calm. "Mr. Jones died early this morning. And I need some questions answered. Can you drive down here or should I send a cruiser to pick you up?"

"I'll drive. Where is the morgue?" Gene was dressed in sweat pants, yesterday's t-shirt, and Nike running shoes.

"We're at University Medical Center," Stanton said. "How long will it take you to get here?"

"Ten minutes." He grabbed his suede leather coat.

"Make it fifteen, Mr. Martine. You can't help Lisa if you die too. I'll meet you out front."

It was Saturday. In two days, Gene Martine would turn fifty. Evaluating his accomplishments was not hard.

He was an equal partner of the largest advertising agency in West Texas and Southern New Mexico. He wanted for nothing and owned two homes. His large El Paso home was in the upper valley on three acres where he kept two Appaloosa trail horses. The other home was in the mountains of Ruidoso, New Mexico, a two-hour drive northeast of El Paso.

Gene rarely stayed at the Ruidoso home. He used it as a base camp. On the occasional free weekend, he loved to pull his loaded horse trailer to the mountains with his Ford F-350 crew cab. He would park his truck and trailer at the house, saddle a horse and ride the trails to campsites that only a handful of people knew existed. It was one of Elliot's favorite things to do, too.

He could reflect on his accomplishments with a smile except for one regret. He had only loved and lost once.

Marlene came from old money. She was the daughter of Roy Whitaker. Her family owned River Rock Boots, the nation's fourth largest boot company. Traditionally, every U. S. president since Kennedy had been presented with a custom pair of River Rock Boots with the United States Seal stitched across the instep. Ironically, most of the boots were made in Mexico.

Gene's relentless desire to build an advertising empire was to the detriment of his relationship. He was obsessed with the success of the agency. Even with the threat of Marlene leaving, he continued to work on project after project, arriving home after midnight too often. Their sex life became non-existent. Her loneliness grew and she divorced him after nine years of marriage. That regret weighed heavy on Gene.

It was still dark. The snow had stopped and the residential roads were covered with white dust. Interstate 10 had relatively clear, wet lanes with dirty slush on the shoulders.

What a fool I was to complicate their lives. What could've happened last night? He wondered.

The speed limit was sixty miles per hour but Gene's Lexus sedan was at seventy and climbing when he ran over a slick part of the road and began to fishtail. He released the accelerator and slowed down, almost to a complete stop.

The blowing air horn from a semi truck made him flinch and snap his head toward the rearview mirror. Its lights were close and bright. He winced and braced for the collision. The semi quickly swerved to the left and passed the slowed sedan, causing the car to shudder like a boxcar. He let the car roll to a stop on the shoulder where he stopped to gather himself.

At fifty-four, Stanton had a six-foot-four-inch, muscular frame. Even though he was wearing a leather jacket, Gene could tell he was fit. His shoulder-length brown hair was graying. His head was capped with a Stetson cowboy hat. His face was leather with deep crow's feet around his steel blue eyes. He sported an overgrown, gray, mustache with downward turns, giving him a permanent frown along with two days of beard growth on his square jaw. Stanton's arms were folded over his white shirt that was tucked neatly into his Wrangler jeans. His River Rock boots were freshly shined.

"Detective Stanton?" Gene asked. "Will you please, tell me what's going on? Where's Lisa?"

"Mrs. Jones has taken a sedative and is sleeping in one of the rooms. She hasn't had any sleep since the night before last." Stanton's voice was calm and firm, but somewhat hospitable. "Please, let's go inside and sit down and I'll tell you what we know."

Gene followed Stanton through the colorless halls until they entered a sterile waiting room with a long metal table and a dozen folding chairs.

The detective wasted no time and started with the cause of Elliot's death. "He was murdered."

As they sat at the table, Stanton described the stab wound. He described a cut on his hand that indicated that Elliot had tried to defend himself and in doing so, he actually helped the knife find the space between the ribs. He said Elliot apparently lived long enough to crawl and sit against a planter until he bled to death.

Gene listened in disbelief at what he was hearing.

Stanton was using an electronic notebook that was small enough to fit in his pocket. "Where were you this morning at approximately 1:00 a.m.?" he said as he tapped the screen with a stylus, scrolling through his notes.

"You're kidding me?" Gene sounded surprised. "I'm a suspect?"

Stanton's chair creaked when he leaned back. "This is a homicide investigation Mr. Martine. El Paso's entire populations of seven-hundred-thousand and the two million people or so across the border in Juarez Mexico are all suspects. This includes you. It's up to you to take yourself out of the line-up." Stanton's steel blues looked straight into Gene's eyes as if reading his thoughts. "Where were you at one o'clock this morning?"

Gene was sitting on the metal folding chair, leaning forward with his elbows on his knees. "I was at home, in bed, and asleep until Lisa called."

"What time was that?" Stanton asked.

"You were obviously standing there when she dialed the phone," Gene's voice was loud. "What kind of B.S. questions are these?"

A woman with a young boy opened the door and walked in. She was an attractive blonde and appeared to be in her early thirties, even though her face showed deep lines and her dress was shabby. She was about five-foot-seven with a curvy figure. Her son was about five years old and wore a stained, miss-matched outfit. Her face was puffy and swollen as if she had been crying.

She looked at Gene. "Do you mind if we sit in here? My son is tired and needs to rest."

"We were just leaving." Gene walked toward the door. Stanton was right behind him and closed the door when they stepped out.

"We're not finished talking." Stanton followed Gene down a long hallway.

"Where is the morgue? I want to see Elliot."

Realizing that the questions would have to wait, Stanton said, "Follow me."

From the elevators to the lowest level of the hospital, neither man spoke. The elevator doors slid open slowly as if building the suspense about what was on the other side. The floors were white tile and across from the elevator there were two stainless steel swinging doors. Stanton led the way as they went inside and found a male intern sitting at a lab table.

"This is Mr. Martine. He would like to view the body of Elliot Jones." Detective Stanton moved his coat to the side to reveal his badge.

The intern said, "Sure. Follow me."

Stanton's boots echoed low-toned heavy steps. Gene and the intern's athletic shoes echoed squeaks as the men walked to a large, refrigerator door. When the intern opened the door, Stanton watched Gene's face drain of any healthy color. The room was designed to maintain the 37 degrees needed to insure the integrity of the bodies. Three of the four walls were lined with dozens of stainless steel drawers.

"It's been quiet down here." The intern walked to the third drawer on the left. "We only have three today and two of them are bodies donated for research." He pulled the drawer and slid the table out that supported a black body bag.

"Sorry for your loss," the young man said. He unzipped the body bag, peeled it open and stepped back.

Stanton could see that Gene recognized the familiar face of a friend and noticed that the torso was bare. Stanton placed his right index finger over the small cut in Elliot's chest, showing Gene the wound. The skin didn't look real, more like wax.

Gene cleared his throat. "I'm ready to answer all of your questions, but not here." He looked around at the steel drawers. "I feel sick and need to get out of here."

"Then let's go to the police station," Stanton said.

"No. I'll meet you at my office, P & M Marketing Communications. Do you know where it is?"

"Fair enough. I assume that's the same building Elliot came out of before his murder," Stanton said.

"First I want to see Lisa. Where is she?"

Chapter Three

Gene found Lisa sleeping in a converted exam room on a gurney that was equipped with a mattress, sheets, and a blanket. Overworked residency doctors used the room to sneak in fifteen-minute catnaps between emergencies. He didn't want to wake her.

Lisa was lying on her right side wearing a New Mexico State University sweatshirt. Her running shoes were placed neatly by the wall. Her hands were in prayer position, giving her head the needed support between her cheek and the thin gurney pillow. Her legs were bent to a fetal position and a hospital blanket covered her from the waist down. He stared at her. Her relaxed face revealed a juvenile innocence and he could see what had attracted Elliot to her over fifteen years ago.

At thirty-two, her small frame had almost perfect proportions. She kept her shoulder-length, dark blonde hair, straight, framing her face that was accented with deep green eyes.

A small-town girl raised in Farmington, New Mexico, she and Elliot met during their sophomore year in high school and talked about getting married early on. Both sets of parents discouraged their relationship.

"Lisa, you'll never finish college. Don't disappoint me like your brothers did," her mother had said.

"Elliot, don't you think you should date more before you settle down?" Nobody was good enough for his mother's son.

He intended to ask Lisa's father for his blessing. On the day he finally found the courage to do it, tragedy struck. Lisa's oldest brother died that January in a small plane accident. The FAA report only mentioned "iffy" weather conditions and possible pilot error. His single engine Cessna 182 hit the ground with such force that his legs went through the bottom of the plane.

Thirty days later she lost her father to a heart attack.

Gene reflected on Lisa's losses. Now she faced another. He knew she was not emotionally weak, but in her personal life, Elliot was the pillar she leaned on.

"Gene?" Lisa said as her eyes adjusted to the light.

"Hi, Sunshine." Gene pulled a chair close to the gurney and sat down.

He could tell Lisa instantly remembered where she was.

"He's dead," she said in a loud whisper. "They killed him."

"I know," Gene said.

Lisa sat up. "Did you see him? Gene, they put a knife through his heart." Lisa's said, "Why?"

"I saw him and we need to figure out what to do, Lisa. I guess you've already talked with Detective Stanton?"

"Is he still here?" she asked.

"I'm going to meet him at the office as soon as I leave you."

Lisa leaned toward Gene and whispered. "Gene, please don't leave yet. We need to talk. I didn't tell Stanton anything, not about the fights or... I'm scared."

"You didn't do anything wrong." He looked up at the ceiling and inhaled deeply.. "It's going to take time, time for the police to figure this out. Meanwhile, I need you to go home and try to get some rest."

"How do you expect me to rest?" She dug in her pocket for some tissue.

"You just need to go home and rest. I'll call Marlene and ask her to keep you company."

During Gene and Marlene's marriage, Lisa and Marlene had become good friends. Their divorce only meant no more double dating.

"Why can't *you* come over?" Lisa said. "Marlene doesn't know about anything that's been going on over the last five days."

He held Lisa's hand and took the tissue from the other so he could wipe the mascara from the under her eyes. "I have to talk with detective Stanton. I'm going to ride with him to the office. I also need to call Price and tell him what's happened." Gene stood, dug in his coat pocket and pulled out his car keys. He continued patting at his pockets.

"I wish Price were the last to know," Lisa said. Lisa resented him for the way he had held Elliot back. "What are you looking for?"

"I was in a rush to get down here and I left my cell phone at home."

Lisa pointed to a stool in the corner with a small pile of Elliot's belongings; a wallet, wedding ring, pocket change, roll of antacids and his cell phone. "Take Elliot's phone."

He picked up the phone. "The press is going to be all over this and I don't want his friends and co-workers to find out from the media." Gene paused as if thinking about a plan, "They said you took a sedative. You need to sleep it off…"

Lisa interrupted, "No, they offered but I didn't take it. I don't want to sleep."

"Are you okay to drive? Take my car and drive yourself home when you're ready. I'll ride with the Detective. Have you called Elliot's parents or family?"

"Not yet. I don't know what to say," Lisa said.

"Let them know you're okay. When you're ready, call your mom. I know it will be hard but..."

There was a knock on the door. "Gene," said Stanton, "we've got to talk, now."

Gene was kissing Lisa on the cheek when the detective opened the door.

"Have Elliot's parents been notified?" he asked Stanton.

"One of the officers called them after we talked with Lisa," Stanton replied. "Lisa, call me when you get home. Let me know when Marlene gets there." He turned to Stanton. "Let's go, Detective."

The snow clouds had moved on and the morning sun was above the horizon. Winter's brief interruption in the high desert climate of El Paso had ended. Snow was now slush and what had been slush was water, steaming from the roads as the sun warmed the black asphalt.

"Price?"

Price's voice sounded much older and half asleep. "Gene is that you? It's eight o'clock on a Saturday morning and you just interrupted a completely erotic dream of me and one of the girls..."

"Price," Gene interrupted, "something bad has happened to Elliot."

"What's wrong with Elliot?" Price said annoyed because now Elliot was the reason for his rude awakening.

Gene could hear Mrs. Price. She was mumbling something, probably from the other side of the bed. He realized he woke them up.

"Listen, Price. Not over the phone, just get to the office pronto. I'll explain then."

Gene didn't wait for a response and hung up. He dialed Marlene's number. Her phone rang four times, and after the answering machine's message, he said, "Marlene, there's been an accident. Please, as soon as you can, go to Lisa's house." A recording was no way for Marlene to hear about Elliot's murder. "Marlene, it's bad, so don't call Lisa. Just get over there soon."

Gene was surprised that Marlene wasn't home early on a Saturday morning. They had been divorced for a long time, but he always got a twinge of jealousy when he thought of her with another man.

Stanton and Gene were in deep thought for different reasons. Both men barley spoke during the fifteen-minute ride to the scene where Elliot's body was found.

"I didn't have any breakfast and I'm pretty sure you haven't either," Stanton said, "Is there any place we can get a bite to eat?"

Gene rubbed his unshaven face with both hands to wake himself. "There's a little café in the building that has breakfast on Saturdays. I'm sure we can get something there."

P & M shared the building with a few other tenants but was surprisingly vacant for such a large building. The first floor was elegant with a security desk on one side of the lobby and elevators in the center. On the other side was Diego's, the building's café.

Stanton was anxious to see Gene's reaction to the crime scene as they pulled into the parking garage. The murder took place near the west side of the garage on Kansas Street, so Stanton entered from the east side and drove up to the second level.

They got out of the car and walked side by side. When they approached the stairs, Gene looked over the edge to the street below. A circus of people were milling around the crime scene on Kansas Street. Three police officers providing crowd control. Stanton gave him a few seconds.

"Look at all of the Press," Gene said.

"They listen to our scanners. Normally, a stabbing death isn't this big of a deal. Frankly, I'm surprised," Stanton said.

"No," Gene said, shaking his head, "Someone told them it was Elliot Jones. He is well known in the community. This is going to be a media frenzy."

Stanton was still observing his body language and gestures. Gene stood looking over the edge and spoke without looking up.

"I need to schedule a press conference. I don't want them getting the facts wrong or making

shit up. Who is responsible in the police
department for releasing the facts?"

"Usually our Public Information Officer, but
on this case, it's me," Stanton said. "I'll join you at
your conference, so you don't have to comment if
you don't want to."

They made their way down and exited the
garage to cross the street toward the crowded crime
scene. Gene squinted into the bright, cool, clearness
of morning sun.

Mid way across the street, someone from the
press recognized Gene. "There's Gene Martine."

The crowd of reporters and cameramen tried
to move toward Gene but were stopped by police.
Gene ignored their plea for answers.

"Is it true?"

"Was it Elliot?"

"Is anybody in custody?"

With Stanton leading the way, Gene ducked
under the crime scene tape and walked past the
marked outline of Elliot's body. The press didn't let
up.

"Come on, Mr. Martine, what's the story?"

They walked through the turnstile doors into
the lobby. José, the day security guard, was sitting
behind the oversized desk, cluttered with monitors
and clipboards. José was a retired assembly line
worker, but in his heavily starched uniform, he
exuded a strong sense of authority as the head
security guard for the building.

"Mr. Martine," José said as he stood up. He held out his hand to shake Gene's. "I'm sorry about Elliot."

Stanton noted how sincere he looked.

"This is Detective Stanton. He's with me." Gene took a magnetic security card out of his wallet and passed it through a card reader on the desk.

Stanton was ready for answers.

"When did your shift start, José?"

"I been here since six this morning." José spoke practiced English with a thick Hispanic accent.

"Who's here before you and what time does their shift end?" Stanton already knew the answer because he had interviewed Roger at the crime scene.

"Roger Thatcher is the night shift desk clerk," José said. "His shift end at three in the morning, but actually he left about an hour ago. He's shook up about all this."

"Why is he shaken up?" Stanton asked.

José said in his heavy accent, "I don't know why you ask this question. Mr. Jones was killed last night. That is why he's shook up. Roger was suppose to protect him, and didn't."

Stanton had pulled out his notebook and moved his stylus around the screen, presumably writing notes about Roger and José. "What do you mean by 'protect him'?"

"Roger suppose to offer anybody that leaves the building at night an escort to the garage."

"Why didn't Mr. Thatcher assign an escort to Mr. Jones?"

"Roger say he didn't know Mr. Jones left the building?" José said.

"Did he know Mr. Jones was here?"

"Roger say he knew Mr. Jones got here about ten, but he didn't see him leave. Roger say he saw someone on the monitor in the fire escape..." José pointed at the video monitors, "...and went to check it out and maybe that's when Mr. Jones leaves."

"I saw Mr. Martine swipe a security card. Did Elliot swipe his card when he left?"

José pressed buttons on his PC keyboard. "No."

"Was there anyone in the fire escape?" Stanton asked.

"I don't know. Roger didn't say."

"Did Mr. Thatcher say what floor he saw someone on and could it have been one of the other guards?" Stanton asked. "Don't they travel between floors using the stairs?"

"I think he say the eleven floor. Roger say he radioed to the others but all of their positions checked out."

Stanton continued scribbling on the small screen. "José, I didn't get your last name."

"Cordero."

"I'll be in touch if I have any further questions."

Detective Stanton walked from the desk to follow Gene.

"Detective Stan-tone," José called out. "You can't go any further."

"I'm a detective investigating a crime," Stanton said with an arrogant tone. "I can go where I please."

"Not in my building," José said. "You must fill out the visitor's clipboard."

As he finished filling out the visitor form, he grinned at José.

"Professional courtesy, right, José?"

José handed him a visitor's badge.

At Diego's Café, Stanton chose a bagel with cream cheese while Gene reluctantly picked up an orange. Both men filled large Styrofoam cups with regular coffee. Mrs. Diego was standing behind the cash register and handed Gene the bill. She was almost six feet tall and about seventy pounds overweight. Mr. Diego was tall and heavy, like his wife, and was standing behind her.

Gene signed the receipt.

"Mi corazon, we are so sorry about Elliot," she said with sadness.

"Thank you, Mrs. Diego." Gene said.

Gene and Stanton selected a table close to a window and sat down. Stanton pulled his electronic notebook from his coat pocket and moved his stylus around the screen.

Stanton said, "I'm going to record our conversation. Okay?"

Gene sipped his coffee, and shrugged.

"Who is Marlene?" Stanton asked.

"She's my ex-wife."

"What is her relationship to Lisa and Elliot?"

"When I met Elliott, I was married to Marlene," Gene said. "We all became good friends. Our divorce didn't change that fact. Marlene and Lisa are still friends."

"When did you divorce Marlene?"

"A few years ago?" Gene fidgeted with the orange.

"Why did you get divorced?"

Gene's voice rose. "That's none of your business and it's not relevant."

"Was Elliot close to Marlene?"

"They are..." He cleared his throat. "...were friends. You could say that."

"Was Elliot, to your knowledge, having an affair with Marlene or any other woman for that matter?"

Gene finished peeling the orange, pulled off one slice and ate it. He seemed to be mulling the question over in his mind. "Stanton, you're a real jerk. Elliot did not, and would not, *ever...*" he said with emphasis "...cheat on Lisa."

Stanton said with a firm voice, "Is Lisa having..."

Gene cut him short. "Nobody's having an affair." Gene leaned forward pointing a finger at Stanton. His eyes shifted from side to side. "Elliot wasn't killed because someone is sleeping with someone else. You got that?"

Stanton put his half eaten bagel down, sat back in his chair and folded his arms across his chest.

"Let's take this from another angle," Stanton said with a calm voice. "Did Elliot have any enemies that you know of?"

Gene settled back in his chair and went back to examining his fruit. "Elliot was well-known in a lot of circles and as long as I've known him, I can't remember anyone saying they wanted him dead. Of course, he had business adversaries but not the type that would say 'I'm going to kill you if you win that account'."

"Who would you consider to be his biggest business adversary?"

"That's easy. Joe Garcia. Joe once worked for P & M, but Price fired him for unethical business practices. Shortly afterwards, we hired Elliot. Joe always thought that Elliot was the real reason that he was fired."

"Was Elliot the reason?"

31

"No. We discovered that Joe was taking money under the table from the media," Gene said. "Since then, Joe opened Garcia Advertising and has weaseled his way into every new business pitch Elliot has developed." Gene sucked the juice from an orange slice. "Over the past couple of years, it has driven us all crazy. Joe seems to find his way into even our most confidential presentations."

"Have there ever been confrontations between Elliot and Joe?" Stanton asked.

"At social events, they just gave each other the cold shoulder or an evil across-the-room stare."

"How about his clients?" Stanton asked. "Have any of them had problems with Elliot lately?"

"Elliot is involved in decision-making for half of our clients, but it never is…" Gene caught himself again "…was, never was confrontational. He hasn't had any problems with them that I'm aware of."

Stanton was about to ask another question when Gene said, "Wait, come to think of it, Julio Rivera called yesterday with a complaint. With everything that's happened I almost forgot about it."

"Who is Julio Rivera? What was the problem?"

"Julio is the CEO of VoiceComm, our largest client. Elliot neglected to send Julio the latest brand recognition market reports."

"Did Elliot always communicate with CEOs?" Stanton asked.

"Most of the client contact is with the marketing director or their staff. But this was important information that Julio needed for a board meeting that could affect the stock prices of the corporation."

"Why do you think Elliot didn't send them? Were the reports harmful in any way?"

"The reports weren't great but not bad either," Gene said. "P & M would have to face some heat from the board of directors of VoiceComm about lagging consumer recall but it's nothing that Elliot would try to hide."

"What did you tell Julio?"

"I covered for Elliot. I told him that he was having some personal problems over the last few days and must have forgotten to send the reports. I emailed and sent Julio hard copies of the report over night." Gene had finished his orange and sipped the last of his coffee.

"Was Elliot having personal problems?"

"What?" Gene's mind seemed to be wandering.

"You told Julio Rivera that Elliot was having personal problems."

Gene started breaking bits of Styrofoam from the coffee cup and dropping them into the cup.

"Was he or was he not having personal problems?" Stanton asked.

"I was just covering for Elliot. I don't know why he didn't send the reports."

Stanton's furrowed his eyebrows in disbelief.

"Detective," a voice called from across the cafe. A uniformed police officer was walking toward them.

"What is it, Davis?" Stanton asked.

The officer glanced in Gene's direction signaling the need for a private conversation. Stanton and Gene stood up.

"Are we done, Stanton?"

"For now. I may have more questions later and I'd like to question some of P & M's employees."

Stanton didn't know why, but he shook hands with Gene before walking away.

A uniformed police officer was guarding the double doors with the agency's logo engraved into the fireproof glass.

"Excuse me, sir. No one is allowed inside," the officer said.

"Maybe you're not allowed in, but I own this place. My name is Gene Martine. Do you see the big 'M' on this door?" Gene pointed at the logo on the door. "That's me. So if you don't mind..."

As Gene reached for the handle the officer blocked his reach.

"I'll need to see some I. D."

He dug in his coat pocket for his wallet, pulled it out and held his driver's license three

inches from the officer's face. The man in uniform
stepped aside. Gene pushed through the doors and
walked down the long hall heading to Price's office,
noticing three more uniforms in Elliot's office.
Price was sitting behind his desk writing on a
document. He was dressed in a white shirt and tie.

"Price, what are all the cops doing in Elliot's
office?"

Price sat back in his imported leather chair
and crossed his arms over his heavily starched shirt.
"You should be telling me what's going on, Gene.
You mind filling me in on the demise of our best
new business man?"

"Price, you are such an ass." Gene dropped
himself into a large leather guest chair and propped
his feet up on the glass coffee table.

"Pull yourself together, Gene. Use your
head. The cops are investigating Elliot's death. It
happened right outside of our office, doesn't it
make sense that they would need to search the place
for clues or evidence?"

Gene was exhausted from lack of sleep. He
took his glasses off and flung them onto Price's
oversized mahogany desk.

It was only ten-thirty in the morning, but
Price got up and walked to his wet bar. He poured
two straight bourbons and handed one to Gene.
Gene went over the details of the morning with
Price. He started with the call from Lisa, then his
near miss with a semi, Elliot's body, and concluded
with Stanton's questioning.

"I'm calling a press conference down in the auditorium at twelve o'clock," Gene said, "Have you heard or seen anything on the news?"

"No." Price walked to his television, turned it on, and changed the channel from CNN to a local station. They saw the reporter in the foreground as the camera panned back to a wider shot of their office building.

"...His body was found here, just outside of his office, P & M Advertising, early this morning. Later, we'll discuss the effect that the growing unemployment rate has had on local businesses. It's all here on News at Twelve."

"Okay, the news is out. I want to activate the calling tree. Price, do you know who is already here?"

"Do you think that's necessary, Gene? The press has already broken the news and it's sure to spread like wildfire. You know, it may not be the best thing for our image." Gene wasn't listening, but Price continued, "I think it's best if we just let it lie."

"Forget it, Price, I'll handle it myself." He picked up Price's office phone and dialed the intercom number. "This is Gene Martine." He wasn't sure how many employees were there. "Everyone, please report to my office right away."

Only five employees were in the office. Mike Kieslowski, Norman Miller, and Karen Scott from the art department were working on the newest campaign for VoiceComm. Madeline Rodriguez from bookkeeping was catching up on time sheets

36

and Joyce Elder, Price's personal secretary, came in because she heard the news.

Gene greeted each one as they came to his office. Madeline was crying, sobbing. Elliot had been her mentor. At twenty-seven years old, she had aspirations of moving out of bookkeeping into account service. Madeline was good with clients and showed intelligence in her work.

"Any of you know why I've called you in here?"

"I assume it's about Elliot," Joyce said.

Everyone's eyes were on her. In her late sixties, she was the most respected employee of P & M. She was old school and had earned respect from Price and two other CEOs before him.

"Mr. Martine, can you tell us what happened?" Madeline asked.

"I will when everyone gets here."

Chapter Four

Gene had just placed the receiver in the phone's cradle when Stanton knocked on his office door.

"Gene, I need to ask you a few more questions."

Gene gestured toward a chair.

Gene's office was large but modestly decorated. His passion for nick-knack antiques helped fill his display shelves where his prestigious awards collected dust and were buried behind antique radios and old newspapers. Two barber chairs had been refurbished that dated back to the early 1800s.

Stanton sat in one of them. "We've recovered some evidence at the scene."

"Did you find the murder weapon?" Gene asked.

"We found two things. First, Elliot survived long enough to pull himself up and sit on the side walk next to the planter."

"He did?" Gene's eyes grew wide.

"Apparently Elliot used a rock we found by his body to scratch a message on the sidewalk. We didn't see it early this morning because it was too dark and wet. We wouldn't have noticed it if the water hadn't evaporated. We could only make out "M", followed by an "a" or "e", then a "d", another "a" or "e", and finally an "l". At first, we thought it might be his assailant's name. Then another officer found this." Stanton dug in his coat pocket, pulled out a zip-lock and tossed in on Gene's desk. "One of my officers noticed something shining in the gutter drain close to where Elliot was standing when he was stabbed."

"What is it?" Gene asked.

"It's one ounce of pure silver. We think that's what Elliot was trying to write "M-E-D-A-L" or "medallion." Stanton's voice had a hopeful tone. He had finally found a lead, "Do you recognize it?" Stanton watched Gene closely.

Gene picked up the zip-lock and opened it. "Can I take it out?"

"Yeah. We've already lifted the fingerprints one on each side, most likely the index finger on one side and the thumb on the other, which will certainly belong to Elliot or his killer."

Gene turned the bag over, letting the medallion drop on the desktop. The silver made a distinct sound as it hit the desk. He studied one side

39

that was embossed with a waving American flag at the left that faded in the middle to become the Mexican flag to the right. He had seen the flag symbol before and his mind raced to remember, but nothing clicked. Then he flipped it to the opposite side that was embossed with a figure of bull's head and horns. A marijuana leaf was upside down where a cowbell would hang. "I've never seen anything like it. Why would this be important and why would Elliot write 'medallion' while he was lying there dying?"

Stanton looked relieved that Gene didn't recognize it.

"That medallion belongs to the largest drug ring in this part of the world. I've heard about it and seen a picture of one, but this is the first time I've come across one." He leaned back in the barber chair and stretched his legs. "Just my bad luck, now the damn thing and the people it represents are part of my case." Stanton sounded concerned.

"Why would you connect Elliot's murder to drugs, much less a gang? That's ridiculous. Elliot is the last person I know who would ever try drugs or be tied up with dealers."

Stanton said, "This isn't some little gang of thugs selling bags of pot on a street corner. This is serious organized crime that involves possibly hundreds of influential people and billions — with a capital B — of dollars. They call themselves Free-Landers. The name originates from the arrogance of their ability to transport tons of cocaine and marijuana from Mexico to the U. S., virtually undetected. They rotate shipments between every border crossing from California to El Paso and every bridge between here and the most southern tip of Texas."

"Elliot just wouldn't be caught up in drugs," Gene said. "I know him *that* well."

"El Paso is their favorite destination because we have four border bridges to choose from and because we're in the South Central U.S. It makes it easier and quicker for the Free-Landers to distribute the drugs throughout the States."

"If you know all of this, why is it so hard to catch them?" Gene asked. "I mean, isn't the FBI or DEA involved? How does all of this tie together with the medallion and Elliot?"

The detective stood from the barber chair. He was quiet and appeared to be distracted as he walked across the plush carpet to the shelves.

"Stanton?" Gene said. "Answer my questions for once."

"Look, Gene. Every law enforcement agency is involved, some more than others. We've been chasing these people for years, and we've nailed small groups when we get a tip on a stash house."

Stanton turned a plastic knob on a 1942 Clarion radio sitting on one of the shelves.

"I've heard of those. That's where the drug dealers buy or rent a house and store their coke or marijuana, right?" Gene said.

"But that's where it stops," Stanton said. "We catch the local bad guys, but we can't figure out where a handful of jerks get a ton of coke with a street value of over eighty million dollars. The shit is coming in from Mexico, sure enough. We believe the medallion is used as some sort of payment. An I. O. U. perhaps, we're just not sure." Stanton looked at the entire showcase of awards and antiques. "Gene, all of the security guards I've interviewed say that one of the tenants in the building is a cleaning company. Is that right?"

"Clean Sweep. And?"

"They trade office space from the building for the service of cleaning the leased offices. Is that also correct?"

"What's your point?" Gene asked.

Stanton looked at his fingers, the ones he used to turn the knobs on the antique radio, and brushed them off. "Why are your shelves so dusty? They don't show any signs of dusting."

He said, "Maybe they just don't like touching my things. Come on, Stanton, stay focused."

"If Elliot was trying to write 'medallion,' then that tells us the killer might be a Free-Lander. If the killer is a Free-Lander, then..."

"Then you automatically assume Elliot was dealing drugs," Gene cut Stanton off. "That's ridiculous."

"Maybe you're right, but people have gotten caught up in stranger things. We suspect that a Free-Lander killed Elliot. Finding out why they killed..."

"Detective Stanton." A uniformed cop was standing in at the doorway of Gene's office. "There are a bunch of people standing in the hall wanting to come in."

"I'm sure they're just reporters. Keep them out."

"No, sir. They all claim to work here."

"They are all employees, Stanton. I called them in to tell them about Elliot." The bourbon was catching up to him.

Stanton could tell Gene was tired and he wasn't feeling much better. "Are the officers done with Mr. Jones' office?" Stanton asked the cop.

"They're wrapping it up right now."

"Go ahead and let them in."

As Stanton walked toward the door, Gene stood from his stool. His head became light and his vision blurred. As the room spun for a few seconds, his hands held the edge of his desktop to control his balance.

"You okay, Gene?"

Gene closed his eyes and let the head-rush clear.

"I'm fine. I just got up too fast."

At 11:45 Gene addressed his staff and delivered the truth about Elliot's death, leaving out specific details. More than a hundred people stood shoulder to shoulder in the room. Price and Madeline met him at the podium. Price was starched and pressed. Madeline hung onto Gene's shoulder and dabbed her nose and eyes.

She appeared overly distraught, but she was the one to ask the question, "Do they have any suspects?"

"As of right now, I am unaware of any suspects," he said.

Price leaned over the podium and spoke. "Folks, in light of the situation, I am closing the office on Monday. If you have important project deadlines, please come in to handle those tasks only."

The crowd dispersed. Some went straight to the few police officers in the lobby. Others congregated in the halls or offices, discussing the events of the morning.

Gene attended the press conference but said nothing. He was exhausted and desperately needed to lie down. Detective Stanton spent fifteen minutes giving limited facts and ten minutes answering questions. Gene went up to the P & M offices and lay down on a sofa in the game room and slept.

Saturday 8:30p.m.

Roger Thatcher had been the night shift security guard for three years. He was well liked and did a good job sitting behind the big desk in the lobby of the office building, watching monitors and recording activity.

He had a medium skeletal frame. The strength of his youth had all but gone. Gravity had stretched and pulled his skin around his face and arms. At seventy years old, his health was deteriorating.

"Here, honey. Some hot tea will do you good."

Roger's wife of forty-three years placed a cup in front of him and sat down in the dining-room chair next to him. Roger was upset. Five hours of restless sleep hadn't helped. Gloria held his hand on the table. She worried for him.

Roger was a kind and gentle man. His wife had seen this look on his tired, old face before when relatives and friends passed on over the years. But that night, he somehow looked much older.

"Roger, it wasn't your fault."

Roger stared at his cup of hot tea. He was given two nights off with pay to pull himself together. His mind was elsewhere.

Elliot was a friend to Roger. During the day, Elliot didn't have much time to fraternize with employees, but his late work nights were different. He would come in during Roger's shift on many occasions and instead of rushing up to the tenth floor, they would talk about family, work, retirement dreams and the holidays.

Two years earlier, one week before Christmas, Roger and Elliot had been talking about their families. Elliot filled Roger in on Lisa's expensive wish list and they laughed. Roger told Elliot of his five grandchildren and their wish lists. One of the grandchildren wanted a pair of dentures so he could be just like his grandpa. Laughter broke out for a little while until something — a thought — made Roger stop. He looked away from Elliot.

"What's wrong, Roger?" Elliot said as he caught his breath. "You've got some adorable grandkids."

Roger said, "This year will be different."

Roger told Elliot that he and his wife had been ill much of that year. They couldn't afford a Christmas tree much less presents for the grandkids. He was ashamed. The entire family was to arrive Christmas Eve and they didn't have the courage to say "not this year" to their children.

On Christmas Eve morning, before any relatives arrived, Roger had returned home from work at 3:30 in the morning. His heart heavy from knowing how the next couple of days were going to go, Roger opened his front door. Inside, the three-bedroom house was decorated with garland, lights, a handsome tree, and dozens of presents. There was a present for Mr. and Mrs. Roger Thatcher, all their children and grandchildren, each one marked from Dad and Mom or Nana and Grandpa. Roger was speechless.

He closed the door and hung his hat on a hook. He looked around the living room at the spectacle. He noticed a note on the coffee table and read it.

Roger,

A good man needs not presents to show his love . . . only his goodness.

Santa knew you were a little too busy to
shop. He's made an early stop this year.

Merry Christmas

Gloria patted Roger's hand. "Roger, you
need to rest some more, Honey. Come on. Drink
your tea before it gets cold."
        She held the cup up to his lips. His shaky
hands took hold of the cup. He sipped and placed
the cup back on the table. Usually, even when his
blood pressure would get too high, the sound of her
smooth voice could bring it down. But that night,
his mind was flooded with recent events. Gloria was
barely audible. Roger stood up from the table,
walked to the front door, and put on his cabby hat.
        "I'm going to go for a walk," he said. "I
need some fresh air." He opened the door and began
to walk.
        It was only 8:30 in the evening, but the air
had cooled to just above freezing. Roger didn't
think to bring a coat and was beginning to get too
cold. He pulled his hat down tight, lifted his shirt
collar, and stuffed his hands into his pockets. After
walking west for four blocks, he decided walk down
the alley that would take him home. The alley was
dark, but Roger knew it well. Dogs barked as he
passed house after house.
        It came from nowhere. Roger fell to the
ground. The excruciating pain emitting in his left
arm told him it was fractured. He tried to yell, but
the pain was too much and the sound stopped dead

in his throat. Not knowing what had hit him, he tried to lift himself to his knees. He wanted to run.

"God help me," he said.

His assailant hit his side with a shovel, breaking ribs. Roger fell to his back. Crying out from the pain and bleeding from his mouth, he saw the shadowy figure kneel down beside him.

"Tell me what the cops know about Elliot's death, right now, or you die, too."

Her voice was familiar, but she was wearing a black ski mask and black leather coat.

"Oh, God. Don't kill me."

"Do they have evidence? Do they have a suspect?"

Roger's breathing was shallow and raspy, his words barely a whisper. "I don't know what you mean."

"Listen, old man." She pulled out a silver medallion, then held it within an inch of Roger's face. "Do they have one of these?"

"Please don't hurt me anymore. I d-don't know anything." Blood ran from his mouth.

Vapors escaped from the black ski mask as her breathing quickened. She brought the shovel high above her head.

"Gloria, I'm sorry."

He closed his eyes tight as she swung the deadly weapon for the last time.

Saturday 5:00p.m.

Marlene got Gene's message on her voice mail that afternoon. She tried to call him several times from her cell on her way to Lisa's house, but Gene didn't have his phone and wouldn't have heard it if he did. He was in a deep sleep in the break room of the agency.

When she arrived at Lisa's, Elliot's parents were there. Their arrival made things worse for Lisa as she relived the entire experience with them. After hearing the facts behind Elliot's murder and consoling Lisa and her in-laws, Marlene gave Lisa and her mother-in-law each a Valium.

Marlene said she'd been at the River Rock Boot warehouse all morning. There might have been a break-in. The alarm had gone off when a window was broken early that morning. The alarm must have scared off the thieves, as there was nothing stolen and everything seemed to be in good order.

Lisa and Mrs. Jones looked groggy soon after they had taken the medication. Mr. Jones insisted that he and Mrs. Jones go home and rest. He seemed to know the next few days were going to be long. They hugged Lisa and Marlene then left their son's home.

"Have you had anything to eat, darlin'?" Marlene said with a country twang.

"Just a few crackers earlier," Lisa said.

"Here, sit down on the sofa, and I'll make us some lunch."

Lisa, wearing the same clothes from that morning. She sat on the sofa, pulled her legs up to her chest, and rested her red cheeks between her knees. Marlene pulled a throw blanket over Lisa's shoulders and walked to the kitchen. She was Lisa's best friend, and although the home was just one year old, she knew Lisa's kitchen as well as her own.

Marlene spoke from the kitchen. "Lisa, this is the worst thing to happen to anyone. I am so sorry it's happened to you."

Lisa said, "I'm glad you're here. Have you heard from Gene?"

"I've tried to call him several times, but he's not answering. What about you? Have you heard anything new about who and why Elliot was killed?" Considering the Valium, she asked a sensitive question without worry of Lisa's emotional state of mind.

"I haven't heard from Gene, either. I only know what I've told you."

A few moments of silence and Marlene appeared from the kitchen with toasted tuna-fish sandwiches, chips and bottled water. "Here you go, darlin'. I know it's hard to think about the little things like eating right now. But you need to keep up your strength."

Lisa sat up, accepting the plate and setting it on her lap. Marlene sat next to her.

"What was Elliot working on that he had to work so late?"

Lisa swallowed some water and a bite of tuna. Her eyes were fixed straight ahead.

"What was he working on?" Marlene asked again.

"I'm not sure. He just said he was going to the office."

Marlene sensed Lisa was holding back. She put her hand on Lisa's forearm. "Lisa, can I ask you a personal question? I haven't seen you in a few weeks. Have you and Elliot been okay? I mean, you are understandably upset and I don't want to sound like I'm not hurting, too, but..." Marlene's words trailed off.

"But what, Marlene?" Lisa said defensively. "Am I not supposed to grieve for my husband?"

"You seem to be taking it so hard."

"My husband, the man I love, was murdered this morning. Just how the hell *am* I supposed to be taking it?"

Marlene wasn't too surprised at Lisa's reaction.

"What, darlin'? What was wrong?" Marlene held both of Lisa's hands.

"Oh, God, Marlene. I feel so horrible." Lisa put her face on Marlene's shoulder. "We had a fight again, and he left to get away from me. I didn't get to tell him I loved him and that things would be all right. Oh, God. He's dead. They killed him."

Marlene hugged and slowly rocked Lisa. "What are you rambling about, child? You and

Elliot hardly ever argued. And what do you mean *they* killed him?"

"It's a long story, Marlene. This whole week has been miserable"

"I'm listening."

She took a deep breath. "Monday night Elliot told me he was running to the store for some milk and eggs. He was gone for an hour. I was concerned and tried to call his cell phone, but he didn't answer. Then it dawned on me. I had just gone grocery-shopping Saturday. We didn't need anything."

"Where did he go?" Marlene asked.

"When he got home he said he didn't want to talk about it. We argued for two hours. He just kept telling me that it wasn't anything that concerned me. He did what he did last night. He just grabbed his keys and left again. I was so upset, I called Gene."

"Why didn't you call me?" Marlene asked. "I would have come right over."

"I would have, except Gene knows Elliot better than anyone and I thought maybe he could tell me what Elliot's problem was," Lisa said. "We talked for an hour and he assured me he would find out. Anyway, he called P & M for me and found Elliot. I guess he must have said some really harsh things to Elliot because when Elliot got home, all he did was slam doors until he went to sleep on this sofa. On Tuesday, he claimed to have to work late as usual. But I was still pissed, so I called Gene. He said he didn't know what Elliot could be working on. So, when Elliot got home it started all over again. We argued for hours."

"Another woman?" Marlene asked.

"At first, I didn't think so. But, on Wednesday, he left the house again and was gone three hours. I felt helpless for whatever he was going through that he couldn't, or wouldn't, confide in me. When he got home, he plopped down in his recliner without saying a word. I wish you could have seen the look on his face." She sipped the water.

"Was he mad or upset?" Marlene was anxious to hear the rest of Lisa's story.

"It was more like he was really worried about something — or someone — as it turned out. Just as I was about to say something to him, he put his hand up to stop me. Then he got out of his chair, dropped to his knees in front of me, took my hands and said, 'Lisa, what I am about to tell you might upset you.' Then he made me promise to try to understand and not overreact. The words that came out of his mouth shattered my heart. 'Lisa, about a month ago, I met a woman.'"

"Oh Lisa, I'm so sorry, honey. I had no idea."

"I didn't even give him a chance to explain. He tried to tell me more, but I wouldn't listen. I just packed an overnight bag, grabbed my keys and left." Lisa stared across the room. "God, I was so stupid."

Marlene took Lisa's hands into hers, "I would have done the same thing. Where did you go? Why didn't you come to my house?"

"I was just so upset. I went to Gene's house," Lisa said. "He knew we were having these problems and at the time, I wanted to hurt Elliot in the worst way."

"Oh, goodness. Tell me you didn't sleep with Gene."

"I thought about it. That night, Gene and Elliot got into a huge shouting match over the phone. I could only hear Gene's part of the conversation, but it was ugly. At the time, I thought Elliot was a real son-of-a-bitch."

"He was, don't you think?"

Lisa thoughtfully bit her lower lip. "I had all of Wednesday night to calm down and all of Thursday to think. Elliot was trying to tell me something about this other woman. I didn't keep my promise about not over-reacting. I should've listened for five more minutes and maybe, just maybe, he might be alive today."

"Don't you start blaming yourself. He got himself into something he couldn't handle. If he would have just minded his own business none of this would have happened." Marlene stopped talking abruptly.

"What?" Lisa asked.

"I'm just rambling. Finish telling me what happened Thursday."

"I gathered the courage. I needed to know if our marriage was over. I made his favorite dinner. When he got home from the office, we embraced for what seemed like forever. I told him I would give him a chance to explain but it would be after we had a nice dinner."

"I can't wait to hear this one," Marlene said.

"You're judging Elliot before you know the facts, just like I did. He told me the woman's name was Samantha. I've got to tell you, when he said her name, my heart broke again. But then he told me that she was a junkie. He met her one night a couple of months ago in the parking garage across from the agency. She had been panhandling. She had a four-year-old son and looked totally out of place."

"There are women begging with children downtown all the time."

"He told me she was a white female in her thirties and except for being a little dirty, she and her son were dressed in newer clothes. She hadn't been on the street too long. You know Elliot. He would give the shirt off his back to a stranger if he thought it would help their situation. I don't know what she said to him but he was compelled to help her." Lisa's fondness of Elliot's character showed.

"But why didn't he tell you about her sooner?" Marlene said.

"He said it was because this Samantha was in trouble. She owed a lot of money to a drug dealer. He didn't want to tell me, 'Hi, honey, guess what? Today I'm helping a druggie pay off her debt to her dealer.'"

"You got a point there."

"He got her into a shelter and every now and then he would check in on her. He said some days she was sober and others she was so out of it she didn't recognize him. On her good days, he would give her money that she promised was to pay off her dealer. If Elliot had a fault, it was being naïve."

"You know that money was going right up her nose or in her arm." Marlene seemed perturbed.

"But Elliot is, I mean, was the eternal optimist."

"Earlier, you said 'they killed him.' What did you mean by that?"

"I guess he realized his visits and his money weren't helping Samantha. He convinced her to set up a meeting between Elliot and the supposed dealer. He wanted to pay off the debt and get her cleaned up. Elliot hoped together we could give her and her son a new start."

"How much did she owe?"

"Elliot said a few thousand dollars. But something went wrong right before the meeting. Last night he got a call on his cell. I didn't hear what was said, but Samantha apparently pissed off the dealer. She also told him that what she was involved in was more than Elliot could handle. He said it was some kind of drug ring that involved people he knew. That's why I said 'they' killed him. I think he was going to meet with them last night."

"Did he tell you any names?" Marlene needed to know.

"That's when he stopped talking. He got really distant, fast. Hell, it almost started another argument between us. Instead, I just stopped asking him questions and made passionate love to him. At the time, I was just so relieved that he wasn't cheating on me."

"Have you told the cops or Gene any of this information? I mean, it might be helpful to their case. Did Elliot tell you anything else?"

"I've been so upset and I didn't want anyone to know that Elliot was on his way to meet a drug dealer."

Marlene noticed Lisa yawning with exhaustion and moved over on the sofa as Lisa laid her head on the armrest. Her eyes slowly closed as she mumbled, "Free-Landers."

"What did you say, Honey?" Marlene said, but Lisa didn't respond as the cell phone rang in Marlene's purse on the kitchen table. She walked to purse to retrieve the phone.

"Hello?" she said as she walked into the kitchen so Lisa couldn't hear the conversation.

"I know I haven't called. It took me longer than I expected but she told me what she knows."

"Oh, God. Did you have to? Son-of-a-bitch."

"Look, she knows about Sam, even so, only her first name. She's never met her or the kid."

"This is getting out of control. You guys don't do another thing until we talk about our options tonight. You got that?" Marlene hit the 'end' button and placed the cell back in her purse.

Chapter Five

It was almost 9:30 in the evening and Gene was the only one in the P & M offices. Aside from his fifty-year-old muscles that ached from sleeping on a couch, he was alert and feeling better. At least emotionally, he felt in check. The initial shock of Elliot's murder and the anxieties that followed were gone. He lay on the sofa staring at the ceiling but looking at nothing.

Gene was startled when Elliot's cell phone vibrated against the hard wood of his desk.

"This is Gene," he said with a yawn as he stretched his arms above his head while holding the phone between his cheek and shoulder.

"Gene?" It was Lisa and she sounded groggy.

"How are you feeling?"

"All right, I guess. I just realized you didn't have a way home after I saw your number on my caller ID," Lisa yawned. "I guess you need a ride?"

"Only if you feel up to it. I can call a taxi."

"I'll come get you. I need to get out of this house. I'll leave right now. Will you be outside?"

"That's fine. I'll..." But Gene didn't finish.

For the first time since they had moved the agency downtown, he was afraid to leave his own office.

"Gene, you there?"

"Park in the underground garage where the delivery trucks park. Do you know where that is? I'll meet you down there. And, don't turn off the motor or unlock the doors until you know I'm by myself and standing next to the car."

"Gene, now you're scaring me."

"I've just got the spooks. Everything's okay, but let's do it that way okay?"

"I'll be there in twenty minutes."

The call ended, but Gene pushed the end button anyway. He inhaled hugely, looked at his watch, 9:45 at night, and then his computer screen. Instead of shutting down, Gene slipped on his coat, stuffed his phone into his coat pocket, clicked off his desk lamp and walked out of his office.

Gene felt chilled. He was leaving, but only after stopping briefly at Elliot's office. The door to Elliot's office was closed and the cold air reminded him of Elliot's lifeless body in the stainless steel drawer at the morgue.

He locked the large glass door with the big "M" etched on it and walked to the elevators as Elliot had done just the night before. He pushed the button summoning a ride down. The wait seemed longer than usual. He pushed again.

"Working late?"

Gene jumped.

"It's just me, Gene... Al," Al walked into the dim light where he could be seen. "Relax."

"Damn it, Al."

"Just walking my rounds."

"I'm just a little jumpy with all that's gone on, you know? What's taking the elevators so long?"

"We've had some problems with them. Hold on." Al lifted his radio to his mouth and it clicked. "I need an elevator on the tenth. Alex, please check on it, over."

"Who's Alex?" Gene asked.

"He's the guard responsible for the floors above us."

"Why would he be the one to call?" Gene asked just as the elevator behind him dinged and the doors slid open.

"Here's your ride," Al said and motioned Gene inside. The doors closed. Al disappeared.

Gene pushed "LL" for lower level and the elevator lumbered down. As expected late at night, it didn't stop until it reached its destination. Down in the basement, the walls were asylum-white and the floors dirty gray. The exit to the underground garage was only sixty feet from the elevators but it seemed like a mile to Gene.

His fears were growing by the time he reached the double steel doors that would lock behind him when he walked outside. Gene pushed the left one open, walked out and let it close. It didn't latch. He shoved it, but something was keeping the spring-loaded bolt from entering the catch on the frame. At closer inspection, Gene found a folded piece of paper stuck in the bolt-hole. Someone was trying to keep the door from locking.

The sound of tires squealing on the painted driveway broke his concentration. He turned to see the car's headlights bobbing up and down when Lisa drove over the speed bumps too fast. His heart raced as she pulled up to the loading dock. He took the small flight of steps down and walked around to the passenger side. Lisa pushed the unlock button, but Gene didn't open the door. Lisa lowered the power window.

"Come on, Gene. Get in."

"Shhh," Gene whispered. "Listen."

Gene heard the distinct sound of sneakers squeaking on the painted floor. He looked in the direction of the squeaks, but the sound stopped. The place was empty except for a fifteen-passenger van that belonged to El Paso Electric and a box-type delivery truck parked in the darkest area of the garage. It was a Clean Sweep truck. Except for the sound of the car's hum, it was quiet. He opened the door and got in.

"Get me out of here," he said.

She shifted into reverse, backed up ten feet, shifted to drive, and shot forward causing the tires to break traction. After they sped away, a dark figure of a man stepped from behind the box truck.

They exited, turning south onto Kansas Street, sped to the red traffic light and stopped.

"What was all of that?" she asked. "Did you see anyone?"

"No," Gene said. "But this has been the strangest day of my life."

Lisa had been through enough for the day. He decided that they would discuss it in the morning.

"Let's just go home."

It was after 10:00. The ride to Gene's house was quiet. It wasn't an awkward silence. He was lost in thought and he honestly didn't know what to say.

There were only a few homes on Morningside Drive where Gene lived but the street was well lit. Except for one black sedan and two pick-up trucks parked curbside in front of his neighbor's home, the street was vacant.

The headlights flashed large white circles on Gene's garage as Lisa pulled into the driveway outside of the first stall that was reserved for the

Lexus. The second stall was for his pick-up and the last was for his horse trailer. Inside, Gene kept a master mechanics toolbox that stored every tool a professional auto mechanic could wish for. Among them were his leather-working tools, including hole punchers, scratch awls and engravers. Working raw leather into fine western belts was his hobby. Gene did most of his leatherwork at his house in Ruidoso or while he was camping in the New Mexico mountains.

"You going to be alright tonight, Lisa?"

"I thought I might stay here," she said. "I just don't think I can sleep in my bed tonight. I packed an overnight bag and…"

"You can sleep in the guest room again," reminding Lisa of the night she wanted to hurt Elliot.

Although she didn't say it, he could tell he unintentionally hurt her. It showed in her face. Lisa got out of the car, walked to the back, opened the trunk, and retrieved her bag. When she closed it, Gene was standing next to her.

"I'm sorry," he said.

"For what?" she asked, without looking at him.

"For everything." He pulled her tight against his chest.

"There is so much…" Her words trailed off.

Gene took her face into his hands, "Let's go inside and talk." He kissed her cheek, picked up her bag and walked with her arm wrapped around his.

Much like his office, Gene's home was filled with antiques, awards, and Southwest style furniture. Unlike his office, it was clean and kempt. Gene turned on lights as he walked to the guest bedroom and dropped her overnight bag onto the bed. Lisa walked into the den and collapsed on a leather sofa in the middle of the room facing an oversized stone fireplace that was capped with an oak mantel. On top of the mantel sat two antique radios and an expensive Remington sculpture. A large bundle of cut firewood was neatly stacked to one side of the hearth.

"Why don't you start a fire while I make some drinks?" Gene said walking into the kitchen.

"It is kind of cold in here," Lisa replied.

The kitchen had a large Sub-Zero refrigerator. An island highlighted the center of the room. Pots and pans hung above it. Gene placed ice-cubes in two double-shot glasses, and then poured Kentucky bourbon into each.

Lisa placed three logs in the fireplace, a starter cake beneath them and lit the block with a long match.

"Here you go."

Lisa sat on the floor as he handed her one of the glasses. Gene sat on the sofa.

"Whoa, Gene. Trying to get me drunk?"

"I thought you might want to do that all by yourself."

"I don't know what I'm going to do."

"I loved him, too, Lisa."

"That's not what I mean. Gene, there's something I need to tell you." She sipped her drink. "I found out what was going on with Elliot over the last several days. I believe it has everything to do with his murder."

Lisa told him about Samantha, what Elliot was trying to do for her, and how she thought the drug dealer was probably the killer.

Now, the medallion, the drugs, and the Free-Landers started to make some sense to Gene. Nevertheless, it still was far-fetched that a billion dollar organization like the one Stanton described would kill a man over some low life junkie woman who was into them for a few thousand dollars, especially if he were actually attempting to pay off the debt.

"This is unbelievable. Did you tell Stanton any of this?"

"No. I almost didn't tell you." Her face was getting flushed from the alcohol.

"Why not? The detectives need to know this stuff."

"I can see the headlines now," Lisa said, gesturing. "Ad Man Elliot Jones Killed Over Sex and Drugs. You know as well as I do, that the press wouldn't actually print the truth. Besides, there's more."

"How much more can there be?" Gene finished his drink and got up to pour another.

Lisa followed him into the kitchen. "Apparently, Elliot knew some of the people involved. He told me the problem was bigger than he could handle and that I could be hurt if he didn't do what he had to do."

"Who are they?"

"He wouldn't tell me. You see? That's why they killed him."

"We have to call Stanton and tell him everything you know."

"I won't do it. I won't have my husband's name drug through the mud. He was loved and respected, and I'll be damned if anyone is going to hear it any other way."

"Don't you want the son-of-a-bitch who killed him to pay?"

"Of course, I do. And maybe you and I can figure out how and when to tell Stanton the truth. But right now, I'm going to mourn for my husband and give him the funeral he deserves."

"After his funeral we'll go straight to Stanton. We'll get in trouble for withholding information but we'll work it out then. Okay?"

Lisa hugged him.

They walked back to the den. Gene sat on the sofa and Lisa next to him.

"Now tell me what happened to you today."

While he talked, she laid her head on his shoulder. The fire blazed for an hour.

It was 8:00 Sunday morning. Detective Stanton was racing through the streets of El Paso toward Gene's house. Stanton had tried to call Gene at home, work, and on his cell. He would normally be simply frustrated but Gene was a person of interest. Stanton's fuse was getting short.

Stanton's car was a brown, police-issued Chevy Caprice. The paint was coated with dirt from the rain, snow and slush. Except for some mud on the rubber floor mats, the interior was clean and his case files were neatly stacked. Unlike most overworked detectives, Stanton was orderly.

He was forced to learn good business habits and organizational skills during his third year as the owner of a small beef ranch. He started with five hundred head of cattle in east El Paso. At the time, he and his wife were planning for his retirement from the police force. Through trials and tribulations, they grew the ranch to more than one thousand head and were making a good profit. Still, Stanton was a detective first. Balancing his private life with his career in law enforcement wasn't easy.

The cattle were young and he overestimated his return on investment the first two years, almost forcing him into bankruptcy. Evelyn, his wife of eleven years, couldn't handle the stress and left him. She came back three months later, but during that time he was suspended from duty for not filing the right paperwork on a drug dealing arrest. The dealer was thought to be part of the Free-Landers and was willing to trade testimony for lesser jail time. He got off because of Stanton's mistake. Wisely, the detective used the suspension time to get his affairs in order. He hired a financial consultant and a respected foreman to run the ranch and he proved to Evelyn he was serious about fixing his bad habits.

      Stanton sped up on I-10 on the west side of the city. The weather was cool, the sky was clear and the sun promised a beautiful day. Gene was becoming a prime suspect in Elliot's murder case. As he drove, he dialed Gene's home number again. After six rings he hung up and dialed Gene's cell; still no answer.

      That idiot, he thought. He knew I was going to call him. Where the hell is he?

      After several turns, he found Morningside. Unlike the rest of his trip, Stanton drove slowly, studying the unfamiliar street, looking for Gene's home and anything suspicious or out-of-place. Two pick-up trucks were in front of Gene's neighbor's house. An older Hispanic man wearing khaki pants and a V-neck T-shirt with tattoos on his arms, from gangs of long ago, played with two kids in the front yard. He caught Stanton's eye. The man knew a cop when he saw one. Both nodded to each other out of respect. Stanton blew a sigh of relief when he saw the Lexus in the driveway. A quick deduction told him that Lisa must have picked Gene up and Gene drove her home the night before. The detective parked behind it out of experience, making any attempted getaway impossible.

      He got out of his car, placed his cowboy hat on his head, walked to the front door, rang the doorbell, knocked hard and waited. Nothing. He pulled his gun out of his shoulder holster, held it with both hands low by his waist and stood with his back against the wall by the door.

"Gene?" he yelled. "Gene?"

Stanton looked in windows as he scooted down the stucco wall to each one. The Hispanic man watched with a stone-face.

A muffled clatter came from the back of the house. Crouching and running with his gun still drawn, Stanton went through an open gate at the side of the house. Pipe and cable-type fencing created a corral over a half-acre of land that surrounded the back of the house. He heard the familiar sounds of horses neighing and equipment being moved.

"Police," he yelled as he pointed his revolver.

Gene was standing next to his two Appaloosas that were tied to a hitching post ten yards away. He was adjusting leather straps on a bridle when Stanton spooked them.

Gene dropped the bridle and raised his hands.

"What are you doing, Gene?" Stanton said, still pointing the gun and walking toward Gene.

"I'm getting riding gear ready. What the hell are you doing?"

"Why haven't you answered your phone?" Stanton said "I've been calling your ass for the last two hours."

"I've been out here since six this morning," Gene said. "I didn't hear the phone ring. Put the damn gun down."

"Everything all right here?" said a third voice.

Stanton pointed his gun directly at the voice. It was Gene's neighbor. The gun in his face didn't make him flinch.

"My name is Ricardo Escobar. I saw you with the gun creeping around the home of my friend Gene and came to check it out. I wouldn't want to see my friend hurt, you know?"

Gene stood with his hands up at shoulder-height and Ricardo stared past the barrel of the gun straight into Stanton's eyes.

Stanton holstered his gun.

"Why is your gun drawn anyway?" Gene said. "You were worried about me, weren't you? Aww, how sweet."

"Kiss my ass, Gene."

"None of this concerns you," Stanton said to the neighbor.

Ricardo waved his hand at Stanton, "I see some guy carrying a gun and sneaking around my friend's home, damn if it's not my concern."

"Ricardo, it's okay," Gene said.

Ricardo said, "I knew you was a cop the second I laid eyes on you. You're all alike." He walked away, disappearing around the side of the house.

Gene asked, "What do you want, Detective?"

"I want you to tell me what you think you're doing."

"Getting my riding gear together."

"You're not thinking of leaving town are you?"

"That's exactly what I'm doing," Gene said. "I need to get out of here for a couple of days, so I'm going to my home in Ruidoso where I can get my head together."

"And I suppose you weren't going to let anyone know."

"Lisa knows where I'm going and Price will know when I call him. They both know how to get a hold of me if they need to."

"And what about me, Gene? Were you planning on including me on the list of privileged people that know where Gene is?"

"Am I a suspect?"

Stanton controlled his urge to grab Gene by the shoulders and shake the stupidity out of him.

"Well, you can bet your ass." Stanton said.

"I need a drink of water. Let's talk inside."

Inside, they walked into the kitchen where Stanton sat on a stool near the island. He evaluated his surroundings, surmising that Gene was indeed well off.

"What do you want to drink?" Gene said.

"Water's fine. You have a nice house."

"Gene handed Stanton a glass of iced water and sat on a stool across from him. "What do we need to talk about?"

"I'm going let you go to Ruidoso," Stanton wanted to re-establish any authority he may have lost earlier. "But I will have all of your phone numbers, the address and directions to get there. I also expect to talk to you once a day while you're gone. How long will you be gone?"

Gene looked relieved. "I'll be back Tuesday, before the funeral."

"Tell me everything you know about Joe Garcia." Stanton switched gears.

"Stanton, we've been through all of this."

"I need to know everything you can possibly tell me about him and his agency."

"Like I told you, Elliot and Joe were just business adversaries. Joe could never murder someone. He's a coward."

"I didn't say he's the murderer. Late yesterday, one of my guys ran a check on him. Except for two unpaid parking tickets that the chief of police wrote off, he's clean."

"I'm not surprised," Gene said. "He's a real ass-kisser, alright."

Stanton retrieved his electronic notepad, pulled the stylus out, and scrawled on the screen. "Joe's name did come up on some court documents. Over the past three years he was apparently a character witness on two separate occasions for two separate employees."

"What was their crime?"

"Drug dealing. Your name came up as a character witness for one of your employees for the same crime last year. And we know you're so clean, you squeak. Right? "

Stanton had waited all night and that morning to tell Gene what he knew about him.

"Tell me about Madeline. Why did you stand up for her?"

"It was a stupid charge. She was at a bar in the central part of town. She was drunk and smoking a joint when she walked up to an undercover cop and tried to sell the joint she was already smoking for twenty five bucks," Gene said. "She was just joking."

"Obviously the cop didn't think so. But why did you stand up for her?"

"She'd been with our agency in bookkeeping and was doing really well. The clients liked her and Elliot was mentoring her. I thought she needed the break."

"How close were Elliot and this Madeline?"

"They were co-workers, nothing more. Come on, Stanton. We're supposed to be talking about Joe. Right?"

Stanton rubbed his unshaven chin in thought. "Our guys picked up Elliot's office phone and hit redial. Joe's number flashed across the screen and the recording on the other end was for

Joe Garcia Advertising. According to the phone records, the call went out at 1:05 Saturday morning." Stanton drank more water and crunched ice. "That's why I need to know more about Elliot's relationship with Joe."

Gene said, "That doesn't make sense because he really hated Joe. He didn't want anything to do with him except to beat him when it came to getting new client."

Stanton poked around on his electric note pad searching for something. "Yesterday you told me that Joe seemed to know about all of your new business pitches, even the ones that were supposed to be confidential. How do you suppose he did that?"

Gene didn't respond.

"Gene, how do you suppose he does that?" the detective repeated.

"Believe me. If I knew that, we'd all live happier lives."

Stanton rubbed his chin again. "It seems you have a mole inside your own agency that's feeding the information to Joe."

"No one is privy to what we're working on. I guess friends inside the agency could pass along the information in casual conversation over a beer, but it's unlikely. We have an automatic termination rule if information is leaked. We keep our client information confidential much like a doctor or lawyer."

"Have you ever lost an employee or client to Joe's agency?"

75

"We've never lost an employee to Joe. We did lose a big client to him."

"When?" Stanton scrawled more notes.

"Stanton, do we have to do this now? I'd like to get on the road. How much more do you need to know?"

Stanton looked at his watch. It was 9:30. "I have to meet with Joe in thirty minutes, anyway. I'm just going to ask him about it?" He stood and swallowed the last of the water from his glass. "You mind if I use your restroom before I go? The water, you know?"

When Stanton reached the bathroom, he found the door closed and the sound of a blow-drier behind it. He turned the doorknob and pushed it open. Lisa was standing in front of the mirror, wearing only a man's shirt. Her eyes were shut as she stroked a brush through her hair. Stanton watched her for a few seconds. When her eyes opened, she screamed. He slammed the door.

Chapter Six

      Garcia Advertising was five miles east of Downtown El Paso in the twelve-story Reddington Building at the Hawkins Exit and Interstate 10. With thirty-five employees, that agency was much smaller than P & M and only occupied two-thirds of the seventh floor. Stanton arrived five minutes early.

      "Detective Stanton to see Joe Garcia," Stanton pointed to his shield clipped to his belt as he addressed the receptionist.

      She was a Hispanic girl that looked to be in her early twenties, dressed in tight stonewashed jeans and a red halter-top that she tugged in an effort to cover the tops of her large breasts. The halter didn't cover the weight that was hanging over the top of her jeans where the seams miraculously held together at the sides of her heavy thighs. She sported a stiff, brunette hairdo, red fingernails and shining glittered lipstick that opened wide revealing the piece of white gum, rolling over her tongue with every chew.

"I know who you are. He's on the phone,"
She picked up a fingernail file and went to work on
her nails as if Stanton had just disappeared.
"Would you mind letting him know I'm
here?" he said in an overly polite voice. "We have
an appointment at ten o'clock."
She rolled her eyes then got up and
disappeared down a long hallway.
Although the lobby was more contemporary
than Stanton's taste, it was apparent that no expense
had been spared. Other than three tabletop lamps,
track lighting was the only other source of
illumination, but it was sufficient enough to cast
large circles of light onto three oversized oil
paintings on the bright yellow wall behind the
receptionist's desk and the red wall in the guest
area. Four modern leather guest chairs were situated
around a large, glass coffee table. Crisp trade
publications and a book titled *Hispanic Americans
Making it in Media* were on top of the table.
    Stanton sat in one of the uncomfortable
chairs, picked up the book, and flipped through
pictures. He remembered Gene's words; 'we
suspected Joe was taking money under the table
from the media...'

    February, four years earlier, it had been
seventy-two degrees on the course and the air was
perfectly still. The sky was God blue. Only the
occasional vaporous cloud gave it any dimension.
    "Are you going to putt it or make love to
it?" radio station manager, Doug McDonald said to
Joe.

Joe was the business director for P & M and the account supervisor for River Rock Boots owned by Roy Whitaker and his daughter Marlene. With media billings of three million dollars a year, River Rock Boots was the agency's number one local media client and the largest advertiser in El Paso. Every media salesperson wanted a piece of the action.

Joe was tall with a clean look. He dressed like a PGA professional on the golf course and played almost as well. He struck the dimpled ball and they both watched it roll ten feet into the heart of the cup.

"Nice putt." Doug said as he'd done the previous eight holes.

Joe pulled the ball from the cup. They placed their clubs into their bags, sat in the golf cart, and lumbered down the cart path. Doug weighed three hundred pounds and made the cart lean to his side as they rounded the corner to the number ten tee box. The par-four hole was four hundred ninety-two yards away. Joe grabbed his driver and approached the tee box.

"You should manage your client's budgets as well as you play."

"What are you getting at, Doug?" Joe said.

"I don't think we're getting our fair share of the River Rock Boots account."

Joe repeated Doug's words in disbelief. "Not getting a fair share..." and then he hit another 300-yard drive down the middle of the fairway.

Doug sliced his drive 150 yards into the number nine fairway.

"I don't hear Marlene or Roy complaining about sales," Joe said.

"If you give us more money, I know we'll sell more boots than all of the local stations combined." Doug's fat face turned red when he was upset and Joe could see it changing colors.

"Hey, it wasn't that bad of a shot, Doug," Joe said, trying to shake Doug up even more.

They drove to Doug's ball where he used a four-iron to hit it another 155 yards, five yards in front of Joe's first shot. When they reached Joe's ball, he pulled an eight-iron from his bag and laid the ball four feet from the pin. After two more shots, Doug was finally on the green with a fifteen-foot putt still in front of him.

"Tell you what I'll do," Joe said. "If you make this putt, I'll see if we can feed you a little more money now and then. What do you say?"

Doug crouched and closed one eye to line up his putt. "I'll do better than that. Not only will I sink this putt, I'll pay you fifteen thousand dollars at the end of the year if you'll increase your budget with our station another ten percent."

"How the hell? Just putt the damn ball." Joe knew Doug was serious but considered how illegal and unethical it was to accept bribes.

Doug struggled to stand. "We pay finder's fees to lots of people. We cut them a check at end of the year based on the size of the account. It's the least we can do. They appreciate it and keep an eye out for more new business. It's legal and everyone wins," he said as he stood over his ball, brought the putter back and sank his putt. Joe stood quiet, staring at the hole.

"Do we have a deal?" Doug asked.

"Doug, you're crazy."

"Think about it. But first, quit standing there like you just lost your virginity and putt your ball," Doug said.

Joe had lost his concentration and three-putted the hole. "I'll see what I can do for you."

"Mr. Garcia will see you now," the receptionist said.

Stanton followed the receptionist down the long hallway, noticing more original paintings and commercial print advertisements. Next to each framed ad was a gold Addy award, the highest award offered in local advertising competition. Five small offices were along the hallway that lead to Joe's office. The door was open, and the receptionist stepped aside to allow Stanton to enter.

The office was large and bright. The light came through the exterior wall of windows from floor to ceiling. Heavy purple draperies were sash-tied at each end, capped by thick ballasts that ran across the top of the panes. A sixty-inch flat-screen television was mounted at the far end of the room, where a white leather sofa and a glass table were parallel in front of it. To either side of the table sat two more leather guest chairs. That end of the room was sterile, lacking any wall hangings. At the opposite end of Joe's office were his oversized glass desk, oak credenza and a wet-bar. The shelves and credenza were filled with family pictures, awards, plaques and sports memorabilia. It had the traditional look of any executive office. But the detective noticed something odd.

Joe was already halfway across the floor with his hand straight out as Stanton came through the doorway. "I'm Joe Garcia. Sorry to keep you waiting." It was Sunday and Joe was dressed in a light tan Armani suit, white cotton shirt, and blue tie. His hair was greased back and he his teeth were noticeably white. Stanton assumed they were capped. He smiled as he greeted Stanton.

"Let's sit over here," Joe said, directing Stanton to the sofa and chairs.

Stanton sat in a chair, Joe on the sofa.

"Where were you late Friday night and early Saturday morning?"

"Whoa. You get right to the point, don't you, detective?"

"Knowing you bill by the hour, you appreciate how valuable every minute is in a murder case. And you've already wasted over thirty minutes of my time."

Joe grinned, revealing his bright white teeth. "I apologize, detective. I was on the phone with a very important client. It couldn't be avoided."

"So it's true then?" Stanton took his electronic notepad from his pocket and poked the screen with the stylus.

"What's true?" Joe said.

"The fact that you hated Elliot Jones. So much so, that finding and bringing his killer to justice as soon as we can doesn't interest you. Am I right, Joe?"

Another grin, "Who's spreading rumors about old Joe?"

"Is it true or not?"

"Well, it's no secret, I guess. Elliot and I have had our differences. But I sure don't want a killer on the loose. Let's just say we were good competitors."

Stanton had dealt with Joe's kind before, cool, smooth talkers that thought they were invincible. To the detective, Joe was just a jerk who needed a dose of humility.

"I understand you use to work for P & M?"

"What a joke they are."

Stanton poked around on his notepad. "You were fired for taking bribes."

Joe's smile disappeared. "That's bullshit! You've been talking to Gene Martine. And you can tell that son-of-a-bitch I said he better stop the slanderous accusations or I'll slap him with a lawsuit."

"I didn't say I talked with Mr. Martine. Any problem you have with him, you can tell him yourself."

Joe tugged at his tie and sat back on the sofa.

"Let's talk about River Rock Boots," the detective said. "They're a client?"

"They are one of many, yes."

"How many clients do you have?" Stanton was trying to keep Joe's thoughts off balance.

Joe was grinning again and talking in a confident tone. "That's none of your business, detective, now is it?"

"Is River Rock Boots your largest client?"

"Again, that's none of your business, but everyone knows it's the largest local client of any El Paso agency."

"I understand you have an uncanny ability to be competitive in almost every new business pitch P & M makes," Stanton said.

"Just lucky, I guess." Joe smirked.

"How does your luck get you into competition on accounts that started off being private and uncontested for P & M?"

"I have a good research team. We all have our resources."

"Tell me how you got the River Rock Boots account," Stanton said. "I mean, isn't Marlene Whittaker Mr. Martine's ex-wife? She must have also thought you were taking bribes during that time. Out of all the agencies in town, why yours?"

"I don't see what any of this has to do with Mr. Jones."

"You tell me what I need to know and I'll make that decision."

"When I worked for P & M, I wasn't the bad guy. I was very well-liked by Price, Gene, employees and clients. Hell, I helped them make a lot of money. Isn't that what life's all about — money?" Stanton didn't answer. "Anyway, while I was the 'good guy'," signing quotations with his hands, "I built a good relationship with Roy Whittaker."

"Marlene's father? What do you mean by 'good relationship'?" The detective scrawled digital notes.

"We played golf, had lunch, took trips to Vegas," Joe said. "He was, and is, a good friend."

Stanton knew there was more to this story. Things weren't adding up.

"You took trips to Vegas? How often?"

"Maybe four or five times a year. We've been to California on business a few times too, but I still don't see the relevance to your case, detective."

"So, you and Mr. Whittaker were friends," Stanton said. "But doesn't Marlene own a large part of River Rock Boots and subsequently make management decisions like what advertising agency they use?"

Joe's smile twitched. He pursed his lips, stood up and walked to the wet bar by his desk. "Want a drink, detective?"

"Bourbon. Three rocks."

Joe dropped three large pieces of ice into two glasses and poured the bourbon. Stanton walked across the room and picked up the glass. Then he walked behind the desk to look at Joe's memorabilia.

"Sure is an impressive collection of autographs, Joe," Stanton said.

Joe stood on the opposite side of his desk and watched Stanton closely as the detective touched a Drew Pearson football, Pete Rose bat and a plastic case that held an autographed boxing glove signed by Cassius Clay. Stanton had noticed the case when he first came into the office. It was odd because it was dusty like the antique radios in Gene's office. Yet Joe's glass desk was freshly dusted. Stanton stepped back and looked the shelves up and down.

Joe said, "Yeah, I know. It's hard to find good help these days. Can't get the cleaning crew to do anything around here."

"You were about to tell me about Marlene?" Stanton responded.

"What I have to say is off the record, detective. Got that? I'm sure it has nothing to do with Elliot's murder because it was so long ago. However, I think you should know about Elliot's so-called friend."

"Let's hear it," Stanton said. He knew he was obligated to use the information.

"Off the record, detective?"

Stanton took a good sip of bourbon. "Off the record."

"There is another reason I picked up the River Rock Boots account. Let's sit back down," Joe said guiding Stanton to a seat. "Before I was fired from P & M, Marlene suspected Gene of having an affair because he spent so much time at the office and not enough at home taking care of business."

"With whom was he having this supposed affair?"

"She didn't know," Joe said. "The problem was that Gene thought I was the one that told Marlene of his infidelities."

"Did you?"

"I didn't know if he was or wasn't. I do know he was spending a lot of time with Elliot's wife, Lisa before Elliot was hired."

"Gene knew Lisa before Elliot was hired at P & M?"

"They were seen hugging and kissing at parties. Hell, stranger things have happened." Joe sipped his drink to help hide another one of his grins. "Anyway, it wasn't long after Marlene and Gene started having problems that I was accused of taking media bribes. The next thing I knew, I was fired and Elliot was hired."

Stanton said, "You think Gene was sleeping with Lisa. Gene thinks you ratted him out to Marlene. Gene fired you over trumped up accusations and hires Elliot because…?"

"Because he is Lisa's husband," Joe finished the sentence.

"That's why you hated Elliot so much?"

"Well, wouldn't you, detective, if your life got turned upside down because your boss couldn't keep his pecker in his pants?"

"And I suppose Marlene gave you the River Rock Boots account to get back at Gene."

Joe didn't respond.

"I don't believe a word you just said." Stanton said.

Joe's grin vanished. He finished his drink, leaned forward on the sofa and stared Stanton in the eyes. "You believe what you want to believe, detective. I don't know if Gene was having an affair, but I do know Garcia Advertising has handled the River Rock Boots account ever since."

Stanton's cell phone rang. He looked at the phone number on the display, but he didn't recognize it and hit a green button.

"This is Detective Stanton."

"Stanton? This is Gene." He was talking loudly over his truck and road noise.

"I'm standing here in Mr. Garcia's office and you wouldn't believe the great conversation we're having. Where are you?"

"Just south of Alamogordo. You told me to check in so I thought I'd do just that. What's the weasel have to say for himself?"

"Well, that would be between Joe and I wouldn't it?"

"Aw, still mad at me for what happened at my house? I told you, I thought she was still sleeping or I never would have sent you to that bathroom."

"Joke all you want. You're not off my shit list yet. In fact, you just moved a few notches higher," Stanton said. The detective became distracted, having a hard time forgetting Lisa standing in front of the mirror with only Gene's shirt on.

"What did Joe tell you detective? You can't trust him," Gene said.

"You just keep checking in. And make damn sure you go where you said you were going."

"Right." Gene ended the call.

"Was that Gene?" Joe grinned.

"No."

Stanton walked to the wet bar to put his glass in the sink. He turned toward the glass desk and something caught his eye. A small piece of white chalk, not much larger than a crumb, sat on the corner closest to him.

The detective pressed his left index finger on the chalk. "You still haven't answered my first question. Where were you late Friday night and early Saturday Morning?"

"I was home with my wife and three kids."

"Can they corroborate that?"

"Would you like me to call them for you?"

"If you say you were there, then I should believe you were there. Right?"

Stanton showed himself out, noticing the receptionist had already left. Once outside, he inspected the white substance on his index finger that was now just fine powder. As soon as his finger touched his tongue he knew it was cocaine. He walked back into the office where Joe was on the phone. Joe hung up without saying good-bye.

"What more can I do for you, detective?"
Joe stood and grinned.

Stanton tossed a small evidence bag on the glass. "Have you ever seen one of these or any of its markings before?"

Joe opened the bag and the medallion hit his desk, making the distinctive silver jingle. He picked it up and inspected both sides closely staring at the side with the flags the longest. "I've never seen a coin like this before. Where did you get it?"

"Why do you ask?"

"I recognize the logo of the fading country flags," Joe said.

"Logo?" Stanton retrieved his notepad.

"Didn't Gene tell you? He designed it about twenty years ago. It was the first logo he designed for River Rock Boots. They haven't used it in years. Where did you get it?"

"A friend gave it to me. Thanks for your help," Stanton said as he took the medallion and left.

The director of the funeral home was a short frumpy looking man wearing a black suit. He had a beer-belly that made his tie point to 6:30 like hands on a clock. "Do you have any questions, Mrs. Jones?" he asked.

"She's still deciding," Marlene said.

Lisa knew she couldn't make all the arrangements alone. She had asked Elliot's mother to help but when she called, his mother was still distraught and declined. With Gene gone, Marlene was the next best choice. She let Marlene think she was her first call.

"I see you're looking at the Dynasty Collection," the director said. "It is one of our finest designs."

The solid oak box was handcrafted with pearl handles. Detailed carvings of mountains and pine trees were along the sides.

"Do you have a budget in mind?" he asked.

"I want something nice."

"Not to offend you, but these are expensive."

Lisa was dressed in a cotton-jogging suit. She had her hair pulled back in a ponytail and wore no make-up.

"Maybe you'd like to look at something over here?" He gestured toward the middle of the room.

"Well, she does take offense, you insulting little man," Marlene said as she stepped between the director and Lisa.

"I'm sorry," the director said. "I was only... I mean it's just that..."

"For your information, Mrs. Jones can buy and sell you," Marlene said.

"It's okay," Lisa interrupted. "I'll take this one." She left the room. Her cell phone rang in her purse. She dug for it, pulled it out, saw Elliot's name remembering she gave it to Gene, on the display and sighed a relief as she answered. "Oh, thank God it's you. Where are you?"

"I'm passing through Alamogordo," Gene said. "Where are you?"

"I'm at the funeral home with Marlene," Lisa said. "I sure wish you were here to help me. Why are you still using Elliot's phone?"

"I guess I just wanted to have a piece of him with me." Gene actually had his own cell phone, too, but both were identical VoiceComm phones.

"I just needed to get away from there. Do you understand?"

"This is so hard for me, and Marlene's not much for compassion."

"Tell me about it. I was married to the woman, remember?"

Lisa smiled at his comment.

"I talked to Stanton and I kept my promise. Anyway he was at Joe Garcia's office."

"Was he okay with what happened at your house?" Lisa asked, remembering her bathroom scream.

"Yes, I just think we caught him by surprise. He may have had a hard time believing us."

"What did Joe tell him?"

"Stanton wouldn't tell me, but whatever it was moved me up on the list of suspects."

"You?"

"I don't know what he could have said, but I'll find out."

"How? When you're in Ruidoso?"

"I'll call Joe tomorrow," Gene said.

"Lisa, the director needs to talk to you," Marlene said from the casket room doorway.

"Gene, I have to go. Will you call me later?"

"I'll call after I get to the house. Keep your spirits up, Lisa. You need to stay strong right now."

"I will." She ended the call.

At 12:30 in the afternoon, Stanton was sitting at his desk downloading his notes from his electronic notepad to his computer and eating a cold roast-beef sandwich. He knew Joe did cocaine and he couldn't get it out of his head. He also had to digest that Gene may be having an affair with Lisa. The dynamics of the case were taking shape but Stanton was far from making any conclusions.

"Stanton, you need to see this."

Homicide Detective Manny Ortega was Stanton's friend. Although Manny was six years younger than Stanton, they had risen through the ranks together, starting from their police academy days and were promoted to each level in their careers almost simultaneously. It surprised Stanton that Manny was there on a Sunday afternoon. He was unaware of any other cases that would require work on Sunday.

Stanton asked, "What's got you here today?"

"Some old guy got capped last night." Manny sat on the corner of Stanton's metal desk.

"You need my help on it already don't you, rookie?" Stanton laughed.

"It's me who's always helping you, old man." Manny said. "In fact, that's why you need to see what I'm working on." Manny placed a file on Stanton's desk.

Stanton took another bite of his sandwich, put it down on his desk, dusted his hands and spoke with his mouth full. "What do we have?"

"Take a look at these pictures." Manny pulled out six eight-by-ten glossy pictures of an old man lying in an alley. The first two pictures were taken several yards away from the body to establish its location. The next two were taken closer. The broken body of the man filled the print. The last two

92

were close-ups of the man's crushed skull. The face was broken, bruised and covered with blood.

"They look like any other homicide pictures," Stanton said. "What's the problem?"

"Look at them closer, Stanton. Especially these two," Manny said touching the two close-up pictures.

Stanton studied the victim's face. "Oh, no."

"It's Roger Thatcher, the..."

"The security guard at P & M," Stanton finished the thought.

"Who found him?"

"His wife. She said he went for a walk and didn't come back, so she went looking for him in their car. When she couldn't find him on the streets, she took the alley."

"I suppose there aren't any witnesses."

"None that we can find, but the uniforms are still canvassing. It was about 10:00 in the evening when we got the call. He left their home at about 8:30"

"That poor woman," Stanton said. "Cause of death was the crushed skull? Blunt force."

"It appears that way. The murder weapon was a shovel. We found it about three feet from the body. The geeks at the morgue are doing an autopsy, but I can already tell you the murderer broke Thatcher's arm and ribs before killing him. What does that tell you?"

"Somebody wanted something from him."

"His wallet was on him and still had twenty-five dollars in it."

"I'll bet it has everything to do with my case," Stanton said as he stood and stretched his long arms over his head. "Maybe the killer thought he saw Elliot get killed and tied up the loose ends."

"But doesn't your report say he didn't know Elliot Jones had left and didn't see anything because he wasn't at the desk?" Manny said.

"That's what has me puzzled. Unless..." Stanton reached into his pocket and handed Manny the evidence bag.

Manny said as he emptied the medallion into his hand and recognized it, "You think the old man was killed over this?"

"I don't know, but doesn't it make sense. The killer knows he dropped it at the murder scene."

"You think the killer thought the old man picked up the medallion and kept it? Sounds like a stretch. I could believe the killer wanted the medallion. But kill an old man just for information?"

Other than several people milling about the back, Stanton and Manny were the only two detectives at the station when the door to the street opened. A poor-looking Hispanic kid, not more than twelve years old, walked in carrying a large manila envelope.

"Que pasa, niño?" Manny asked.

"Are you Señor Stanton?" The kid spoke broken English.

"I am," Stanton said.

The kid walked to him and handed the detective the envelope.

"A man pay me and say to take this to you," the kid said.

"What man?" Manny asked.

The kid turned and ran.

Stanton sliced open the envelope with a pair of scissors. He shook it until he could grasp its contents with the tips of his fingers because wanted to make sure he didn't contaminate possible evidence. He looked at three eight-by-ten photographs. Then he handed Manny the pictures.

"Who are they?" Manny studied the pictures which showed Gene's car, a duffle bag and his house in the background. In the foreground of the first one were Gene and Lisa standing close together. The second and third pictures showed Gene kissing Lisa's cheek.

Chapter Seven

Stanton filled Manny in on Gene, Lisa, Joe and a half a dozen other people connected to Elliot's life and possibly his death.

"So, it is possible these two are having an affair?" Manny asked.

"Somebody sure wants us to think so. It would give them a motive to kill Elliot." Stanton took the last bite of his sandwich. "Neither Gene nor Lisa have someone who can prove their whereabouts at the time of the murder."

"These pictures are enough evidence to bring them both in for more questioning. Are you going to?"

Stanton paced from desk to desk thinking then said, "If Gene and Lisa had something to do with Elliot's death then you've got to rule out the medallion. Now, we got fingerprints off of it, but we won't know to whom they belong until tomorrow. I just don't believe it's a coincidence that some Free-Lander dropped one of these things in the drain next to the victim on the same night Elliot was killed."

"How do you know that thing wasn't there for days?" Manny asked.

"That's just it. I do know, for two reasons. First, Elliot tried to scratch the word on the sidewalk. Second, the snowfall."

"I don't get it."

Stanton pulled out a file from under a small pile of paperwork, opened it and pulled out several pictures of the murder scene. "There it is. The medallion and it proves my theory."

Manny studied the picture. "It's just a picture of the medallion and a bunch of trash at the bottom of the drain where you found it."

Stanton pointed to the picture. "The medallion was situated at the high end of the drain on top of these twigs and cigarette butts. The bottom of the drain slopes downhill with the street in a way that the water run-off doesn't touch the upper third of the drain's slope. That upper third was dry except for the snow that fell through the drain grate. Yet, there is nothing on the medallion. It's sitting there like it was dropped on top of the snow."

"Why do you suppose the snow in the drain hadn't melted yet?" Manny said.

"I guess it's just colder below the street because the sun doesn't get to it."

"So, if the medallion had been there before the snowfall it would have been covered with snow. You're right. It couldn't have been there very long. What about Gene and Lisa? If they were having an affair and wanted to get rid of him, what better person to pay off than a Free-Lander?"

"I guess that's possible, but I don't think so. I've got another interview. I think my case is connected to your Roger Thatcher case. We'll talk about it later." Stanton put on his coat and hat, grabbed his pile of paperwork and left the office.

Just outside of Ruidoso a light snow fell over Gene's truck. At 1:30 in the afternoon the temperature had reached its high for the day of twenty-nine degrees. The road was wet and he knew there would be patches of ice. He wasn't a stranger to the road conditions and drove forty-five miles an hour. No other vehicles had been on the road for the last ten miles.

Something was in the rearview mirror. It was an older black and it was catching up fast. It wasn't dark outside but the front headlights were on as were the four larger spotlights on top of the truck. It didn't take long before the truck was tailgating Gene's horse trailer.

"Idiots," Gene muttered. "Stupid kids."

But the truck's lights flashed on and off. Gene became concerned for his horses. The trailer must have a flat or maybe one of the doors had come open. Worse yet, maybe the hitch was coming undone between the trailer and truck. He tapped his brakes several times bringing the rig slowly to the shoulder of the road without stopping. The black truck raced up to the driver side. Two large dirt bikes were tied down in the bed and the windows were tinted dark. The passenger window rolled down so Gene did the same. There were two Hispanic men wearing T-shirts and jean vests. The passenger was wearing a blue bandana on his head. The man's right arm was covered in tattoos.

"What's wrong?" Gene asked.

"Nothing man. What's wrong with you?" The man replied in broken English then smiled revealing rotting teeth.

"Why did you pull me over?

"We didn't pull you over, Man. What's yo problem, Vato?" He said then took a drink from a paper bag and handed it to the driver.

Gene realized the guys were just drunk jerks. He wanted them to take off and let him back on the highway, but they wouldn't move on.

"Let me back on the road."

"Hey, Vato, you should go back home before you get hurt."

"Kiss my ass!" Gene said.

The two men laughed and sped away, letting Gene return to the road and back to forty-five miles an hour. Gene tried to keep his distance but eventually caught up with them. The passenger of the truck climbed up and out of the window and threw the paper bag and the rest of its contents. The bag hit Gene's hood and sprayed whiskey over his hood and windshield.

Furious, Gene slowed his rig while the black Chevy raced out of sight. He safely pulled over, got out and inspected the scratches on his hood.

"Unbelievable!" he yelled and kicked the front tire. "Just once I wish…" he finished his sentence in own mind, cursing them and imagining beating them up as he climbed back into the truck.

Gene drove thirty-five and had been somewhat successful clearing his mind after assessing the damage and cussing for several minutes. Thoughts of sitting in front of a roaring fire while hand-working some saddle leather in his mountain home and concentrating on the icy road kept his mind busy. Then his cell-phone rang. He fumbled with both cell phones, looked at the display of his. The number was from P & M.

"This is Gene."

"Gene. Price here. Where you at, son? How's the weather in Ruidoso?"

"It's cold and snowing." Gene was somewhat distracted.

"Have you made it to the house?"

"The roads are kind of icy. I'm just on the outskirts of town. Why?"

"You haven't heard yet?"

"What's wrong now?" Gene knew Price wouldn't be calling him if it weren't important.

"Well, I wasn't sure I'd reach you on your cell so disregard the messages I left at your house," Price said. "I just got a call from Pinkerton Security and they've got a problem with one of the guards that was on duty when Elliot was killed.

"Roger Thatcher? What's wrong with him?"

"He was killed last night. Murdered."

"What the hell?"

"Did you know him well, Gene?"

"We've talked a few times when I had to work late. Elliot knew him better. Do they have any suspects in custody?"

"No, but they're certain it's connected to Elliot's murder."

"What is going on, Price? Who's doing all of this?" Gene asked not expecting Price to respond. He thought about calling Stanton, breaking his promise to Lisa.

"I don't know what Elliot got himself into. This is all happening way too close to home. You should take some time off and stay in Ruidoso for a while, at least till all this blows over."

"Elliot's funeral is Tuesday. I'll be back then."

"Didn't you read the front page of the paper this morning? You didn't come off sounding too good. The pictures they used are the worst I've ever seen of you. You need some time off."

"What do you mean, I didn't 'come off sounding good?'"

"You know newspapers," Price said. "They write what you tell them, but they don't write it the way you tell it. Listen, Son, when you get to Ruidoso, pick up the Times and read it for yourself. Then consider what I said. Take some time off. At least a week, Gene."

"Fine. I'll read it."

"And guess who else called me this morning? The CEO of VoiceComm."

"Julio Rivera called you on a Sunday morning? Why?"

"Well, apparently one of his district managers is here in El Paso. They told him about Elliot. At first he was very sympathetic. But then he told me about some reports Elliot screwed up. I understand you were involved?"

"Hell, Price, it was just the brand awareness reports."

Price's voice grew louder. "Gene, what's wrong with you? Those reports are important to their shareholders and you know it."

"That's why I took care of it personally with Julio himself. We'll talk about it next week."

"You can bet we'll talk about it."

Gene had listened long enough. "I can't hear you. What was that?" Gene ended the call.

Just one month before the VoiceComm pitch, Madeline Rodriguez had been hired in the bookkeeping department. In her interview with Price and Gene she said she wanted to be an account executive, where she could make a decent salary.

Price studied her résumé, "It says here you graduated from San Diego State University with a B.A. in marketing and minor in accounting." Price moved his eyes from the paper he was holding to Madeline and back to the paper. "Were you raised in San Diego?"

"I was raised by my dad in San Francisco."

She crossed her legs. At twenty-four years old, Madeline was about five foot five with a firm curving figure that was accented by her short black skirt, tailored jacket and red silk blouse. Price made several efforts during the interview from his side of the desk to see her long legs.

Price said, "You haven't been out of school very long, but I see here you have some experience selling television time for an independently owned station. Were you any good at it?"

"Well, I never lost any clients. I serviced them all very well."

Gene was noticeably irritated by the tone of her sultry voice.

"Ms. Rodriguez, Gene said.

"Oh, call me Maddy," she said, now turning so that Gene could see her shapely calves and thighs that were almost completely uncovered. Her short skirt had worked its way up even higher as she forced her hips to the edge of her seat.

"Ms. Rodriguez." Gene began again. "We don't have any positions open in account service right now."

"Are you sure, Gene? Just the other day we were talking about adding..." Price said.

"I'm sure, Price." Gene interrupted. "We have too many people on that account as it is."

Madeline lowered her chin and bit her lower lip.

"Madeline?" Price said.

"Maddy."

"Would you be willing to take an entry-level position? It won't pay as much as what you're looking for. But when a position opens in account service, you'll be the first person I'll consider for the job."

"I was really looking for something that pays me what I'm worth," Madeline said as she tilted her head like a Barbie doll and fluttered her eyelashes at Price.

Price leaned back in his chair, cleared his throat and crossed his arms confidently realizing the pretty Madeline Rodriguez was about to come on board.

"How about bookkeeping? Your résumé says you have a minor in accounting."

To her credit, Madeline worked hard on the VoiceComm account planning. She proved to be a real asset during the actual pitch when Price, Gene, and Elliot were visibly caught off-guard at the end of the presentation. In front of six VoiceComm executives including CEO, Julio Rivera, Price had just finished his closing statements and asked for the business.

"Mr. Price, I believe I speak for all of us when I say that your team has put together a very fine presentation," Julio said. "You demonstrated your understanding of our business, developed a sound marketing plan and presented us with some of the best creativity we've seen yet."

Price said, "Shall I have our attorneys draw up the contracts for you?"

"Well, I've promised another El Paso agency that we would drop by their office before we made our final decision."

You could hear stomachs churning bile from the A-team. Price knew Joe found a back door, again.

"We understand," Price said. "Who?"

"Joe Garcia," Julio said as he and the other five executives put on their suit coats, and began packing briefcases.

Price could feel the blood coursing through his veins, but kept his composure.

"Your agency has done a fine job, Price, but we need to make sure we've done due diligence for our corporation."

"Mr. Rivera." Madeline stood. "May I have a word with you?"

"What are you doing, Madeline?" Price glared at her. "I'll handle this. Please sit down."

"What's on your mind, young lady?" Julio asked.

"Well, it seems to me that you have already done due diligence for your corporation by looking at only the best agencies." Madeline walked toward Mr. Rivera. "You just said we demonstrated our ability to handle your account." She placed her hand on his lapel and seductively traced his tie with her finger.

"I'm listening."

She leaned into Mr. Rivera's ear and whispered so that no one could hear, then turned, and walked back to her seat as the whole room watched in anticipation.

"Price," Julio said holding his hand out for Price to shake.

Price was dumbfounded.

"Price, as I said, we haven't made up our mind. We'll let you know soon." Julio and the other executives shook hands with Price, Gene, Elliot, and the rest of the A–team and left.

The A-team sat around the conference table without saying a word. All eyes were on Price, as if waiting for him to take Madeline apart.

"Everyone, please leave," Price said.

Everyone except Gene began gathering notes, briefcases and storyboards. Elliot stormed out of the room.

"Leave it. Get the hell out of here." Gene blew up. "Madeline? Where the hell do you think you're going? Sit down."

The room was empty in seconds.

"I don't know what's wrong..." Madeline started. "I mean, we're getting the account." Madeline said as she leaned back in her chair and crossed her feet at the ankles.

Price said, "You just pissed away eighty-five million dollars in billing for this agency. You're lucky if I don't kick your ass out of my agency and making sure you never work at anything higher than flipping burgers."

Gene said, "Madeline, you better start explaining yourself. What was that all about?"

"You put me on the A-team to do research."

"You're not on the A-team. You're not qualified and you definitely proved that today," Price said.

"Well, you may not think I'm qualified, but you'll see. I won that account."

"You mean blew it. What did you tell Mr. Rivera, anyway?" Price said.

"Let's just say I did more research than the request for proposal required."

The receptionist opened the door. "Mr. Rivera is on the phone for Mr. Price."

"Put it in here on the speaker phone," Price looked at Madeline then Gene. "Here we go. The big kiss-off, thanks to her. Don't say a word, Madeline. You hear me?"

Price let the phone ring twice before pushing the speaker button.

"Hi, Mr. Rivera. This is Price and I have Gene with me on the speakerphone. Is that okay?"

"I'm calling you from the car. We're on our way to the airport. I just wanted to let you know we're giving you our business," Julio said. Silence followed. "Hello? You there?"

"Yes. I mean, thank you. I mean..." Price was lost for words.

Gene asked "What about Joe Garcia?"

"We thought about it on our way over to his office. That young lady you got there has a good head on her shoulders. You are the best agency for the job. I'll have our legal department get in touch with yours."

"Thank you again," Price said. "We're looking forward to the relationship."

"Great. We'll be in touch," Julio said, and hung up.

Madeline smiled as she gathered her papers and left the room.

Stanton rolled his eyes as he spoke on the phone. He wouldn't dare do so in front of his wife. "I don't see any reason why I won't be home early tonight to help." Stanton's wife was planning a reunion. "But right now I am in the middle of the Jones case."

The only sound in the car was his air-conditioning as she spoke on the other end of the phone.

"I'll only put in a half-day tomorrow. I'll come home, cook a big barbeque, and sit around the rest of the evening, drinking beer and playing dominos with your brother and sister." Stanton's big moustache raised and he grinned. "I'm not being sarcastic. I promise. I'll be there. Okay. I love you."

He hated family reunions. He was always volunteered to do the cooking. Sometimes he wished he owned a flower shop instead of a beef ranch.

He exited onto Hawkins Ave. and turned right. After several blocks, he reached River Rock Street and turned left. It was a short dirt and gravel road that led to the sprawling two-hundred-thousand-plus square-foot River Rock Boots warehouse that was cut into the desert landscape.

It was Sunday, but old cars and trucks belonging mostly to illegal Mexican workers filled twenty to thirty spaces. In the space closest to the entrance of the building was a new, red top-of-the-line Mercedes. Stanton parked in the next space reserved for Mr. Whitaker. As he stepped out of his car, dust was still swirling around from his drive in. He replaced his leather jacket with a tweed sports coat. The gravel under his boots popped and crackled as he walked to the entrance, opened the door, and walked in.

The floor of the reception area was unkempt cement with chips and holes. There were two metal folding chairs and two old wooden chairs for guests. The wooden coffee table was held over from the seventies. Cigarette burns dotted the dark wood finish. Nothing decorated the paneled walls except spider webs stretching from the ceiling to the corners. It was hard to believe this was a company that was worth tens of millions of dollars.

"Welcome to River Rock Boots, Sugar." Marlene said as she came through a doorless threshold.

"Marlene Martine, I presume?" Stanton smiled, tipped his hat and shook her hand. Stanton was never short of a little Southern hospitality.

"You're Detective Stanton?"

"Yes, Ma'am."

Stanton smelled cigarette smoke. "Quite a place you have here."

"It's not the Taj Mahal, but it pays the bills," she said.

"Is there someplace we can talk?"

"Follow me."

Marlene looked good for her age, aside from the little extra weight she carried on her thighs and hips. She was wearing tight faded boot cut jeans and a blue polo shirt that sported the River Rock Boots

logo above her left breast. Her snakeskin River
Rock Boots were new, with three-inch heels and cut
sharp at the toes. When she walked, her thighs
rubbed together, making a soft sweeping sound with
every step.

She led Stanton down a hallway that was
also cement and paneling. At the end of the hallway
to the right was the entrance into the warehouse.
Large clear plastic strips covered the doorway that
she and Stanton pushed aside and walked through.
Hot air hit his face.

"Sorry about the heat," Madeline said. "The
swamp coolers are either disconnected or just not
working. I'm not sure which."

They walked through the warehouse that
was busy with workers driving forklifts up and
down aisles of twenty-foot racks filled with
hundreds of boxes. Each box contained a pair of
River Rock boots. Three semi-trucks were backed
up to loading docks on the south side of the
building. Each one was busy with the activity of
either loading or unloading the boxes.

"Is this place always this busy?" Stanton
asked.

"Sugar, this ain't busy," Madeline said.
"These guys are just getting ready for the week
ahead of them."

They had reached a wooden staircase.
Marlene raced up to the top as if she had done
hundreds of times before. The wooden planks
creaked and squeaked as Stanton kept up with her
pace. At the top were three offices that looked in the
same poor shape as the reception area, except the
floors were wooden and the inner walls had glass
windows that overlooked the warehouse. Marlene

led the detective into the first office, which was decorated with an old green vinyl sofa, two wooden chairs, a metal desk and grey metal shelves.

"Have a seat, Sugar," Marlene said as she sat behind the desk in an old roller chair, opened a drawer and pulled out a pack of cigarettes.

"Isn't it against the law to smoke in a place of business in El Paso?" Stanton said as he took his seat in one of the wooden chairs closest to the window that looked into the warehouse.

"You going to arrest me if I do?"

"You ought to be able to make that call, not the politicians." The detective was seasoned at dealing with women. He felt the more apathetic you were to their sense of being in charge, the more comfortable they felt talking to you. In most cases, women would eventually tell Stanton more than he cared to know.

Marlene stuck the butt of the cigarette in the corner of her moist lipstick lips, grabbed a lighter from the top of the desk and lit the end. Her lips pursed, dragging clean air through the burning tobacco. After a single long puff she sat back in the chair, crossed her left arm over her stomach, rested her right elbow on the arm of the chair and pulled the cigarette away from her mouth.

"Detective, you called this meeting. I assume you want to know what I know about Elliot Jones." Smoke floated from her mouth and curled slowly from her nostrils.

The detective retrieved his electronic notepad from his sport coat.

"I'm interested in your relationship with Mr. Martine."

"Gene? Our marriage? Why in Sam Hill would you want to know about us?" Marlene said. "What does that have to do with Elliot's murder?"

"Well, Ms. Martine..."

"Call me Marlene."

"We need to establish Gene's credibility."

"What does Gene have to do with any of this?"

"It's my understanding that Gene and Elliot were friends even outside of the workplace," the detective said.

"Friends? Hun, they were more than friends. They were like brothers. Everyone who knows them knows that."

"Were you close to the Joneses when you were married to Gene?"

"Gene and I had been married several years before Elliot went to work for P & M. It wasn't too long afterward that I met Elliot and Lisa at a client party." Marlene took another drag of the cigarette. "Lisa and I hit it off just grand."

"Did you get along with Elliot?"

"Elliot was a great guy."

"Tell me why you and Gene got divorced," the detective said.

Up to that point, Marlene had remained poker-faced. Then her eyebrows, which were painted on, furled and her eyelids narrowed. Her twisted skin revealed deep wrinkles in her forehead and crow's feet at the corners of her eyes. She sat up in her chair, leaned forwarded, took one last long hit of the cigarette and smashed it in an old beanbag ashtray sitting on the desk.

"Detective, I want to make something clear to you before we continue. My marriage to Gene and subsequent divorce are none of your damn business. Nor is any other relationship I may have had before or after Gene. You're here to figure out what happened to Elliot, not to discuss my love life. If you approach my personal life with your questions again, I will not only ask you to leave my office, I will physically throw your ass out of here myself. Do we understand each other?"

Stanton was caught off-guard by Marlene's reaction and as he struggled to keep from laughing out loud, he could only think of one response.

"Yes, Ma'am."

Marlene's face relaxed as she sat back in her chair. Stanton was amazed as the wrinkles in her face disappeared without a trace. The detective needed to regain his composure and control of the conversation. He cleared his throat, stood from the chair and faced the window overlooking the warehouse and all of the activity down below.

"Tell me, Marlene, what percent of your boots are made in Mexico?"

"With today's labor costs, we really can't afford to make boots in the States. Almost one hundred percent are assembled across the border."

"I like some of your advertisements, at least what I've seen."

"The damn stuff costs enough."

"Is it really that expensive?" The detective was slowly getting back to the topic of Gene. However, this time he would approach Marlene differently.

"Honey, try two words: 'mucho dinero'."

Stanton was relieved that she was back to calling him 'Honey'.

"I once saw the police department's advertising budget. It was thirty-five thousand. I couldn't believe it." Stanton just knew that would get him a 'Sugar' and hoped it would get her to tell him what her budget was.

"Thirty-five thousand? Sugar, that ain't enough to pay our agency's receptionist." Marlene lit another cigarette.

Got the 'Sugar,' he thought. "You're kidding?" He smiled as he turned to face Marlene. "Do you mind if I ask what your advertising budget is?"

She took a hit of nicotine and thought about the question without looking at him.

"About ten million," she said.

"Wow."

"Uh huh. Can we talk about the case, please?"

"Sure. Tell me about Joe Garcia and his relationship with Elliot."

"Here you go again, Detective. What does Joe have to do with Elliot?"

"The same as Gene, we need to establish Joe's credibility. He does handle your advertising account, doesn't he?" Stanton watched the workers through the glass.

"He is our agency of record. So?"

"You and I both know why Gene hates Joe."

"We do?"

"Come on, Marlene. You took your ten-million-dollar account from your ex-husband and handed it to the person he most despised. And since we can't talk about your love life, I can only assume you did it out of pure spite toward Gene. Hell, I'm surprised he still talks to you."

"That's not fair, Detective. The decision to hire Joe Garcia Advertising was a good business decision. It just happened at the same time as our divorce. Yes, I know how much I hurt Gene, but he doesn't understand what was going on here at the time." Marlene's hand was quivering as she puffed away.

"What was going on here that made you change agencies if it wasn't to get back at Gene?"

Marlene smoked and took some time before answering. "Detective, our business affairs are not for public record. I shouldn't have told you what our advertising budget is. Our decision was for the good of the company."

"Okay. Fair enough." It wasn't fair, though. As a man, Stanton found himself feeling for Gene and thought he should know the truth. But the detective knew it was none of his business and moved on.

"Marlene, do you trust Joe Garcia?"

"Of course we do."

"I'm not asking your board of directors. Do *you* trust Joe?"

"We wouldn't have given him our business if I didn't trust him."

"Joe told me that he's seen Gene and Lisa alone at different events. Is there or has there ever been anything more than friendship between Gene and Lisa?" He fully expected Marlene to wrinkle her pretty face and chase him out of the building, while yelling obscenities.

Instead, she calmly put out her second cigarette, leaned to her right and plucked a bottle of water from a small ice chest. "I never wanted to believe that Gene would ever cheat on me during our marriage. Much less, I would have never believed he would sleep with his best friend's wife."

Marlene cracked the seal on the bottle of water. Stanton watched as she wrapped her full lips around the opening and watched the condensation from the bottle drip down her left collarbone toward her cleavage. His mouth was now dryer than ever.

She continued, "But, toward the end of our marriage, Gene was working later and later. Sometimes he never came home. Our sex life was nonexistent."

"I thought we were prohibited from talking about your relationships," the detective said.

"Honey, it's not polite to interrupt."

"Yes, Ma'am. Please continue."

"Gene and I fought like cats and dogs for a long time. He claimed to be building an advertising empire. I said screw your empire. I want you home. I want sex. Heck, I'm an attractive woman now. You should have seen me then. And we were good in bed."

T. M. I., Stanton thought. Too much information.

"Anyway, I knew there were times that Gene and Lisa went to business functions alone. But I really never thought anything of them. I trusted Gene and I really trusted Lisa.

"You think there is, or was, something more than friendship between them?"

"They are the only two people that can tell you that."

Stanton scribbled notes into his computer.

"Marlene, is there anything else you think I should know that might help me solve Elliot's murder?"

"No, Detective. And please, Sugar, everything we said here stays here. Lisa and I are still good friends. Gene and I have buried the axe a long time ago and I'd like to keep it that way. Okay?"

"It only becomes an issue if what you've said becomes important to the case. Otherwise, I will keep it confidential."

"One more thing." He pulled out the plastic bag holding the medallion. "Have you ever seen one of these?"

Marlene took the bag and gestured as if asking to empty its contents. She dropped the medallion onto the desk and Stanton heard the familiar sound of pure silver. She picked it up and studied the bull's head and marijuana leaf on one side for several seconds.

"Flip it over," the detective said.

Marlene turned the medallion over revealing the American flag fading into a Mexican flag. Her eyes squinted and the crow's feet appeared. "Where did you find this?"

"You recognize it?" Stanton knew the next few words.

"This is an old logo of ours," she said. "This flag design. I've never seen this medallion, but that sure is our logo. In fact, Gene designed it for us years ago."

"Do you know anyone, including Gene, Elliot, Joe, or anyone else that uses or sells cocaine?"

"Detective, I'm a self-respecting woman. I would never associate myself with someone that was involved with any kind of drugs."

"So your answer is no?"

"My answer is no."

Chapter Eight

Gene arrived to Ruidoso hungry. His mountain home was only nine miles away, but he knew his supply of food consisted of canned soup, crackers and an assortment of prepackaged, stale cookies. He wanted to eat a hot meal and shop for riding supplies. He also wanted to get an El Paso Times newspaper and read the story. He drove North on Highway 54 until he reached the first set of stoplights, drove through and stopped at the local Denny's, where he'd eaten many times before.

He needed to let his horses stretch before going inside. He parked his rig at the North edge of the parking lot and backed both horses out of the trailer. After leading them several laps around an empty lot adjacent to the restaurant, he tied the horses to the trailer and went inside.

He sat in a booth with a window where he could keep an eye on the horses.

"Hi, Gene," a waitress said as she approached. She put a hand on his shoulder and said, "I'm so sorry about Elliot."

"You heard?"

"It's in the papers and it's all most of us can talk about. He was always so sweet."

"Sally, I've been so busy that I haven't read the story. Do you have a copy of the paper?"

"Sure. What else can I get you? Hungry?"

"Let me have an American Omelet with bacon, wheat toast, orange juice and coffee."

"It'll be right out."

Sally returned with a newspaper that had been read and put back together out of order. Gene thanked her and began organizing the pages. There it was on the front page. LOCAL ADMAN MURDERED. The main photo was taken at the murder scene with yellow crime scene tape in the foreground and Gene standing with Stanton's hand on his shoulder in the background. As he stared at the photo, his stomach knotted and the blood left his face.

In the photo, Gene was looking at the exact spot where Elliot's body was discovered. Stanton's badge prominently displayed on his hip and Gene's disheveled look in the picture made Gene look like he was the primary suspect about to be arrested.

He read the story that peppered quotes from Price, Gene, Lisa, Stanton, and to Gene's shock and dismay, Joe Garcia.

"What the hell?" Gene mumbled aloud.

"Here's your omelet." Sally said. "What's wrong, Gene?"

He folded the paper and put it next to his leg on the seat. "I just can't believe they used such a horrible picture of me."

As Sally placed a coffee cup on Gene's table and poured the hot brew, Gene glanced around. He noticed some of the wait staff suddenly looking away as others continued to stare at him.

"Is there anything else I can get you, Gene?"

"I have everything. Thanks."

Instead of eating, he picked up the paper and found his place.

"Elliot was a good friend and competitor," Joe said. "He will be missed by the entire advertising community."

The reporter had then asked Joe if he had any theories about why Elliot was murdered.

"No. But I hope they question all of the people that surrounded Elliot. They might know if anything wrong was going on."

Gene felt nauseated. Joe made innuendos that Elliot's murder was more than just being at the wrong place at the wrong time. He felt implicated by Joe.

He folded the paper and laid it on the table. He felt as if suspicious eyes were burning holes in him from all directions. He poked his omelet and nibbled his bacon. The nausea wasn't getting any better as he thought about Lisa's secrets about Elliot.

Outside the window, the black truck with the motorcycles was parked behind his trailer. Gene looked around the restaurant scanning for the two Hispanic men. He spotted them, sitting on stools at the bar counter. His first instinct was to approach them, but he knew he would end up on the wrong end of a beating. He motioned Sally over to his table.

"I'm ready for my check, Sally."

"Are you sure? You really didn't eat anything."

"Have you ever seen those two guys at the bar counter?"

"Nope. And I hope I don't see them again. They demanded sandwiches and called Mary a bitch."

"I had a run-in with them on the highway."

"You going to say something to them?" Sally asked.

"No way. They'd surely beat the hell out of me." He handed Sally a twenty-dollar bill.

"I'll be right back with your change."

"Keep it and keep them distracted for me. Will you?" Gene took the paper, and walked out of the restaurant. He was sure they didn't notice him leave. In fact, they seemed to be so drunk on the highway that he doubted they even recognized his rig.

Gene had to pull his trailer forward to load the horses. With his truck running, he took a pocketknife from a saddlebag in the trailer, made sure they didn't see him hiding behind it, and crouched down. He looked toward the restaurant's glass door just in time to see the men headed out. Then he saw Sally call them back in.

"Hey, guys, wait," she yelled.

"What, Chica?" one said.

Gene slashed the front tire of the black truck and ran to his, but he dropped his knife as he got in and drove away.

At four o'clock on that late winter afternoon, the El Paso temperature had dropped to sixty-nine degrees, but the large building retained its heat like an oven does an hour after its been turned off. Five people were in the room. Three of them were sitting. The other two were standing about but the only sound came from the whir of an oscillating fan that did nothing more that stir the stale air.

The male voice came from a speakerphone on the middle of the table. The voice was business-like and authoritative. "I cannot believe how screwed up you people have gotten things. What the hell is wrong with you?" The voice was loud and angry. "You're the biggest bunch of screw-ups. I can't believe this."

"You told us to clean up the problem," an older deep male voice from the room said. "So it didn't get done like we wanted. But it got done just the same."

The voice from the phone spoke again. "You idiot! It's done but now we've got a whole new set of problems. You were supposed to be watching out for my little girl. How in the hell did you let this happen?"

"That's easy," a female voice spoke from the room. "She's a spoiled little brat that does whatever the hell she wants. She's uncontrollable."

"You bitch," said another female voice in the room. "It's not my fault. If you would have had Elliot do what you were supposed to, none of this would have happened."

"Cut it out. The last thing we need right now is a catfight," the voice from the phone said. "I take it the old man didn't have the medallion?"

"No, sir. A Detective Stanton has it," another male voice said from the room. "He's been showing it to people all over town asking them if they've seen it."

"What are we doing about Gene and Lisa?"

"Lisa doesn't seem to be a problem. However, we are taking care of Gene as we speak, just like you and I discussed earlier and the detective is being sent on wild goose chases. It's complicated, but there shouldn't be any more screw-ups. He will take the fall for all of this. That, my friend, is my promise to you and your lovely daughter."

"You make me sick," said the second female voice.

"There had better not be any more problems, for the sake of all of you. This operation is too big to let some idiots like you bring it down. Am I clear?"

All of the voices in the room said a resounding "Yes" or "Yes, sir".

"I will be in El Paso Tuesday. This better be cleaned up by then."

With a click, the voice on the phone disappeared. The room fell silent except for the fan.

As promised to his wife, Stanton made it home by 6:30. By 7:00, he had eaten dinner, washed the dishes and was now sitting in his home office. His desk was cherry-wood, antique roll-top that he found at an estate sale in good condition. It had fifteen drawers and dozens of nooks and crannies, which he used to stuff notes and envelopes. There were also hidden compartments. He couldn't find more than the five, but he liked to think there were more. He kept two handguns, one nine-millimeter on the left and a Colt .45 in another on the right.

Several vertical slots for files and envelopes were built into the upper half of the desk. Panels behind two of them could swivel and open to compartments large enough to stash a pint of Kentucky Bourbon in each. If his wife ever found one of the bottles, she would never suspect there would be another. Of course, he used the bourbon strictly for medicinal purposes to get rid of headaches and as flavoring for weak coffee that his wife would bring him late at night. Other than his modern leather office chair, the only other thing that didn't fit the rustic décor of his office was the laptop computer on his desk.

Stanton began downloading his notes from his electronic notebook. He knew from experience that one interview alone would not solve the case, but it was the inconsistencies of all of them together that would stand out and give him direction for tomorrow's work. He reached and pulled the top file from the stack next to the computer.

"By the looks of things, you're settling in here for the evening. Is this going to be a tough one?" Stanton's wife asked as she walked in wearing only an extra large nightshirt and began massaging his shoulders.

Stanton pulled out the first set of eight by ten glossies. The first few were of Elliot's body leaning against the planter on the sidewalk. Being married to a homicide detective, she had seen her share of murder victims lying motionless in color on two-dimensional sheets of paper. Stanton knew some bothered her more than others.

They looked through several more pictures of the murder scene until he came across Elliot's etched word, MEDAL.

"What's that?" she asked.

"The victim was trying to tell us something by scratching it into the cement."

"What does it say? It looks pretty diluted because of the water."

"It's faded, but we were able to make out an 'M', an 'E' or 'A', a 'D', and an 'E' or 'A'. We think he died before he finished the word 'medallion'."

"What does a medallion have to do with it?"

Stanton spent the next few minutes explaining the medallion's connection.

"Oh Lord, I'll make some coffee," she said as she walked down the hallway.

Stanton tacked the glossies side by side on a bulletin board hanging on the wall to the left of his desk. After studying them for a few moments, he opened a file marked 'Copies - Thatcher' that Manny had provided. Stanton posted those shots of the Roger Thatcher crime scene on the bulletin board below Elliot's.

Stanton studied each picture. He would break each picture down to one-inch grids. By the end of the night he would know every part, every piece of debris, every relevant and non-relevant detail of both murder scenes. Would there be anything in common? Would there be anything that tied the two murders together other than the fact the two victims knew each other?

Stanton's wife returned carrying two cups of fresh, black coffee. "What are you looking at now? Oh my God." She gasped at the photo of the crushed skull of Roger Thatcher and spilled hot coffee on Stanton's legs. "Oh, I'm so sorry. I'll go get a towel," she said as she hurried down the hallway.

The coffee soaked Stanton's jeans, which held the heat of the scalding liquid. He hopped up and down, cursing under his breath, removing his boots and jeans. When his wife returned, he was standing in his briefs, white socks, and polo shirt. His thighs were bright red where they had been scalded. As she entered the room she began laughing at the pitiful sight.

"What are you laughing at?" he said with a twisted brow and grin under his big mustache, realizing how silly he must look.

"And I thought you were going to be too busy for me tonight." Stanton's wife blotted his thighs, closing the distance between them.

"Unfortunately, I *am* too busy. I need to study this stuff." He placed his hands on her shoulders.

She dropped the towel and her hands began tugging at his briefs.

"What are you doing, baby?" he whispered.

She lowered his briefs to mid-thigh and began caressing his butt cheeks.

"Honey, I really need to work."

"Mr. Stanton, those guys are dead. They aren't going anywhere. They can have you when I'm finished with you."

"Something tells me you spilled the coffee on purpose."

"I'll never tell."

After Lisa left Marlene at the funeral home, she drove home for the first time since Elliot's death to find dozens of flowers in her doorway, wilting as the midday sun illuminated her approach. Being alone from then on was starting to sink in. Her stomach knotted and her head swirled. She leaned down and gathered an arm full of floral arrangements, opened the door, and walked in. As she put her keys, purse, and flowers on the kitchen counter, she heard a familiar beeping sound. Her answering machine was a good distraction. It was full. She pushed the 'play' button.

"Lisa, we're so sorry about Elliot... Let us know when you're ready for visitors... We'll come by." They were all condolences. She thought about returning each call but she really didn't want to talk to anyone. Instead, she got an idea. She grabbed her keys and went to the movies where she sat for more than five hours watching the same movie twice and waited for it to start a third time. She needed to be alone and the noise of the movie blocked negative thoughts. She dreaded the moment when an usher might kick her out.

It was 7:00 in the evening when she returned home. She walked into the kitchen and gathered all of the flowers, potted plants, and bouquets and took them back out front. She suspected more people would be dropping by and leaving the same types of gifts. Why not let them build up out front for everyone to see? Lisa needed the inside of the house to be as it was before to make it through the night without a nervous breakdown.

She walked around the house, picking up throw pillows in the living room and some dishes in the kitchen. When she reached the bedroom, she picked up the socks, underwear and nightshirt she was wearing when the call came about Elliot. She could pretend he was still alive. She held one of his shirts to her nose. She gave in. The smell would get her through the night.

She walked to the bathroom, pulled the full laundry basket into the bedroom, and sorted the clothes. When she finished, there were three piles of her and Elliot's dirty clothes. She gathered the largest pile and walked down the hallway to a large laundry room that had the washer and dryer at one end and a large basin sink at the other. She didn't care for the sink as the hot water heater was just on the other side of the wall. The hot water from the faucet was immediate and scalded her hands before she could get it adjusted. She had complained to Elliot about it.

After starting the load of clothes, she went into the kitchen. She made a turkey sandwich, removed the crust, and placed it on a plate with a sliced pickle. She opened the refrigerator and removed a cold bottle of water.

The lights were dim and the house was quiet. Lisa sat on the sofa with her sandwich plate on her lap and her bare feet curled beneath her thighs. She turned on the TV. The screen lit up with a re-run of Lucille Ball. She could barely follow it as her mind began filing, sorting, and cataloging all of the events of the past six days.

The sound of the phone ringing seemed to be off in the distance, like one of the thoughts being mentally sorted. But the next ring was louder and closer somehow. Then a third and a fourth. Lisa blinked and she felt the burn of her dry eyes causing her to shut them tight, forcing tears to erupt.

Looking through fluttering, wet lashes, she found the handset lying on the cushion next to her feet, picked it up, and hit the TALK button.

"Lisa? It's Gene."

"Gene? Oh, I just dozed off," convincing herself as much as him, as her vision cleared.

"You okay?" he asked in a fatherly voice.

Lisa looked at her watch; ten o'clock at night. She couldn't remember the last thirty minutes.

"I was just eating a sandwich and watching TV." Her half-eaten sandwich had fallen out of her hand onto the sofa cushion. "It's just nice to hear your voice."

"I've settled in and made a fire and put the horses away. I did have a little run-in with some drunken cholos on the highway," he said.

"What happened?"

"Nothing, it was no big deal." He caught himself.

"But after I got into town, I stopped at the Denny's and that's when things got strange." Gene described the article, how the photograph made him look bad, the glares he had gotten from the people in the restaurant and the statement given by Joe Garcia.

"I'm going to call him right now and give that jerk a piece of my mind. Where does he get off saying stuff like that?"

Gene said, "Don't call anyone. Imagine how I felt reading it. I want to do a lot more than give him a verbal thrashing. I know the great Detective Stanton is looking at us as suspects. The last thing I want to do is give Joe something like our idle threats to twist and pass on to Stanton."

"Why would you say that?" Lisa was offended. "We haven't done anything wrong. How could I be a suspect?"

"You're kidding, right?"

"I'm not kidding and you're starting to piss me off."

"The man caught you, the morning after your husband's murder, in *my* guest bathroom virtually nude. I had an entire conversation with him and conveniently forgot to mention that you were there didn't help."

"But we explained all that."

"It doesn't matter. He's suspicious that we're having an affair," Gene said. "When we do tell him about Elliot and this girl Sam, Stanton will have no doubts about us and that won't be a good thing."

There was a moment of silence as the realization of what Gene just said set in. They were suspects in the murder of the man they both loved. No one could have predicted they would ever be having this conversation.

"What makes you think Joe would play games with Stanton?" Lisa broke the silence.

"He's an ass, for one thing. Plus, I called Stanton while I was on the road to check in. He met with Joe and said Joe told him some interesting things that moved me up on his suspect list. That's what made me start thinking about our situation." Gene's voice had dropped half an octave. "Anyway, maybe I'm just over-thinking things and got myself worried over nothing."

"I wouldn't put anything past Joe," Lisa said. "He is a sick man who would do anything to hurt you and Price."

"Lisa, something is bothering my horses. I better check on them. Can I call you later or will you be in bed soon?"

"I'm going to bed. Call me in the morning."

The horses became louder than usual and he hung up on her.

He walked to the kitchen window. It was too dark to see what was bothering them. Gene's mountain home sat high upon two acres on the side of one of the peaks that circled the town of Ruidoso. Surrounded by thick pine trees, the log home was built in its location for the seclusion, not the view.

For the most part, the house, work shed, stables, and corral were on flat land. The driveway in front was merely a circle around six large pine trees of shallow ruts of dirt and pine needles that had been shaped over the years by vehicles. Gene's truck and trailer were parked at the side of the house.

The steep dirt road leading up to the home was a quarter mile long from the main road. In wet weather four-wheel drive was a must. At the mouth of the road was a magnificent log gate that he and Elliot built to keep out wandering cattle. It was always closed but not locked. He would simply place a loop of wire over the end of the gate and pole.

The corral and stables were on the opposite side of the circle driveway, close enough for Gene to hear the excitement, but far enough for the reach of the light illuminating from the house windows. He watched through the kitchen window but still couldn't see through the darkness. He walked through the kitchen to the den where a fire in his large fireplace worked on five logs. After slipping into his wool coat, Gene opened the front door and stepped out onto the wooden deck and into the bitter cold air. He immediately understood the problem with the horses; motorcycles.

The sound seemed to be coming from the bottom of the steep road but then it would change. The sound moved from where the road was and traveled to his far right and back again. The deep sound of four-stroke motors grew closer. Both horses were running back and forth in the corral, neighing and kicking. The louder the sound became, the angrier he became.

"Probably just some kids."

Gene stepped down the stairs of the deck and into the driveway. Ready to kick them off of his property, he picked up a baseball bat-sized tree limb. Just as the motorcycles sounded like they had reached the top of the road, their motors went silent. Gene couldn't be certain exactly where they were. He knew they were close enough to see his silhouette cast from the lights of the house behind him.

"Hey, you idiots, what the hell do you think you're doing?" he yelled. "Don't you know this is private property?"

There was no reply.

"How stupid do you think I am? I know you're there and if I have to come down there to prove it, I'm going to kick your asses. Get off my property."

Gene realized he might be dealing with something that he couldn't handle alone.

"Elliot?" Gene yelled to the house. "Elliot, we got some real jerks out here. Get your rifle. We need to get rid of some trash."

He took three steps toward the road, pounding the wooden club in his hand. But his threat had no effect on the mysterious bikers. It was time to get back inside and just wait for them to go away, or call 911. Just as he turned and started toward the house, a motor kicked on, then a second. He stopped and turned to see them, but there were no headlights on the bikes, only sound. He strained his eyes, trying to cut through the darkness. The bikes revved louder but didn't move. The horses were restless again.

"What the hell do you guys want?" he said more to himself as he started walking backwards in the driveway.

He heard the gears of both bikes engage then peel dirt and twigs into the air as they shot toward him. Gene only took two big steps before the first bike reached his deck and cut him off. The bike was blue, and the rider was wearing dark clothes, a ski mask and carrying a black duffle bag. Gene stared at him as the rider held his front brake while letting his rear tire throw dirt against the house.

The second bike came from behind. The rider kicked Gene in the ribs, knocking him to the ground. He was able to get up quickly and moved toward the center of the pine trees as the riders on identical bikes rode slowly around the circular driveway. The only difference between the two was the duffle bag the first rider was carrying. Gene's heart was racing and beads of sweat broke out on his forehead.

These were those cholos from the highway and restaurant. They must have seen me slash their tire, he thought. But how did they know where I live?

They were riding slow and apart. Gene leaped toward the deck, hoping to make a quick dash into house. The second rider immediately cut him off. Gene wasn't about to show his fear. It was time to fight. He chased after each bike as they toyed with him by speeding up and slowing down.

"You want me to buy you a new tire? Just ask. You jerks started this crap," he said as he grabbed the back of the second motorcycle, which accelerated throwing dirt over Gene's entire body. Infuriated, Gene ran across the driveway, through the trees to the other side meeting the same bike. In one long leap, he tackled the rider. The bike kept going another twenty feet before falling on its side and stalling.

They wrestled on the ground in front of the deck. Gene pinned him to the ground and kneed the rider in the groin.

"Gene punched the rider in the face with a nose-crunching blow. The rider struggled with wheezing breaths as Gene struck his stomach and face. The ski mask was soaked with the rider's blood that splattered with every blow. Gene fully intended to beat him unconscious. With his left hand wrapped around the rider's throat, squeezing, Gene looked around for the other biker. There was no sign of him or his bike or the duffle bag.

"Where are you?" he yelled. "Your friend left you to take a beating," Gene gasped as he struggled to stand over the rider. With one final kick to the head, the rider fell back to the ground.

Gene bent over to catch his breath and began heaving until he threw up on the rider lying motionless but gurgling blood. He wiped his mouth with the cuff of his wool coat and scanned one more time for the other rider. Still no sign of him. Gene staggered up the steps of the deck to find his door open. He couldn't remember if he had left it open, or did the other rider go in?

He stood outside with only his head looking in, slowly looking to the left, then right and listening. He decided the other rider must have left, the one he just beat up wasn't going anywhere and now he could call the sheriff's office. Gene walked to the kitchen and dialed 911. While he was talking, he grabbed two long zip-ties from a kit in his saddlebag on the table.

By the time he finished his call his adrenaline had waned. He walked back through the den and out onto the deck. The rider was still down but groaning. He secured the rider to the deck support posts with the zip-ties.

Gene walked back into the house, put three more logs on the fire, and fell back in a chair constructed of wood and cowhide. A sudden flash of light and the excruciating pain in his head lasted only a second before he passed out.

Chapter Nine

The only one on duty that Sunday night, Deputy Ronald Culver, was sitting on the toilet in the only stall of the men's room, located twenty feet from the front desk of the sheriff's department. He left the bathroom door open in case the phone rang. He was reading the forum section of UFO Magazine, fully engrossed in the alien abduction story and on the edge of his proverbial seat. At ten thirty three, the ringing phone startled him.

He tried to stand, but he'd been sitting in the same position for too long and his legs had gone numb causing him to fall forward on his knees and hit his cheek bone on the stall door. The phone continued ringing as the deputy scrambled to his feet. Holding his pants up by the belt with one hand and clutching the bruised side of his face with the other, he stumbled out of the bathroom to his desk and picked up the receiver.

"Sheriff's office." The deputy winced in pain. "Deputy Ron Culver speaking. What can I do for you?"

"My name is Gene Martine and I want to report an assault."

Gene woke up from the shock of cold water thrown in his face.

He shook the water from his cheeks and tried to stand, but his hands were tied, no, handcuffed to the arms of the chair he was sitting in.

"What is going on?" Gene said. He was barely able to focus on the deputy standing in front of him. The fireplace was burning low. Deputy Culver stood with an empty glass in his left hand and a nine-millimeter handgun in his right, the barrel of which was pointed at Gene's chest.

"You've got the wrong guy, you idiot. The other one is still out there somewhere."

Deputy Culver said, "I got the right guy, all right. Calm down, Mr. Martine."

Gene's head was beginning to clear.

"Are you crazy, man? I called you, remember?" He vaguely remembered the flash of light before going unconscious. "The other guy knocked me out and now he's getting away." He struggled with the cuffs.

Deputy Culver's gun clicked. "Mr. Martine, I'm not going to tell you again. Calm down, right now."

Gene stopped struggling. He was breathing hard as his heart pounded at his ribs. He noticed the intense smell of cheap whisky. It was all over his shirt.

"Now, Mr. Martine, I'm not surprised at your reaction. I'm sure you didn't expect things to end up like this, did you?" Deputy Culver said.

Gene could only continue staring at the deputy in front of him. A bruise was on the deputy's cheek. Maybe the deputy captured the other guy on the bike, and the deputy got the shiner from a struggle with him.

"Come on now, Mr. Martine. Tell me what happened. Did the deal go bad so you lost control of your senses? Or, maybe you were so drunk and coked up you just lost it, beat the crap out of your buddy outside and then killed him?"

"What are you talking about?" Gene was confused and the strong smell of the whisky made him want to puke. Then he saw something on the heavy wooden coffee table. There was the black duffle bag the first biker was carrying, an empty bottle of whisky, a razor blade, three lines of cocaine, and Gene's wallet.

"What's happening here?" Gene said.

"Don't act stupid. You know exactly what's going on. Why don't you just admit it?"

"Ask the guy, the guy outside?" Gene stuttered.

"You mean 'corpse'."

"What? Corpse? He's not dead. He attacked me but I didn't kill him."

"Man, you must have been really screwed up," the deputy said. "If you didn't kill him, why is your buck knife sticking out of his chest? The knife with your name engraved on it."

"What?" Gene said in a dry whisper. The pounding in Gene's head stopped. He turned cold with fear of the realization of what was happening. He remembered losing his knife at the restaurant.

The deputy picked up the duffle bag and tossed it onto Gene's lap. "The way I see it, your buddy shows up for some kind of drug deal, you two partied a little too hard, and a fight broke out. Looks like you won."

Deputy Culver swapped the gun from hand to hand. "Then you decide the only way out is to call the sheriff's department and claim self-defense, right? But your mind was fried and unfortunately for you, you passed out before you could hide the evidence," the deputy deduced.

"You're wrong," Gene said.

"Because there's a dead guy out there with your knife sticking out of his chest, I had to wake up the sheriff. He's on his way over here right now. It sure would make me look good if you would just tell me what happened. Comprende? If you don't, I might be inclined to beat it out of you. After what you did to the guy outside, nobody would think you came out of the fight unhurt." Culver's eyes were glistening.

"I'm not telling you a thing. You don't have a clue." Gene said angrily.

The back of Deputy Culver's left hand hit Gene's right temple. The hit stunned Gene as his head fell forward. He shook off the blow and saw what was in the bag; bundles of bills and a large plastic bag of white powder.

The high-pitched, rhythmic sound of sirens from at least two vehicles filled the air and got louder as they reached the top of Gene's driveway.

Ron walked to the den window and looked out. "Seems your luck is changing."

"Kiss my ass. Let's see how yours holds out when..." Gene yelled as Deputy Culver kicked Gene's shin with his steel-toed boot.

"Shut up, you scum. You're in enough trouble."

The deputy opened the door for Sheriff Wilcox and Deputy Mansfield. Both men were below the deck surveying the body of the victim. Deputy Culver left the door open and joined the others.

They spoke too low for Gene to hear but he listened to the low mumblings of the men as he watched the red and blue lights move across his walls in a hypnotic pattern. The fireplace was no longer putting out any appreciable heat and the door was open. Gene was wearing his wool coat but his hands and face were cold. Gene twisted his wrists as the cold radiating from the handcuffs pierced his skin like needles.

Maybe he wasn't being framed. Was his assailant still in the house doing the drugs and counting his money when the deputy got there?

Gene heard the sound of leather utility belts and boots as three officers walked up the stairs and across the wood deck to the doorway. The sheriff and his two deputies walked inside.

"Mr. Martine," Sheriff Wilcox said. "You're in a bit of a pickle here. Please don't make matters worse for yourself."

The sheriff was in his late fifties. He was of medium height and sporting a large beer belly that caused the buttons on his freshly starched uniform shirt to pull to their limits.

"Deputy Culver tells me you have so much as admitted to killing the man outside your home, something about beating the crap out of him? I'm advising you that you have the right to remain silent." He gave him the Miranda rights, and said,

"You are under arrest for murder, possession of a controlled substance, drug dealing, and assaulting a police officer."

"I called 911 for help," Gene said.

The sheriff scribbled in a notepad. "You told me you understood your rights. So, now I'm going to let you talk. Do you still want to talk, Mr. Martine?"

"I haven't killed anyone. Two men on motorcycles came to my house."

"You took on two men by yourself?" Sheriff Wilcox said.

"They were circling my driveway and had me trapped in the middle of the trees. When I realized there was no other way out, I tackled one of the riders and beat him up."

The sheriff scribbled on his notepad as Deputy Mansfield walked through Gene's house from room to room taking pictures and Deputy Culver listened, ready to step on Gene's words if necessary.

"Is this the guy you beat up?" the sheriff said, showing Gene a picture.

"But, I didn't kill him."

"What happened to the other guy?"

"He just disappeared," Gene said. "When we stopped fighting, I looked around for him, but he was gone. At least I thought he was. I tied up the guy outside. He was very much alive when I called 911. Then, I put more wood in the fireplace and sat down. Apparently the second guy was in my house and knocked me out. I've got a goose egg on the back of my head that proves it." Gene leaned forward to show the knot on the back of his head.

The sheriff showed no interest in Gene's scalp. "Ron, get me a chair from Mr. Martine's kitchen. My feet are killing me. Mansfield?"

Deputy Mansfield was in Gene's bedroom in the back of the house.

"Bring me a mirror."

Culver appeared from the kitchen carrying a chair from the dining room table and put it in front of Gene.

"Gene, everything you've told me is intriguing. For now, let's assume I do believe you." Wilcox picked up the black duffle bag from Gene's lap and put it on the table. "How do you explain the fact that the guy outside was killed with your knife?" The sheriff leaned forward as if he didn't want to miss a word of Gene's explanation. "And, why would someone leave a duffle bag full of money and drugs on your coffee table?"

Gene lowered his head. "I don't know,"

"You don't have any ideas?"

"I don't know," Gene said, "after I was knocked out, the second guy decided to do some drugs and have a drink before you guys got here. But your deputy surprised him. The guy is out of his mind from the coke, and didn't have time to put away his stuff or rescue his friend." Gene realized, even he didn't believe what he was saying.

"And then?"

"Then I guess he decided it was better to kill his friend and frame me for it rather than risk letting his friend get caught and turning on him," Gene said.

Mansfield had returned from the back of Gene's house and handed the sheriff a lady's mirror that he had found in Gene's bathroom. It had belonged to Marlene during better days.

Gene's hair was a mess and his eyes were bloodshot. Cocaine was inside and around his nostrils and he smelled like cheap whisky. "Let's do a drug test right now. I may have it on my face but I'm not high."

"We'll do just that back at the station."

"I want to talk to my lawyer."

Mansfield snapped a picture of Gene's face. Deputy Culver unlocked Gene's right arm and placed it behind Gene's back, forced Gene to his knees, unlocked his left arm and finished by cuffing it to Gene's right arm.

Two more vehicles approached Gene's home. It was 1:15 in the morning as Gene was lead out of his home by Culver and down the deck steps.

The coroner was taking pictures of the body that was still zip-tied to the deck. Gene noticed that the ski mask had been removed. The man's nose was shattered and twisted to the left and his jaw had been dislocated.

"You sure did a hell of a job on him, didn't you?" Deputy Culver said as he shoved Gene in the direction of the SUV.

When they reached Culver's vehicle, Gene stopped short forcing Culver to take a wide-leg defensive stance.

"Come on," Culver said.

With one swift motion, Gene's boot hit the center of the wide stance taking Culver's feet out from under him. Then he kneed the officer in the head, knocking Culver unconscious. Gene frantically searched the deputy's pockets for the keys to the handcuffs. His hands were cuffed behind his back making it difficult to see and feel at the same time. He scrambled to the shirt pockets.

Bingo. Using his thumb and middle finger of his right hand, he fumbled the keys twice before freeing his left hand.

Once the cuffs were off, Gene maneuvered the deputy's body and used them to cuff Culver to the trailer hitch of the SUV.

He ran, slipping and falling into the mud. He got up again and limped five more yards to hide behind the house. He crouched there, head in his hands, and waited to catch his breath.

"Oh, my God, Lisa." Gene said low, but aloud to himself. "If they're after me, there's a chance they're after you."

He put his back against the wall, and then crept from window to window surveying the sheriff and his deputies in the house. Eventually Culver would come to and yell or someone would radio him to make sure the prisoner was locked up. He decided that the only way out of this mess would be to get back to El Paso, find Lisa, and go straight to Stanton to tell him everything.

He knew there was no way to drive out. Even if he could get his truck out through all of the cop cars, it would be the first thing they would look for and he wouldn't make it as far as Alamogordo before he was caught. There was no chance of stealing his attacker's motorcycle because it was lying close to the body.

Gene crouched and moved behind trucks, SUVs and finally the coroner's van. He was able to reach the horse trailer undetected. The only person within earshot was the coroner. The corral was thirty feet away. Both horses recognized Gene and began neighing lightly as they walked over to his side of the corral. The coroner looked at the horses. Fortunately, the coroner had set up bright lights directly over the dead body, which destroyed any ability to see out into the darkness.

Gene waited until he went back to work collecting evidence. He took great care not to make any noise as he lifted each door pin on the back of the trailer. There was squeaks and scrapes against metal as he opened both doors. He continued to watch closely as the coroner and assistant continued working.

Gene stacked one saddle, two bridles, a bedroll, and his saddlebags inside the corral without making enough noise to cause suspicion. Time was running out. Before saddling the oldest and more experienced of the two horses, he looked to check on the coroner one more time, but he was gone.

A chorus of laughter broke out from the house and a few seconds later the sheriff and two deputies appeared on the Gene's deck with the coroner. Gene's hands were spastic with cold and his jaw clinched. The overweight sheriff and the other men rolled the dead man onto a black plastic body bag.

As the four men lifted the body bag, Gene realized they were coming his way. He ran into the trees on the far side of the corral, but the horses followed his path around the corral neighing.

"What the hell has gotten into those horses?" Sheriff Wilcox asked.

The coroner said. "They're probably just spooked with all of the activity up here."

The sheriff slowed down the group of men carrying the body bag and squinted in Gene's direction.

"This guy is heavy," Deputy Mansfield said.

"Remind me to get Animal Control out here in the morning to take care of these horses."

Knowing the horses would follow, Gene used them for cover and slowly walked the corral fence around to the opposite side. From there, except for the trees in the middle of the circle driveway, there was nothing to hide behind. But it was the darkest corner on the property until he reached the house.

He waited until the van doors were opened and their attention was on the task of getting the corpse into the van. He ran, slipping once but recovering and made it to the deck. Crouching, he looked toward the van, but his vision was limited just as the bright lights hindered the coroner's vision.

He climbed the edge of the deck with two steps and walked into his house. He hid behind the door waiting for someone to yell. Gene exhaled, as he heard nothing but their low voices coming from the direction of the van.

He surveyed the ransacked house. Every cabinet and drawer in sight was open and their contents strewn about the floor. He went to the kitchen looking for his portable cell phone charger in a drawer but spotted them on top of the counter along with papers, dishtowels and cooking utensils. He walked back to the den. On the coffee table, there were dozens of zip-lock type evidence bags, each containing his personal things.

As he rifled through the bags looking for his phone and glasses, he was startled by the sound of the van doors closing.

He could hear their voices become louder and footsteps closer. He remembered his glasses falling into the black duffle bag. He grasped the bag from the leather chair. When he heard the first boots step onto the wooden steps of the deck, Gene crammed the battery charger and one of the two phones into the black bag and made a quiet escape through the back hall to the back door. He waited to close the door until he heard them laughing.

With everyone in the house, Gene made little effort to hide as he ran back to the corral. He slid on his knees just outside of the corral's fence, dropped the black bag, and retrieved his glasses. He zipped and tossed the bag into the corral and climbed through the piping. The horses came to his rescue.

It was easy for Gene to saddle his horses in the dark. He threw a blanket and the saddle on the back of the eldest horse then worked the buckles and straps. He tied their reins to the fence and finished loading the bedroll, saddlebags and duffle bag. Gene led the horses to the corral gate that faced the house.

Even though the trees in the driveway obstructed the view of the corral from the deck, it would be easy to see him and the two horses riding off. Gene's heart was in his throat as he lifted the leather strap that held the gate closed, walked the horses through, and closed it again. If he had any luck, the closed gate could buy him more time. He hoped that once they discovered he was gone, they would assume he was on foot.

Before Gene could mount his horse he heard something. It sounded like someone was rattling a chain in the distance followed by moaning and cursing.

"Sheriff. Somebody. Help me."

Deputy Culver was conscious. Gene jumped on his horse and leading the second horse, trotted into the darkness and safety of the trees.

"Would somebody get out here?" Ron yelled as loud as he could.

The sheriff and his men were packing up the last of the evidence inside Gene's house. Each had taken a couple of shots of Gene's bourbon by the time the coroner went into the house to ask for help with the body. And now, the coroner and his assistant were partaking of the libations, joking and laughing until a window in the back of the house shattered.

"What the hell was that?" Mansfield said as they all rushed to sound with their guns drawn.

When the officers reached the spare bedroom from, there was glass scattered on the bed under the broken window the sheriff turned the light out. With it dark inside, whoever was outside could not see in. Three flashlights turned on almost simultaneously as they gathered around the window in silence. The sheriff's flashlight shone on a pair of boots below the window and Deputy Culvers SUV still parked out back.

"Come on, somebody." The words came from behind the vehicle.

"It's Culver's unit," Mansfield said.

"And that's Culver's feet hanging out from behind it." the sheriff said, then ran out of the room to the back door. The others followed.

Gene was headed for the trails that lead to higher ground, but was still close enough to hear the sheriff screaming at Deputy Culver and barking orders to the other deputies. He laughed at the sound but the crooked smile on his face disappeared when he thought about the trouble he was in and the thought of the long journey in front of him.

Chapter Ten

Gene fell in and out of consciousness. At times, his horses would stop and wait for his instructions to continue. He slapped his own frozen face with the leather glove on his hand.

The tops of his thighs and boots were frosted over and he shivered. He was cold to the bone. Just as his eyes began to close again, the sound of a helicopter snapped him to attention. He saw the low-flying police helicopter shinning a spotlight along the trail ahead.

He grabbed a tight hold on the reins, kicked his horse, and galloped both horses blindly off the trail into the darkness of thick trees. Branches, thick and thin, snapped on his shoulders and his face as he tried to escape the spotlight. He could barely see in front of him to guide the horses through the trees. It was like trying to thread a needle in a dark room with a piece of thick yarn.

The sound of the helicopter faded in and out and changed direction. Its pattern was erratic enough that Gene knew he hadn't been seen, but one thing was clear; they were looking for him. He knew that when the sun came up, there would be plenty of law enforcement obstacles in front of him.

The helicopter went north into the distance and Gene stopped the horses. They needed a rest as much as he did. He knew it would be necessary to stay off the trails for a while. Finding a path between the pines was tough. He dismounted the Appaloosa and tied the reins to a branch.

Gene was hungry and regretted not finishing his last meal at Denny's Restaurant in Ruidoso. The lack of sleep and the hunger were no match for the cold.

He removed the bedroll from his saddle, leaving it rolled up, placed it next to a tree, and sat on it. Leaning back against the bark, his vertebrae cracked from top to bottom as he stretched. His attempt to rest his head against the bark proved painful when the bump on his head touched the tree.

The sound of a branch breaking came from his left. A doe looked at Gene, then leaped away.

He dug through his saddlebags only to find an extra pair of wool socks and underwear, his leather working tools, an unfinished belt, and one box of matches.

Gene lifted the duffel bag from the saddle horn, sat back down on the bedroll, and unzipped it. He took out one item at a time and only what was most familiar to him. He put on his glasses and then took out the phone charger and set it aside. Then he retrieved the cell phone. He pushed the send button to see the screen light up the last number he dialed.

He was confused only for a moment when he realized it was Elliot's phone and was happy to see it had almost a full charge. He had grabbed the wrong phone by mistake. He set it aside and became even more perplexed when he emptied the rest of the bags contents. There was one sandwich bag half full of white powder, five thick bundles of hundred dollar bills, and two silver medallions.

He pulled out the medallions for closer inspection. By the light of the moon, his numb fingers caressed the silver embossed medallions as if they were Braille. The designs were identical; a bull's head on one side and the fading flag on the other. He realized what Stanton had meant when he said Joe's interview moved him higher on the suspect list.

Great, Joe told Stanton I designed this. Gene's heart picked up its pace. I'm already guilty by association. He became angry. He knew then that the guys from the past night were sent to frame him for Elliot's murder.

And it almost worked, he thought. I'm now wanted for two murders in two states and possession of cocaine. And I assaulted a police officer and now I'm an escaped fugitive on the run. And these babies--he jostled the medallions in his hand--these babies tie me to the largest organized drug ring in North America. Hell, I'm a Free-Lander.

He knew time was against him. He began filling the duffle bag. He might need the money but he had no use for the cocaine and left it on the ground. He placed the bag back on the saddle horn, and adjusted the straps on his horse. When he reached down for the bedroll, his boot smashed and grinded the bag of cocaine causing it to spill.

The cocaine could get him through. He had learned about the affects of cocaine years ago in a college chemistry class. Just a couple of snorts and his mind would become more alert, his pains might disappear, and he would be numb to the cold and hunger. He didn't have to worry about the legalities of it, not that night.

Gene kicked some of the powder to the wind and diluted the rest in the dirt with his boot. He tied his bedroll to the back of the saddle and mounted his horse.

Lisa's phone was on its fourth ring as she rolled over and looked at the clock that read 7:14.

Her first night alone without Elliot was everything she was afraid it would be. She tried pretending Elliot was only out of town, but reality kept setting in. She called Marlene and talked until 3:00 in the morning, when Marlene finally convinced Lisa to hang up the phone. She fell asleep about 5:30.

At six rings, Lisa remembered the voice mail was full. On the eighth ring, she picked up the cordless phone from its cradle on Elliot's nightstand.

"Lisa?" The voice on the other end was familiar. "This is Detective Stanton."

"Detective, do you have news about Elliot's murder?" She was suddenly alert and hopeful.

"Not this morning. Things have gotten more complicated."

"*More* complicated?"

"Have you heard from Gene?"

"Of course. Why?"

"When was the last time you were in contact with him?" Stanton asked.

"I don't know. Yesterday? Last night?"

"Lisa, I don't have time for games. Gene's in trouble."

Lisa sat up in bed. "It was late last night. What's wrong?"

"Some men may have attacked Gene at the cabin after he talked to you."

"This can't be happening...." Lisa whispered as she pulled her legs to her chest and rocked back and forth.

"Don't get excited. He's okay."

"Why?"

"Was there anything wrong when you and Gene talked?

"He was just letting me know he was at the cabin and checking on me."

"Are you sure he didn't say anything to you that would cause you to think he might be in trouble?"

"Why are you asking me? Why aren't you asking Gene these questions?"

"Gene's in real trouble right now, but you have to think about your conversation with him last night. Think hard. What did he tell you?"

"He arrived at the house and, and..." she said, and began to rock faster.

There was a long pause.

"He told me he ran into some trouble with a couple of Cholos on the highway but it was no big deal."

"That's perfect, Lisa. That's just what I wanted to know."

She sounded credible.

"Detective, that may be fine with you, but I'm still lost. Where is he?"

"I can't talk about it right now, Lisa. You're going to have to trust me. However..." There was a pause. "Listen, you'll probably be hearing from Gene real soon. When you do, please have him call me."

Lisa hit the 'off' button on the phone and threw it across the room.

Gene knew the trails. Gene had decided two hours earlier that the main trail would be his best bet in avoiding anyone with a badge. If he were looking for someone that was familiar with the terrain, he would start on the rarely and mostly-hidden trails, assuming the person he was tracking was a fugitive. He had no idea how the police operated. He knew that his plan had worked so far.

He estimated that his first six hours of the *ride and hide* game so far, had put him ten miles north of Cloudcroft; a mountain-top community that was only twenty miles east of Alamogordo, New Mexico. At that pace, he would be in Cloudcroft between 9:00 and 10:00 that morning

From the time the sun came up, he had wanted to call Lisa. He knew it was her first night alone.

"Let her rest," he told himself.

He simply didn't know what to say.

The Appaloosa he was riding threw its head back when Elliot's cell phone rang in the black bag.

"Whoa." He tugged on the reins bringing both horses to a stop.

He opened the flap on the bag and retrieved the phone. He was glad, yet nervous, to see the number on the screen, as he quickly dismounted and answered.

"Hi, Lisa," he said in the most positive tone he could muster.

"Gene, where are you? What's happened to you? Stanton called, and…"

"I'm okay, Lisa." For the first time since the attack, he was talking to a trustworthy voice.

"I've been calling your cell phone for hours but it just goes straight to voicemail. Thank God I remembered I gave you Elliot's."

"Do you remember the two guys I had problems with on…'

"…the highway?"

"They showed up at my house on dirt bikes. That's why my horses were going nuts when I hung up with you. At first I thought they were just a couple of drunks harassing me."

Gene didn't know how much or how little to tell her. If it wasn't already on the news, it would be that night. "Lisa, the cops think I killed someone."

"Gene, we talked about this. After Elliot's funeral tomorrow, we'll tell Detective Stanton everything."

"You don't understand. They think I killed one of the men that attacked me last night. I beat him up pretty good, but I didn't kill him. Now I'm on the run with all this drug money, and I, well, I'm not sure I know what I'm doing."

"Drug money?

"I'm carrying wads of drug money. I had some cocaine but I dumped it." The more he talked the more anxious his voice sounded.

The familiar sound of the helicopter caught his attention in the distance. "Lisa, hold on a second."

"Is that a helicopter?" she asked but got no response.

Gene instructed his horses to follow. The noise was loud as the helicopter hovered directly over Gene then it began to fade away.

"You still there?" Gene said.

"You're scaring me."

"You should be in my position. I've spent the last six hours freezing and hiding from police helicopters."

"We can work this out together. You're going to have to slow down, start from the beginning, and tell me the whole story."

Gene told her an abbreviated version of the last night.

"You believe me, don't you Lisa? You know I wouldn't kill anyone right?"

"Of course, I do. But where are you going? Do you have a plan?"

"I'm kind of working things out as I go. All I know is that I have to get back to El Paso to start piecing things together. I can always call Stanton."

"I almost forgot. That's why I called you. Stanton knows all about last night. He kept asking me about our phone call and if you had said anything to make me think you were in trouble."

As he listened to Lisa, Gene realized that if Stanton knew about Gene's dilemma, then every police department within a hundred mile radius of Ruidoso would be looking for him.

"I didn't remember about your problems on the highway until he started pressuring me. He seemed to be glad when I did remember, but he really pissed me off."

"The sheriff in Ruidoso called Stanton? Did you say he was glad when you remembered?"

"He said it was *perfect* and exactly what he needed to hear from me."

"Do you know what this means?" Gene's voice lifted. "It means the Sheriff told Stanton my story.

"Do you think you should call him? Lisa said.

"There is too much evidence that says I'm guilty. I've got to find a way to turn it around."

"What could Elliot have possibly gotten into that would bring this much trouble?"

"I'll bet the answers to those questions are in knowing where these medallions came from. Remember the Free-Landers Stanton told me about? I think the woman that Elliot was trying to help is wrapped up with them. I'll bet she knows who killed Elliot and who attacked me. If we can find her, she can talk to Stanton."

"But we don't even know what she looks like."

"I didn't say it would be easy. Try to remember everything Elliot told you about her and write it down. It'll help you remember. When I get closer to El Paso, I'll call you and we'll figure out where to start looking. Okay?"

"Okay. I'll try," she said.

"I need to get off the phone. The battery is getting low. I have a portable charger in my saddlebags, but I need to save it. Good old VoiceComm. It's good to have a client that gives you free crap."

Lisa said, "I guess now isn't a good time to wish you a happy birthday but, happy birthday anyway, old man."

"I've got to go. The battery…" The line went dead.

His conversation with Lisa gave him his second wind. He hooked the phone to the charger, mounted his horse and climbed back on to the main trail. Barring any problems, he would make it to Cloudcroft in less than 2 hours where he would try to buy some food and water under the assumption that there would be cops looking for him.

At 8:15 in the morning, the 29th precinct where Detective Stanton worked was already alive with activity. Dozens of detectives and police officers were starting their week where it had ended the week before.

"Homicide," a detective said, answering his phone.

"Boss, we got a problem," said the voice on the other end of the call.

"I told you to never call me here," the detective said in a low voice, as he made sure no one was in earshot of the conversation. "Are you crazy?"

"I have to talk to you and you're not answering your cell phone."

"Hold on." The detective pulled his cell phone from his hip. The display showed fourteen missed calls. He touched a few buttons and remembered he had the ringer set on silent during a morning briefing.

"Jefe?" the voice said.

"I'm here but, make it quick. Did you get it done as planned?"

"Yeah, it worked but..." The detective could hear the stress coming from his voice.

"But what? What happened up there?"

"We did everything you said and he was busted by the local sheriff, but he escaped, and..."

"Escaped?" the detective said in a loud enough voice that two uniformed officers looked at him. They kept walking and he returned to the low voice. "What do you mean, he escaped?"

"I don't know how he got away. I just rolled through a local roadblock, so I asked a cop what was up. He told me to be careful because there was an escaped murderer on the loose. But, it's about Eddie."

Ortega could hear the caller's voice begin to quiver.

"My cousin? What the hell has he done now?"

"He's dead, boss. The guy jumped him on his bike and killed him before I could help. I kicked the shit out of the guy and knocked him out. I didn't know what else to do, so I called the sheriff's department, pretended to be him, left the evidence on the table, and got the hell out of there," the voice finished speaking, followed by a long moment of silence.

"You listen to what I'm telling you and you listen good. Understand? Kill his ass."

"But, we were supposed to just set him up. It worked and he'll pay for both of them."

"Am I not speaking clearly? Who protects your family?"

"You do, Jefe."

"What would happen if I stopped protecting your family? It's a dangerous world out there."

"I'll do it. But it's going to be hard to find the guy. He took his horses and he's hiding in the mountains."

"Then I suggest you dress warm and call me when it's done. I will work things on my end and call you later."

By 9:30 that morning, Gene's luck was still holding out when he was only two miles north of Cloudcroft. His thoughts turned to P & M.

"The Agency," Gene said aloud as an awareness came over him. "Damn it. I've got to call Price."

As he reached for the cell phone, the horses stopped and began neighing and turning. He couldn't get control as his horse reared up and threw him to the ground. The sound of the helicopter surprised him. It was coming from the south, behind the treetops. He jumped to his feet, pulled the reins of the lead horse, and scrambled down the east slope to get back in the trees. The reins of the second horse had somehow come loose from Gene's saddle and the animal stayed on the trail. He quickly tethered the first one to a low hanging branch and tried to get back up the hill, but there was no time to retrieve it.

Do they know where I am? He wondered. He looked up through the branches of the trees to where the sound was coming from. His heart was pounding. It was a smaller, unmarked chopper.

He put one foot in a stirrup, ready to mount and ride east as fast as he could.

The hacking blades were so loud that a piercing ring deafened Gene. He covered his ear with his free hand as the helicopter flew fast and low and in a straight line over the trail, over his stray horse, but it never slowed down. It headed north toward Ruidoso. When it was out of sight, he dropped to his knees in relief, closed his eyes, and ran his hands through his hair shaking his head, trying to clear his ears.

When he opened his eyes he looked for the horse on the trail, but it was gone. He thought the helicopter must have spooked it. He climbed back onto the saddle. He grew anxious that he was going to waste time trying to find it. He turned toward the trail and climbed back to the top.

He jumped down from his saddle running and then slid on his knees to a stop in front of the Appaloosa that was lying motionless on its side in the middle of the trail.

"What happened? Get up, Baby," he said, frantically looking at the horse's motionless body. He put his head to its chest but there was no heartbeat.

Blood was coming from under the horse and was soaking through the knees of his jeans. The horse had been shot.

Gene looked in the direction the shot could have come from. He heard nothing, not even a bird. The helicopter had scared all of the animals away for miles. He could feel eyes on him. The bullet that had killed his horse was probably meant for him. He ran back to the opposite side of the horse he was riding.

The motion of someone in the distance caught his attention. His body tensed when he saw a man running with a rifle through the trees at the bottom of the west slope. Gene was afraid and angry at the same time. He watched the man with curiosity even though he knew he should have been retreating.

"Where are you going, you son-of-a-bitch?" he whispered then looked ahead of the man. His stomach tied into a knot when he saw a parked dirt bike.

Both the man and the dirt bike were too far away to make out details, but Gene knew who it was. That's why the horses got spooked. They heard the motorcycle before the helicopter. The man reached the dirt bike.

Gene mounted his horse and turned in circles as he looked down at the one he would be leaving behind, then back at the man at the bottom of the hill. Gene kicked hard and took off in a gallop down the east slope away from the rider.

"There it is." Sheriff Wilcox said to Deputy Mansfield.

The police helicopter flew low over the top of the pine trees that surrounded a large meadow just south of Ruidoso. It hovered above the landing area before touching down. The wind from its blades blew the hat off Deputy Mansfield's head. While Mansfield chased it, Sheriff Wilcox walked with his chin tucked low to the helicopter. The door opened and Detective Stanton stepped down.

"Sheriff Wilcox?" Stanton yelled over the sound of the blades and stuck his hand out. Stanton had driven his own car to Cloudcroft earlier that morning then took the short helicopter ride to Ruidoso.

Sheriff Wilcox shook Stanton's hand. They walked to the outer edge of the meadow. The helicopter lifted and headed back over the trees.

"Detective Stanton, meet Deputy Mansfield. He was at Mr. Martine's house last night when Mr. Martine beat up another one of my deputies and got away."

"What's the status on the search for him?" Stanton asked.

"Let's drive to the temporary command post we've set up. We'll talk there and I'll show you what we're doing."

The three men got into the sheriff's SUV and drove across the meadow and onto a graded dirt road. After making a series of turns, Stanton saw a set of twenty by ten-foot nylon pop-up covers. There were several SUVs, four-wheel ATVs, motorcycles, and horse trailers. Sheriff Wilcox parked next to the pop-up where two other men, not in uniform, were sitting at a folding table.

When the men got out of the SUV, Stanton noticed the table was covered with topographical maps of the mountains. The main map had been marked with triangles and squares.

"Any luck yet?" the sheriff asked.

"Nothing yet, Sheriff," one of the men replied.

"What are these markings?" Stanton pointed to the maps.

"They are areas we've already covered," the sheriff said. "The way we see it, Martine wouldn't head north. He's probably trying to get back to El Paso. He's riding one horse and leading another."

"How many men are looking?" Stanton wanted to know.

"We've got about ten off-duty Ruidoso police officers here, ten more in Cloudcroft, some border patrol agents and a couple of state police. We don't think he'll ride any of the main trails. It's too risky. From what we know, he's been riding in these mountains for years and knows the trails like the back of his hand. There are hundreds of miles of trails to cover. We're focusing on those that would get him to Cloudcroft the fastest. It's just a matter of time, you know. Detective, when we do catch him, New Mexico gets to try him for murder first."

"What do you mean, first?"

"I know he's just a suspect in El Paso but, isn't this enough to arrest him for your case?" the sheriff asked.

"Can we talk in private for a moment?"

The two men got back into the sheriff's SUV and closed the doors. Sheriff Wilcox started the motor and turned on the heater.

"What's on your mind, detective?"

"I don't think Martine, killed anyone."

"My deputy caught your guy red-handed. He found Mr. Martine passed out in a chair. He smelled to high heaven of whisky. He had coke in his nose, a duffle bag filled with cash and cocaine was sitting on his table."

Wilcox bit down. The El Paso detective questioned his judgment.

"A dead guy was tied to his deck outside. Your guy worked him over good before he killed him. I'd say he tortured the poor bastard first."

"I knew you'd feel strongly about your case and I don't blame you for being upset. That's why I asked to speak to you alone."

"I'm listening."

"As far as I'm concerned you are right about your assessment of the situation last night and yes, he is a suspect in the murder of Elliot Jones. However, Martine has been a well respected business man in El Paso for years."

"I know. It was in the papers. All those big city ad guys use coke."

Stanton winced. "Let me finish."

<u>Chapter Eleven</u>

Detective Stanton unzipped the leather coat he was wearing over a flannel shirt, and retrieved the bag containing the medallion. He opened the bag and let the silver coin drop in his hand. He handed it to the sheriff.

"Ever seen anything like that before, sheriff?"

"Is it solid silver?" the sheriff asked, but Stanton didn't respond.

The sheriff smoothed the engravings with his fingers.

"What is it?"

"It's a medallion that has been tied to one of the largest drug rings this country has ever seen. Notice the bull's head with the marijuana leaf."

The sheriff's weathered-dry thumb caressed the leaf.

"The other side is a flag. Notice how it begins as a U. S. flag and fades into a Mexican flag.

Both designs are logos representing the drugs and the cooperation of people from both countries to move them. They call themselves Free-Landers because they're trafficking the drugs freely across two countries. Even the Feds can't seem to connect the pieces of the drug ring."

The sheriff said, "So your boy is involved with this drug ring. Hell, that's even more of a reason to bring him in. Martine was caught with a duffel bag of cash and cocaine."

"This is the part of my story that you will have to decide what to believe for yourself."

Stanton knew what he was about to say would be hard to believe but Stanton needed an ally. "We found this medallion at the murder scene of Elliot Jones, who tried to scratch the word 'medallion' on the sidewalk with a rock. With so little to go on, we believe whoever killed Jones was a Free-Lander."

"The sheriff tossed the medallion back to Stanton. "Martine is wanted for murdering a man at his house. He had cash and drugs in his possession, not to mention the stuff that was in his nose." The sheriff scratched his chin. "And, he was personally connected with the victim in El Paso. That, to me, adds up to one guilty S.O.B. Let's catch him and lock him away."

"I knew you'd be too stupid to see the big picture." Detective Stanton was losing ground but expected it and went on the offensive.

The sheriff said, "Just what other scenario could there be?" He crossed his arms as if waiting for an answer.

Stanton placed the medallion in the bag and back into his pocket.

"I was thinking, being that you're a Sheriff, you might be a smarter man. I was wrong. I'm sorry for wasting your time." Stanton opened the door, stepped out of the SUV and closed the door.

Wilcox struggled to turn around in the driver seat. He threw his door open, jumped out, slammed the door and moved to where Stanton was standing. Stanton stood with his back turned, but heard the Sheriff's exertions and smiled under the thick mustache.

"Who in the hell do you think you are, detective?" the sheriff yelled as he approached. "I got this position because I call them as I see them, and I am rarely wrong." He was pointing his finger at Stanton's head when he turned around. "In this case, your boy is guilty as sin, and you know it."

The men at the map table stopped what they were doing and stared at the two men.

Stanton held up both of his hands in a weak defense. "You're right, Sheriff. Go get your man."

"Then what the hell was all that back there, Stanton? You're one stupid son of a... Wait."

Wilcox stopped abruptly as he rubbed his face and paced two steps.

"I'm a stupid son of a what, Sheriff?"

"You may not be as stupid as I thought," the sheriff said. He took his hat off and rubbed his head as if his brain had not had this much stimulation in years. You think your boy is being framed. You think these so-called Free-Landers are setting him up for the murder in El Paso."

"It's possible."

"But that doesn't explain anything. There's still the dead guy we found at his cabin and the drugs and the money."

"Did you ever consider what Mr. Martine was telling you was true?" the detective asked.

"How could I? He was sitting there with all the evidence, looking like crap. My deputy tells me he found him passed out from the drugs and alcohol."

"That entire crime scene didn't make sense. Did you take a blood test, Sheriff?"

"Hell, none of it made any sense. I'd have to say the guy being tied up outside was pretty strange and no, we didn't do a blood test."

"I don't want to discredit your investigation Sheriff, but you told me the story Mr. Martine had conveyed to you. Isn't it possible he might have been telling the truth? That's how frame jobs work."

"I still don't believe he's not guilty, but..."

"Isn't that what the jury is for?" Stanton said.

"The only way we'll begin to get to the bottom of this thing is to bring him in."

"I just don't want your boys to get trigger-happy before we do."

Gene rode his trail horse harder than he should have, cutting in and out of trees at full-speed. The horse's mouth frothed with foam. Its chest and back were sweat-soaked.

Gene knew he had a good head start. Even on a dirt bike, the gunman couldn't have followed down the rough terrain. Now that Gene knew the gunman was out there, he just needed to listen and pay attention to his horse's reactions. At the slightest twitch of its head, he would kick his horse and ride like hell.

He dismounted and inspected his Appaloosa. Gene's face had a few burning scratches on his right cheek caused by a tree limb but the horse had blood trickling from the corner of its right eye.

The horse snorted and jerked. On closer inspection, Gene started to gag. He hunched over, heaving several times as he threw up yellow bile from his empty stomach onto the white snow at his feet. He held onto the reins with his left hand and fell to his knees. He filled the glove on his right hand with clean snow and rubbed it over his face, until it was numb. He stood up and stroked the horse's nose, slowly sliding his hand up to the horse's blinded eye, where a broken splinter had impaled itself.

"It's okay, Baby. It's okay. I'm sorry. I'm so sorry," he whispered in its ear. "Shhhh, it'll be all right," he said.

He pulled the twig out with flesh still attached, then hugged the horse's neck. He was disgusted for what happened to his horses but, he saw no other signs of any discomfort or suffering of this one. He mounted and walked the horse slowly at first, making sure it would still respond to his commands.

"First," he whispered. "I'll find a place to rest, eat and figure out how to get home. I'll need to leave you, baby, but I'll come back for you." He patted the horse's face on the good eye side. "The only way out of this mess is to prove my innocence."

The air was cold and the sun was bright. He welcomed the warm rays as his cheeks began to thaw. The pain from the scratches on his face returned in a light, thin throb from the edge of his nostril to his earlobe. As the trail wound around, he could only see pieces of mountain through the trees. It would be hard to see anybody coming his direction, but they would have the same problem seeing him. He glimpsed something through the trees about forty feet in front of him.

"Whoa," Gene whispered, pulling the horse to a stop. He dismounted, walked the horse to a nearby tree and tied the reins to a low branch. His line of sight had changed. Taking one step every couple of seconds, he moved from tree to tree, hiding, looking. When he finally saw it, his heart began racing.

About fifteen yards in front of him sat a riderless four-wheel ATV with camouflage paint on the fenders and an official looking logo on the fuel tank. The green color in the design was pale, distinctive to the U. S. Border Patrol.

Standing behind a tall pine, every muscle in his body tightened. He noticed the vapors from his breath and tried to hold it for seconds at a time. He wasn't sure if he had been spotted.

Gene crouched as low as he could and took four slow steps to his left to another tree, surveyed the area again, then moved to yet another tree that was closer to the ATV. A low groan, as if someone was in pain, came from his right. He saw only pine trees and a shell of a large fallen tree that had been consumed by termites. The groaning started again coming from behind one of the larger trees that stood next to the fallen one.

Gene took three deep breaths for encouragement and then ran as fast as he could. He slipped once just short of the log and scrambled to get up, then dove over the log.

The surprised border patrol agent stumbled and fell backwards to the ground as his pants dropped to his thighs.

"Stop right there, Mr. Martine. You're under arrest." The agent squirmed and slid, fighting his pants that were now around his ankles to get up.

Gene was surprised to be called by name.

The squelch of static from a radio came from the agent's utility belt hanging from a broken tree limb.

"Don't do it. You're in enough trouble. Don't you do it."

Gene grabbed the belt, pulled the standard issued nine millimeter gun from its tight leather pouch, and pointed it at the agent.

"I don't have a choice," Gene said.

"Don't shoot," the agent said. "Please God. Don't shoot me. I've got a family." The agent held up his shaking left hand and kicked, freeing one of his legs from the tangled pants. He began dragging his naked buttocks backward through the twigs and snow.

"I'm not going to kill you." Gene shook the gun barrel at the agent.

The man in uniform complied with Gene's orders.

"Put your pants back on, but take your boots off."

"I'll get frostbite," the agent said.

He rose to his feet, wearing only his green United States Border Patrol uniform shirt, coat, gloves and work boots. He dusted the snow and dirt from his buttocks and legs and pulled up his pants.

Gene was racked with emotions being the first time he had ever held a gun on someone. He surprised himself for having the guts to be so bold. As the situation became more controlled, he started feeling sorry for the poor guy standing in the snow and mud without any pants.

"Why were you groaning before?"

"I have a urinary tract infection and it hurts when I urinate." The agent said. "Listen, Mr. Martine. This mountain is crawling with people looking for you. If you don't do the right thing now, your chances of getting off this mountain alive will be slim-to-none." The agent removed his boots.

"Toss those over here," Gene said referring to the boots.

"You can't expect me to stand in the snow without boots."

"You heard me." Gene shook the gun.

The agent did as he was told and kicked the boots to Gene's feet. "Be careful with that thing. It's got a touchy trigger."

"Sit over here on the log next to this tree."

The young agent took two giant steps in an effort to stay out of the snow.

"What's your name?" Gene asked, as he pulled one of two sets of handcuffs from the agent's utility belt and tossed them to the agent, keeping himself out of his reach.

"Richard."

"How old are you, Richard?"

"Twenty-two. But... Mr. Martine. Don't you understand the severity of this situation?"

"Put your arms around the tree and cuff yourself."

"You can't be serious. You can't leave me out here. I'll die of exposure."

"Well, Richard, it seems to me being exposed is not a real problem for you. But, if you don't cooperate, you're the one who is going to be worrying about the severity of your own situation."

Agent Richard complied with Gene's instructions as he reached around the tree and placed the cuffs on his wrists. Expecting them to be loose enough to slide his hands back through, Gene grabbed each cuff and tightened them. He began walking back to his horse.

"Where are you going? C'mon man, don't leave me out here."

But Gene didn't reply.

"At least take me as far as the edge of town. I got a three-year-old little girl."

Richard's words trailed off as Gene disappeared behind the trees. Less than five minutes later, he looked up to Gene coming back up the trail with his horse in tow.

"Now, Richard, before I leave I'm going to tell you a story and I want you to remember everything I say, so if I don't make it..." Gene paused at the thought. "Just make sure you tell the right people what I tell you. Got it?"

"Whatever, man." The fact that Gene wanted him to tell his story assured him he would survive the ordeal.

Leaving out minor details, Gene explained everything. Richard tried to ask questions but Gene would only shut him down with a harsh 'listen'.

"I'm taking your ATV. When I get to Cloudcroft, I'll tell someone where you are. You shouldn't be out here more than a few hours. And, I'm leaving my horse with you to keep you company." He tied the reins to the links between the handcuffs.

Then he kicked the boots over to Richard's feet where he could slip them on with a little effort.

"If anything happens to my horse, I will break your legs. Do we understand each other?" Gene didn't wait for an answer and began walking to the ATV.

"Mr. Martine, if what you've told me is true, then why don't you just turn yourself in?" Richard said, as he watched Gene toss the gun toward a tree, lay his saddlebags with the agent's utility belt over the gas tank and mount the ATV.

"Just tell it the way I told you," Gene said then he heard a crack.

The horse started pulling at the agent's cuffs, trying to pull away from the sound of the ATV and Richard slumped over. A puff of smoke from the barrel of a rifle rose from a position high on the slope. Gene ducked and bark flew off a tree that was only a foot away, followed the same crack. He pushed the throttle of the ATV all the way, popped the clutch, and took off down the trail.

He went full throttle in the straight-aways and wrestled the machine around the tight turns, occasionally on only two wheels. He imagined he heard the sound of the assassin's motorcycle gaining on him. Finding a place to hide was his only option. He turned left, then right, then left again when he saw a grove of wild bushes about fifty yards off of the trail. He stayed on the trail until he passed the grove then turned off and circled back behind them. Moments later the motorcycle raced by. Gene waited until the sound faded and disappeared. He rode to the trail and backtracked until he was sure it was safe. Then he took another trail that would lead him to the town of Cloudcroft. He never looked back but he was sorry that he threw Richard's hand gun away.

Cords of split pine were stacked five feet tall, two rows deep across the outside of the lowest level of the three-story cabin that stood ahead of him. The second level had a balcony that jutted out over the stacks of wood. Snow had been left unshoveled and there were no tracks from vehicles or humans. On one side of the home was a pile of pine logs. A splitter was covered by a black tarp and sat next to the logs.

There were no signs of human activity or vehicles on the road in front of the cabin. Other than the sounds of a woodpecker chipping away at a tree off in the distance and the radio chatter coming from his duffel bags, it was quiet.

Gene pushed the ATV up the short incline to the pile of uncut wood. He surveyed the property. The brick chimney at the south end of the cabin had once stood straight. The bricks were weathered, broken, and missing in places, absent of smoke rising from its mouth on that cold late morning.

He threw his saddlebags over his shoulder and looked for a way inside, staying away from the front of the home. He peered through two windows that were locked before finding the door to the lower level on the north side. Gene thought the paint on the old warped door might have once been red. The panes of glass in the door were too dirty to see inside and the handle was rusted.

He took off his coat, placed it over one of the panes to deaden the noise and shattered it with his elbow. Reaching through the new hole he found two latches holding it firm to the frame. He slid the first latch free, but the second latch was stuck. He pulled at it until it gave way.

He grabbed the back of his left forearm. When the latch gave way, he cut it on a piece of glass that was still wedged the door. Blood trickled from the jagged glass to the thirsty, dry wood. The bottom of the door scraped the dirt on the threshold as he tugged it open and shut it again once inside.

It was as cold inside as it was outside. There were no interior walls in the large room and the dirt-filtered sunlight shown bright enough through the windows so that the whole bottom level of the cabin so he could see it was used for storage.

An old leather sofa was in the far left corner with two more leather chairs stacked on top of it. Four sets of queen-size mattresses leaned against the wall in the right corner, along with their headboards and frames. In the middle of the room, two or three sheets were used to cover other assorted heavy items. Dozens of boxes filled with someone else's life and memories were stacked along the walls and in the spaces between all of the other junk. Large abandoned cobwebs hung from every corner and ceiling rafters like small sets of draperies from the years of dust that had settled.

Gene found the wooden staircase that lead to the second level. Next to it stood an old refrigerator. The handle was stubborn at first, but he jerked it sharply and it broke loose. The door creaked and squeaked. Something was pushing the door with its weight from the inside as he let go of the handle.

The door sprang open and whatever it was jumped out at Gene and crash to the ground with a loud clatter. He gasped, tripped over his own feet, and fell to the ground. He scrambled to stand up to see an old set of golf clubs scattered about the floor. His nerves rattled, he raced up the dark stairwell to the second level of the cabin. He was comforted to feel the same cold air upstairs as down. No one was home.

He was standing at the edge of the furnished living room, with a pool table in front of him. Beyond that, a rawhide sofa and matching chairs faced the grand fireplace built into the far wall. Including the coffee table and two end tables, the arms and legs of all of the furniture were made from cattle horns tied together with strips of leather. The walls were adorned with pictures of a large family. Most were current photographs and others were dated black and whites. The head of a buck with large antlers hung on the wall across from the head of a mountain lion that stared down, frozen in time with its mouth open in a fierce growl from above the fireplace mantel. Unlike the storage room below, the room appeared to be recently cleaned.

To his right was the continuation of the staircase to the street level, where the front door would be. To the left of the staircase was the entrance to the kitchen.

Like the living room, the kitchen was immaculate with modern stainless steel appliances, a microwave, newer cabinets, and beige stone-colored tile countertops that wrapped around creating a breakfast bar. An eight-seat wooden dining table was on the opposite side. To his dismay, the side-by-side refrigerator was empty of real food. Bottles of ketchup, mustard, and barbeque sauce occupied the door shelves. Three bottles of water, a six-pack of Coors beer sat on the top shelf along with a large note written in black marker taped to the shelf.

The note read, "Anything you don't want, leave behind Anything that will spoil, throw away; anything that can be frozen, put in the freezer." Suddenly it made sense: This was a vacation home.

He grabbed a cold beer, closed the door, and opened the freezer. Inside was a frozen loaf of bread, a pack of assorted sandwich meats, and a half-eaten gallon of ice cream. He took out the bread and meat and placed them on the counter.

Gene had managed to defrost them in the microwave and then found the cabin's thermostat to defrost himself. He constructed two towering sandwiches of warm wheat bread, pastrami, ham and turkey. He consumed the first with big bites and washed it down with half of the beer. He took the second sandwich, his beverage, the cell phone and radio to the living room. He sat on the sofa and sighed heavily before he finished his first meal of the day.

It was 12:30 in the afternoon. Until that moment, Gene had been in a sort of self-survival mode and had not reflected on the morning. To him it felt like a week had gone by in twenty-four hours. He dozed off before he finished the beer.

"Richard," Gene yelled and sat straight up on the sofa. He quickly regained awareness. He picked up the cell phone that displayed the words 'New Voicemail'. He hit the end button once. The message changed to '7 missed calls'.

"Lisa," he surmised. "3:15? Oh, my God. I've been asleep for almost three hours."

He found Stanton's number but just as he was about to hit the send button he realized no one knew he had Elliot's phone except Lisa. If he used it, Stanton would use its signal to find him. He wondered if they were tracking his phone.

Detective Stanton and Sheriff Wilcox had arrived in Cloudcroft in the Sheriff's SUV an hour earlier. Wilcox was dropping Stanton off at his car when they decided to get some pie at a local diner in the heart of downtown. Stanton was surprised to see the phone number with a New Mexico area code of 575 on the display.

"Hello?" the Detective said, as he looked at the sheriff.

"Stanton, you need to listen."

"Bull, Gene. You have authorities in two states looking for you. You're the one that needs to listen and lis…" Stanton's line went dead.

"He's here," Stanton informed the sheriff. His phone rang only once before he answered.

"Gene, where are you?"

"In case you didn't notice, all I have to do is hang up. Now you need to listen. It's a matter of life or death for Richard, I mean, Border Patrol Agent Richard."

Stanton motioned to Sheriff Wilcox for something to write on and took a pen from the v-neck in his golf shirt. The sheriff handed the detective his used paper napkin.

"Gene? Are you there?"

"I just left a border patrol agent handcuffed to a tree. He said his name was Richard."

"You did what?"

"I came across him in the woods. Unfortunately for him I caught him by surprise and cuffed him to the tree then he was shot in the back by a guy trying to kill me."

"What guy is trying to kill you? There's a lot of guys in those woods looking for you. You sure it wasn't one of them trying to stop you from killing the agent?"

The detective covered the phone and spoke to the sheriff. "I thought I told you I didn't want your men to get trigger happy."

Sheriff Wilcox shrugged.

Gene said in an angry tone, "Stanton, you were right about the Free-Landers. They were trying to frame me and now they're trying to kill me. I've got to prove my innocence."

"Where are you, Gene? The only way we're going to get to the bottom of all this is for you to turn yourself in. Let us do our job. I'm in Cloudcroft right now. I can pick you up and we can talk this out."

"Cloudcroft?"

"I'm trying to help. Where are you?"

"I'll find my way to Albuquerque. At least there I know I'll have some time to think things through. Right now, you need to get some guys to the south rim of the Lincoln trails, about three miles north of Cloudcroft. That's where you'll find the border patrol agent."

Stanton covered his phone again, "Have your men surround the Lincoln trails from all angles and tell them there is an officer down below the south rim."

The sheriff began relaying the information over the handheld radio.

"Stanton, I'm gone."

"I still don't know what you're talking about. Who do you think is after you and why?"

"Free-Landers, detective, and I don't know why except that it's all related to Elliot's murder. There's more I need to tell you, but not now." Gene hung up the phone.

"What's going on, Stanton?" Wilcox said.

"He's got a radio," the detective said as he rubbed his chin in deep thought and then handed Sheriff Wilcox the napkin he was writing on. "Get this number traced. He's here."

"What do you mean he's got a radio?"

Detective Stanton stood from the table, reached into his pocket, and then threw a ten-dollar bill on the table.

"I heard your voice delayed through my phone. Come on, I'll tell you on the way," he said to the sheriff then began talking to himself.

"Where are we going?" The sheriff struggled to get out of his seat as if lead weights were holding him down.

Chapter Twelve

When he looked at the VoiceComm cell phone, Gene saw the small icon of an envelope flashing in the upper right hand corner signifying a text message was waiting to be read. He pushed the buttons to read, "I tried to reach you. Call me."

"Gene, I'm so glad you called," Lisa said in an even tone.

"Where have you been, Lisa? I was worried."

"I was out handling more funeral arrangements. Marlene called me a little after one o'clock. She asked me to meet her at your house. She said the police wanted to search it and she said she thought I should be there since you couldn't be. It's strange that they would call her, but I guess it's because she's your ex."

There were four marked police cars parked on the street in front of his home, one unmarked car and a crime scene investigation van parked in Gene's driveway. The front door was open as a stream of uniformed police officers walked in and out of the house. Some officers were interviewing Gene's neighbors, including Ricardo Escobar.

"Lisa, who's around you?" he said.

"I'm in front of your house and Marlene is inside."

"From now on, if anyone comes within ear-shot of our conversations you need to act like you're talking to someone else until it's clear."

"Okay, I understand," she said, and he heard her sniffing to fight back tears. Where are you?"

"I'm still trying to get to Cloudcroft."

As much as he trusted her, he didn't trust the people that might ask her the same question. The less she knew about his whereabouts, the safer she was.

"Gene, none of this makes sense. You've never lied to me. So, I need to believe in you, right?"

"What the hell have they been saying?"

"They found your stuff," Lisa said as she turned toward the house.

Marlene was watching her through the living room window.

"Just tell me you're not involved with those people. I'll believe you, Gene."

"What did they find?"

"Make sure the flowers are arranged the way I told you. Uh-huh, yeah, just like we talked about." Lisa's voice changed to a calm business tone as she walked away from two officers that had stopped and begun talking to each other too close to her.

"Can you talk now? What stuff are you talking about?"

"Your drugs," she whispered. "The cocaine."

"You can't be serious."

"I saw them with my own eyes. There were three large bricks of that stuff under your bed. What are you doing with all that coke?

"I've never taken anything stronger than an aspirin. You know that. Someone is playing you just like they're playing me. Why else would they want you to see it?"

She said, "Marlene told me to come down here, not the police."

"Did she say who contacted her?"

"No."

"Lisa, don't let them get to you."

Lisa cleared her throat. "What do you want me to do?"

"Nothing right now. Don't let anyone know you and I have ever talked, not even Marlene. If everything goes well, I'll be in El Paso before nightfall. I'll call you then, okay?"

"I'm scared," she said.

"I am too, Lisa. I'll call you as soon as I can," Gene said and ended the call.

Lisa turned to see Marlene standing behind her.

"Stanton, your boy is no more than a few miles northwest of here. We traced the call from the phone number you gave me to a house in the woods. My guys will pick him up."

They were riding in Stanton's car.

"I don't believe Martine is dumb enough to stay put for you," Stanton said. "I think he's out here. Just keep your eyes open."

They drove up and down the main street and through the parking lot of Pine Meadows, the town's only strip mall. The number of people milling around the shops on that Monday afternoon were few, allowing both men to study the face of every person they passed as they drove by very slow.

The fact that most men were wearing the flannel shirts and jeans didn't help and many were wearing the same kind of leather coat with wool lining that Gene was last seen in. Stanton knew exactly what Gene looked like as he scanned the small local group of men. Only those few with full beards were ignored.

After striking out there, he drove east toward the cabin neighborhoods where the call was traced. He looked at the caller I.D.

"It's him," he said, gesturing to the Sheriff to pick up his handheld radio. "When I give you the signal, hold the button down for five seconds and release it."

The Sheriff nodded.

"Hello, Gene. Have you changed your mind?"

"I thought you were one of the good guys, detective."

"I'm trying to help you."

"Then why is my house in El Paso being torn apart as we speak? You were just there and I invited you in. You know I have nothing to hide."

"I have no idea what you're talking about." Stanton held up his hand with curled fingers and wiggled his thumb at the sheriff.

"They searched my home and found three kilos of coke under my bed. What do you think of me now, detective? Guilty as charged?"

Stanton was caught off-guard with what he had just heard. He knew nothing about a search warrant and the man he believed was innocent had just confessed to possessing enough coke to put him away in a penitentiary for years. Stanton didn't want the sheriff to know any more than he already knew about their conversation.

"Gene, I promise that I'll check into the situation. All I'm asking is that you talk to me. You've got to trust me."

"That's a bunch of crap, Stanton, and..." Gene stopped talking to Stanton and held the phone away from his ear. "He's back."

"Who's back?"

Gene ended the call.

"What was all that talk about search warrants?" the sheriff asked.

"He's close, Sheriff," Stanton said.

"How do you know he's close?"

"The radio. Gene must be too distracted because he didn't notice my delayed voice coming over the radio. He must have taken it from the border patrol agent."

Stanton took the Sheriff's radio. "How far do these things reach up here?"

"Maybe 7 to 10 miles without obstructions," the Sheriff said, as his bulldog face twisted from a look of bewilderment to a look of satisfaction. "If you could hear your voice over the two-way that means I was right. Your guy... I mean, our guy could be no more than a few miles away."

"Mr. Martine's here, but where?"

"I'll put an all-points call out right now," the sheriff said, attempting to take the radio out of Stanton's hand.

"He'll hear it and disappear for sure. We need him to think we bought his story about heading north again. Maybe Mr. Martine will make a mistake and decide the coast is clear enough to step out into the public."

Through a window on the first floor of the cabin, Gene watched a man on a blue motorcycle ride up the dirt road that lead to the cabin. Instead of feeling the rush of adrenaline and anxiety, his heart rate maintained. It was easy to recognize the rider as one of the two men that attacked him in Ruidoso.

How did you find me? He thought. "Or, did I find you first?"

It was the same man who had thrown the bottle of whiskey at Gene's truck on the highway. If the man entered the home from the same door as Gene had, he could hide behind the door and hit him over the head with one of the golf clubs down stairs or he could simply hide until the murderer was gone.

The rider was wearing a thin black leather coat, a dingy bandana low around his head, blue jeans and black cowboy boots. A gaudy gold ring was on each of his fingers and both thumbs. He had several long gold chains around his neck that bounced on his chest over every bump in the road.

Gene watched him pass all the cabins surveying each one. He passed Gene, but continued down the road passing the last two homes on the road. The rider made a quick u-turn and idled back up the road. It was then he saw the rifle hanging over the man's left shoulder, somewhat hidden under his coat. The barrel of the gun at the end hung several inches below the coat's seam. Gene moved away from the window and listened to the bike's gears go from first to second then to third, then back down to first. The bike rode to the back of the home.

Gene watched from the master bedroom window as the rider cut the motor and rolled to a stop next to the rows of stacked wood under the balcony. He kicked down the stand, dismounted the machine, pulled his arm out of his sleeve and retrieved his weapon. Holding the rifle at his side, he walked a few feet away from the cabin, looking at the ground. The ATV's tracks were visible that led from the forest to the cabin and toward the covered log splitter. He turned back and squinted hard as he looked up at the three story wooden cabin. He ran to the back to the old warped door with the broken glass.

He reached through the broke pane, turned the knob and walked in. He headed to the stairs only to become entangled and tripped over the scattered golf clubs. The element of surprise was gone. He jumped to his feet and climbed to the top of the staircase in four giant stair-skipping steps.

"Donde estas gringo? You ass is mine," he said. "Come on, I'm cold. Let's get this over with."

The killer searched the kitchen, went back to the living room, and crept down the hallway checking the closet and bathroom. As he was headed for the master bedroom, Gene leaped from the balcony.

The man smiled. "Oh no, you don't gringo!" and ran back through the cabin.

The ground was soft. Gene's boots left deep impressions where he landed but the trail of footprints disappeared after Gene's sixth step toward the log splitter that was still covered fifteen yards away.

"So you wanna ride, si?"

He shot through the tarp twice as he approached the splitter. Suddenly, the ATV roared to life from under the pile of wood. The gunman began firing, splintering three pieces of wood before Gene popped the clutch and exploded from the pile.

The flying wood hit the gunman, knocking him to the ground. There were too many things happening for Gene to notice he had run over the man's right knee, ripping his jeans and tearing flesh from his kneecap.

He sped up the hill to the neighborhood dirt road, turned left and headed toward town, continuously looking over his shoulder. He expected the man to appear behind him racing through the gears of the dirt bike. With a maximum speed of forty-five miles an hour, the ATV would be no match for the dirt bike.

Gene knew Highway 82 couldn't be more than a half a mile away and he needed to reach the main road before the assassin caught him. Highway 82 would be the quickest way and the most direct route off of the mountain and to Alamogordo, but it would be crawling with cops. Instead, he planned to turn south again on Highway 24. Without any sign of being chased, Gene reached the highway and turned right.

Detective Stanton and Sheriff Wilcox were headed east on the same highway when Stanton saw Gene approaching them in the distance.

"Hey, Stanton, that looks like a border patrol agent," the sheriff said, as Gene passed them. "Let's stop him and see if he's seen anything."

The detective agreed and flipped a small black switch next to cigarette lighter on the dash.

Gene swerved right, up into the trees.

"Where's he going?" Stanton asked Wilcox.

"Maybe he didn't see your lights."

He lifted his foot from the gas pedal and let the car coast as he thought about what he just saw. Then he turned the steering wheel hard left and floored the gas pedal, leaving behind several feet of tire rubber in a U-shape on the asphalt and a trail of blue smoke.

"What are you doing?" yelled Wilcox.

"I think we found our guy," Stanton said, with a smile under his mustache. "I saw saddlebags lying over the gas tank. Look for him."

They raced westward, passing the ATV's entrance to the trees from the road. If they couldn't see Gene, Stanton wanted to get in front him.

Gene didn't go far before he parked the ATV behind a fallen tree and watched as the car sped past.

"Okay, Stanton, now you know I'm here," Gene whispered aloud. "The good news is, now I know where you are."

As soon as the Chevy had cleared the horizon, Gene started the four-wheeler, rode back down to the highway and crossed it. He drove slowly through the trees until he reached the business district of downtown Cloudcroft. The Ace Hardware store was the first building he came to on the small highway. He parked the ATV on the side of the store and covered it with trash bags taken from a dumpster nearby.

Including the hardware store, there were only four cabin-type buildings between him and the highway he wanted to be on. Next to the hardware store were a bakery, an antique store and a real estate office. A large diner sat on the northwest corner of the intersection and a busy gas station was on the northeast corner.

Like most of the hillside buildings, the front of the hardware store stood on short stilts. The crawl space provided Gene with an ideal hiding place, concealing him but giving him a view of the parking lot on his side of the road and of the busy diner and gas station across the way.

He dropped to his stomach and crawled between the stilts only to come face-to-face with a family of raccoons. The glowing pink eyes of at least four of the animals startled him, causing him to bump his head hard on the wooden floor above him. Gene watched the four of them scamper through the openings of the short staircase in front of the store.

"Look, Mama. Raccoons," a toddler boy said as he ran toward the staircase.

"No. Stop." his mom said as she took a step and grabbed his arm. "They could bite you."

Gene heard their voices, but could only see both pairs of legs. The boy was wearing jeans and tennis shoes. His mom was wearing brown polyester slacks and hiking boots.

"I wonder if there's more, Mama. They came from under there."

Gene didn't move. The little boy walked toward his position with his mom behind him. Just as the boy began to bend over just five feet from Gene, his mom pulled on his arm and dragged him in the opposite direction.

"Awful," she said. "We don't have time. Besides, you're going to get dirty."

Then Gene saw it, Stanton's car parked at the diner across the street. The occasional passing car or semi truck would block his vision for a split second, but he could see a person sitting in the passenger seat while Stanton was standing outside dialing his cell phone.

He wondered who Stanton was calling as he dialed the phone several times, seemingly never making a connection.

It was 4:45 in the afternoon at the El Paso Police Station. Detective Manny Ortega was typing reports. He was detailing the events that had transpired at the Martine residence earlier that day and recording the evidence seized from the bedroom. His desk phone rang twice before breaking his concentration.

"Detective Ortega," he answered.

"Manny, it's Stanton."

Ortega smiled and relaxed back into his chair and propped his right foot over the corner of his desk. "Did you bag your buck yet?"

"Why don't you answer your cell phone?"

"I must have left the ringer on silent since this morning's briefing. Sorry about that."

"Our boy's made it to Cloudcroft."

Manny's smile disappeared. "How do you know?"

"I saw him, that's how. He's riding a stolen a border patrol ATV. Martine seems to be smarter than I gave him credit for, but we'll find him. Tell me, Manny, who trashed Martine's house and on whose authority?"

Manny didn't respond. Instead he rubbed his five o'clock shadow as he bit his lower lip.

"Did you hear me?"

"I did. An anonymous tip came in that there were drugs in the home and I got the warrant signed by Judge Bonner. We found three kilos under his bed. Once we found it, no more bullshitting around, if you know what I mean. We trashed it good, but didn't find anything else."

"Why didn't you call me? This is my case." Stanton yelled.

"You weren't here," Ortega replied. "You're out of your jurisdiction chasing the damn rabbits. I was doing my job."

"I don't give a shit, Manny, and don't tell me how to work my case. You should've called me and you know it."

"Kiss my ass, Stanton. You would have done the same thing. Besides, we got the evidence, didn't we? You've got a case now, right?"

"Did you find a murder weapon or a medallion?" Or did you find anything in his house that would tie Martine to any homicide?"

"No."

"Then we don't have anything. You have three blocks of coke that any public defender could get thrown out."

"I'm sorry I didn't call you, but the results would be the same. Gene Martine is a dealer. We know that now and I think we both know he's part of the Free-Lander organization. It's just a matter of time before we put all the pieces together. Maybe we can't pin the murder on him, yet, but we've got what we need to hold him."

"Yeah, maybe."

"I'm telling you partner, all you got to do is catch his ass."

"And, I'm telling you, partner, don't let anybody lift another finger on this case without telling me first. Got it?"

"Fine," Manny said. "How did you know we trashed his house anyway?"

"Anonymous tip," Stanton said and ended the call.

Gene watched while Stanton finished his phone call then walked back to the car and talked with its passenger. The passenger opened the car door and got out. Gene recognized the sheriff when both men went inside the diner.

Gene waited to confirm it wasn't just a bathroom break for the two men. He surveyed the stretch of Highway 82 from west to east. He didn't see any other law enforcement in the vicinity. The space under the hardware store was too tight to turn around, and crawling out through the front would attract more attention from customers. Pulling with the toes of his boots and pushing with his hands, he worked his body backwards. When he was half through the opening, he stopped at the sound of a motorcycle. He could no longer see the highway to the east where the sound was originating, but he could see the gas station and convenience store across the road and the diner. He watched and listened, as the sound grew louder.

An eighteen-wheeler blocked his view for a moment. Before the truck reached the intersection, it down shifted and slowed before speeding up again as it went through. When it passed, he saw the blue bike. The rider coasted to a stop at the south side of the store in front of a large ice refrigerator. He dismounted, carrying a long object wrapped in burlap. He limped to the refrigerator and placed the bundle on top of it before limping into the store. Gene was too far away to see exactly what the man placed on the cooler, but he was sure it was the rifle.

He backed himself out of the crawlspace and sat back on his legs. He thought about calling Stanton and was about to do just that when another idea flashed in his head. The idea had *Elliot* written all over it.

When Elliot was a teenager, he and a friend had walked to a welding supply shop. 'You had to be eighteen or older to buy the stuff,' Elliot would say. Gene never thought to ask Elliot how they acquired what they needed. They supposedly spent hours carefully grinding the single ingredient into a fine powder. 'The stuff was too combustible straight up and we wanted to make as many bombs as we could, so we diluted it with baby powder, fifty-fifty,' Elliot would tell Gene. He had told Gene the same childhood story several times about going out to the canyons and blowing up large sandstone boulders or causing small landslides or exploding rabbit holes into big craters. Gene had always figured Elliot exaggerated the explosive properties of welding oxide.

Gene took his gloves off. He checked his pockets only to remember the Ruidoso Sheriff's Department had taken all that he had. He walked several feet to the pile of trash hiding the ATV, moved two trash bags and retrieved three hundred dollar bills from the duffel bag under the saddlebags. Lifting his coat collar up to conceal his identity, he inhaled deeply and walked out into the open, up the wooden steps and into the hardware store. He glanced around the small store, seeing only the young boy with his mother talking with an older man in coveralls about small animal traps. It seems raccoons were knocking her trashcans over in the middle of the night.

"May I help you?" the elderly woman behind the counter asked. She looked to be in her seventies, but in good shape, wearing bright pink lipstick on her thin lips and the same type of coveralls as the man describing a trap called 'Critter Gitter'.

"You wouldn't happen to have..." Gene caught himself whispering and cleared his throat to recover. "You wouldn't happen to have welding oxide, would you?"

"We do, but it's really old," she said in a voice louder than Gene would have preferred. "We don't sell much of it anymore. I don't know why. It's back there in the corner." She motioned to the back of the store.

"I'll find it," Gene said and walked away.

"Ronald, go show him where the welding oxide is," she shouted, even though Ronald was just two aisles away.

"Can't you see I'm busy, woman?" Ronald shouted back and continued demonstrating the Critter Gitter to the mom.

"That's okay. I got it."

Gene was relieved that he had seen the four dusty yellow boxes on the bottom shelf without needing assistance. He picked up one of the eight-by-two inch boxes and opened it to see six sticks of oxide, each wrapped in wax paper. He didn't know how much he was going to need and decided to take two boxes. He picked up one roll of duct tape that was two shelves higher. He would need some type of fuse to ignite it. Elliot claimed to use dynamite fuse but Gene wasn't about to ask for it. He looked over his shoulder, then back to the shelves for anything that might work.

"You find what you're looking for, Honey?" the woman hollered from the register.

Gene didn't look at her. "Exactly what I was looking for."

There it was, a twenty-foot roll of waterproof dynamite fuse.

He slid one roll of the fuse into his coat pocket and walked back up to the counter. Through the window behind the counter, Gene could see the motorcycle still parked in the same position, no sign of its owner. He could also see Stanton's car parked in front of the diner.

"You sure must like your welds hot," she said. "Find everything?"

"I need some D batteries."

"We got plenty of batteries." She wrinkled her nose.

Gene smiled, "I'll take twelve please. I've got a lot of flashlights."

Chapter Thirteen

Gene paid for his supplies. "Do you have any matches?"

"There's some complimentary ones right there." She pointed to the end of the counter closest to the doorway.

Gene took two books and walked to the entrance. He stood in the doorway to scan the area. He wondered why the assassin was taking so long in the convenience store. Acting as casual has he could, he walked down the wooden steps and disappeared around the side of the building and squatted behind a brown metal trash bin.

He tried to remember Elliot's description of how to build an explosive device. Although he had enough welding oxide to build several small bombs, he only needed one.

He rummaged through the trash bin and found a wadded piece of blank notebook paper. He flattened the paper against his thigh, rubbing it to loosen the wrinkles. Then holding it by two corners, he waived it like a handkerchief and laid it on the seat of the ATV. Streams of sunlight through the pine trees dotted the paper and the ground around him providing good visibility.

He retrieved one stick of from a yellow box and filed it, using the rough edge of a rock, making sure the filings landed on the paper in a pile of black powder. He remembered Elliot saying how they diluted the oxide fifty percent with baby powder and even then, the explosions were strong enough to cause a small landslide on the canyon walls.

Gene pulled out a pack of four, D-size batteries, then took out his leather working tools from the saddlebags and retrieved a scratch awl and used it to rip through the plastic packaging, freeing one of them. He used the awl to pry the top of the battery off and dig the life out of the casing. He placed the top of the battery on the ground and used the rock to hit the awl through the center of it. Taking the fuse from his pocket, he used a sharp edge of the rock to cut three inches of fuse and stuck one inch through the hole in the battery top and set it aside. He poured the oxide filings into the casing and carefully used the top of the battery to pack the filings as tight as he could, making sure the short end of the fuse stuck.

He wrapped duct tape tightly around the casing, leaving only the two inches of fuse exposed. When he finished, the explosive was a little smaller than a tennis ball, but not as round. He held up the finished product and studied it, then adjusted his focus across the road.

The motorcycle was gone.

Gene scrambled to his feet, gathered his supplies and placed the paper bag inside a saddlebag on the ATV. The bomb rested in his coat pocket as he crept to the corner of the building.

He spotted the blue motorcycle parked at the side of the diner. Stanton's car was still parked in the front.

Another eighteen-wheeler was coming from the east and he decided it would be his cover. Moving as slow as the others did toward the intersection, the truck would block the view from the diner just long enough for him to run across the road to the convenience store. As the truck approached, he walked from the hardware store to the shoulder of the highway and ran across when the truck passed, stopping when he reached the ice cooler. He kept a close eye on the diner doors as he stood on his toes trying to see what the biker left on top. The barrel of a rife was exposed through burlap.

"I thought so," he said.

With a hop off the ground, he shoved the gun hard enough to make it fall behind the cooler.

When he reached the back of the store he made sure the scene hadn't changed again and walked until he was directly behind the diner.

Gene had a unique view through the diner's rear window. He looked and saw the biker sitting across the room from Stanton and the sheriff.

Gene ran in a crouched position to the motorcycle. He wedged the explosive ball of duct tape in a crevice between the top of the engine and the fuel tank. He disconnected the spark plug wire, placed the tip of the fuse on the top of the spark plug and used the wire to hold it in place, leaving a small gap between the spark plug and wire. He heard voices and laughter coming from the front of the diner. When the young couple turned the corner, Gene was gone. They got into a pickup that was parked three spaces away from the motorcycle, backed up and left.

Stanton answered his cell phone. The number was another *505* area code but a different number.

"Gene?" he said and motioned to the sheriff to move to the front windows from their table that was in the middle of the diner.

"Yeah, it's me," he said into the receiver of a pay phone outside of the convenience store.

"I don't suppose you're going to tell me where you are?" The detective waited, but got what he expected: silence. "I didn't think so. What I do know is we are both in Cloudcroft, Gene."

"Stanton, I've done something I know I might regret, but it's the only way..." Gene said.

"The only way to what?"

The assassin was sitting on the near side of the room with his back to the windows, two booths from where Stanton and the sheriff were watching. He was eating pancakes when his cell phone rang, too. Briefly distracted by the ring, Sheriff Wilcox glanced in his direction, then back to the window.

"Stanton, they're destroying my life. In less than three days, they've killed Elliot, attacked me in my own home and framed me for the murder of one of their own."

"I know you're talking about Free-Landers, but I can't help you if you don't let me."

203

"Now one of them is trying to kill me. I've been hunted for the last eight hours. He killed one of my horses and Richard."

"Is Richard the border patrol agent?" Stanton asked.

"He shot him in cold blood and then he took a shot at me. And I don't know how he did it but he found me again."

"We can protect you, but it's up to you." Stanton could hear in Gene's voice the eerie calmness of determination.

"You know as well as I do, detective, you guys can't protect me," Gene said. "You told me yourself the Free-Landers are everywhere. Besides, if I let you guys take me in the chance of me not doing time is zero. And as I see it, my career is all but gone. Even if I were found innocent, the damage to the reputation of the agency would be too much. Price will have to fire me and I don't blame him."

"Focus, Gene. You're over-thinking this entire situation."

Detective Stanton needed Gene to know he was on his side. "We both know the Free-Landers are behind all of this. I want to get those sons-of-bitches myself and you can help me do that. We'll clear you of everything. Tell me what the guy that shot at you looks like and how's he getting around?

The assassin left the diner through the front door and limped up the cement walkway in front of the windows.

"Stanton, he's a Hispanic man about five ten wearing…"

"Wearing what?"

"…a black leather coat, lots of gold chains, and I think he has a hurt right knee that makes him limp," Gene said.

"Stop the guy that just limped his ass out of here." Stanton ordered the sheriff.

"What?" Wilcox said.

"Do it now. He's going to get away."

The overweight sheriff wrestled himself from the booth, ran out of the diner and down the cement walkway.

Gene said, "I'm hitchhiking my way back to El Paso and I just got a ride. I'll call you later."

"Gene, we've got him. Gene? Damn it." Stanton slammed his cell phone closed and followed the sheriff.

The assassin was already on the motorcycle when Wilcox rounded the corner of the diner with Stanton behind him with his gun drawn.

"Freeze right there." the Sheriff said, keeping a safe distance. The biker smiled at the sheriff with rotten teeth and appeared to be about to comply, but the smile disappeared. Gene ran across the street and started pushing the ATV across the parking lot.

"Screw you," the assassin said. "I haven't done anything. I'm out of here." He kicked the starter once without any success, but lighting the fuse.

"Get off the…"

When the bomb exploded, Stanton and the sheriff fell to their stomachs. A woman at the convenience store screamed and bystanders yelled as they watched the man become consumed by flames from the gasoline. The fuel tank exploded blowing the dead, burning body into the street twenty yards away.

Wilcox ran around shouting orders to anyone within earshot making sure everyone stayed back. Stanton was a hundred miles from his jurisdiction and for the first time since beginning his investigation of the murder of Elliot Jones, felt insignificant. He began to realize the enormity of the situation as he analyzed all that he knew about the case, all that he had heard about the Free-Lander organization, and the significance of the ounce of the silver he carried in his coat pocket. He knew the Free-Landers would stop at nothing now. Somehow, one of their own was killed at the prominent creative director's mountain home and now another lay dead on the streets of Cloudcroft. Gene Martine was probably going to die within the next forty-eight hours and there was very little, Detective Stanton could do to stop it. His concern grew, because he knew the Free-Landers believed in an eye for an eye. Someone close to Gene would also die.

"You just going to stand there, detective, or are you going to start investigating something?" Wilcox said.

"Well, like you say, I'm not in my jurisdiction, Sheriff. This mess is all yours, but if you want my opinion, you should stop telling other people what to do and start trying to figure out how that motorcycle over there blew up."

"Aren't you the genius? For your information, I already have."

"Oh, really?"

"It seems someone, and I'm not saying it's your guy..." the sheriff said. "You know, the one that's innocent of now three murders until proven guilty?"

"You're rambling, Sheriff."

"Someone planted an explosive under the guy's gas tank and BOOM!," Wilcox said raising his hands in imitation of the explosion.

"There's probably good fingerprints on the materials used to make the explosive," the detective said.

"We'll send them to Las Cruces to be analyzed in the morning, but I think we already have our answer," the sheriff said.

"I need to call all of this in to my office. Excuse me." Stanton walked away and dialed his cell phone.

"This is Detective Ortega," Manny said. He was in his car driving east on I-10, on his way to a meeting.

"Manny? Stanton."

"Are you back in town?"

"No. How's your case going?" Detective Stanton was ready to talk about anything as long as it didn't include Elliot Jones or Gene Martine.

"I finished my report and checked the three kilos of coke into the evidence locker. We lifted whatever markings we could from the packages..."

Stanton interrupted. "Manny, you're talking about the coke from the Martine residence?" Stanton finished asking the question. He realized Manny was discussing things about Stanton's case as if it were his.

"Why?" Manny said.

"That's my case." Stanton took Manny's answer as a simple misunderstanding. "I asked you to tell me about yours. You know, the old man, the security guard that was beaten to death with the shovel."

"So far, nothing. As we suspected, the killer didn't leave a trace of physical evidence. However, we did find some good footprints. Let me check my notes. Hold on. Here it is. They were women's running shoes with a Nike logo on each sole."

"A woman beat that man to death?" Stanton said in disbelief. "I've never heard of woman that would crush and old man's skull. There had to be other footprints."

"Plenty of them, but they were all made by the old man and the person wearing lady's shoes. Sick, huh? The killer was a woman or a cross-dresser with really small feet." Manny said. "Anyway, we're working on it. His wife hasn't taken it well. She had some kind of breakdown and is at the hospital now. I'll be checking on her condition tomorrow. I want to question her some more on what she knew about her husband's job and his connection to your victim, Elliot Jones."

"They knew each other quite well," Stanton said. "Supposedly, Mr. Jones and this guy talked a lot at night about their personal lives, but I think that's as far as their relationship went."

"You sound distracted, Stanton. What's going on up there? Don't tell me you let him get away."

"This thing has gotten big Manny, and it's gotten dangerous. I'm going to need your help to figuring this one out."

"Anything you need, partner. I thought you'd never ask," Manny said.

"After we found the medallion I suspected Free-Landers might be connected. Hell, I even hoped they were. Who wouldn't want to bring something that big down? But I couldn't connect the dots between organized crime and a clean-cut businessman. Now that all this crap has gone down, I'm convinced. It's got Free-Landers written all over it. If I'm right, they're going to be pissed-off after today."

What's happened? Is Mr. Martine one of them? Did he steal from them? You know, you just don't steal from organized drug rings."

"I'm sure he's not a Free-Lander, but he thinks they're trying to kill him. Remember his story I told you about? The two guys that attacked him at his cabin last night?"

"Martine killed one of them," Manny said. "Slit his throat."

Stanton didn't remember telling Manny how the man was killed. "Gene claims he had nothing to do with killing the guy. He thinks he's being framed and that's why he escaped. He says the other guy had been hunting him ever since."

"You've been in contact with the suspect?"

"I think I'm the only person he trusts right now. He calls my cell phone periodically. Anyway, right now I'm standing in the parking lot of the diner in Cloudcroft looking at a corpse lying in the middle of the road. Someone wanted the gang banger dead and blew up his motorcycle with him on it. When his gang finds out what's happened... Let's just say, more dead bodies are on the way and we have absolutely no way to stop it."

"You can bet on it. By the way..." Manny said. "I've noticed you're calling your suspect by his first name. You're not getting to close to this investigation, are you, detective? Because, if what you say is true, that Gene Martine is as good as dead."

Stanton picked up the angry tone from Detective Ortega. "What's your problem, Manny? Who cares what I call him. You want in on this or not? If you can't handle it, I'll find someone who can."

"I'm in."

"I'll be in the office first thing in the morning. We'll go over everything we've got and figure out where to go from there, okay?"

Manny ended the call with Stanton when a fist hit his window causing him to flinch and duck to the passenger side of his unmarked car. He pulled his gun and pointed it at the person standing outside the car as he scrambled to exit from the passenger side. Outside, he moved the gun from his left hand to his right, slammed the door closed, and walked around the front of the car to his target.

"What the hell do you think you're doing?" he said as he grabbed the man's lapel and shoved the barrel of his gun under the man's chin. "You want me to kill you? Is that what you want?"

"It was just a joke, detective. You can't do it because you don't have the balls."

Manny tightened his grip on the man's clothes and pressed the barrel into the man's chin even harder.

"Keep this shit up and I promise one day I'll cap you with a smile on my face."

Ortega shoved the man toward the warehouse and holstered his weapon. The man straightened his clothes as they both walked inside.

The warehouse was warm but not unbearable. The detective and the man walked up the long flight of wooden steps without paying any attention to the activity below. Three of the loading dock doors were open with semi-trucks backed up to each one and at least a dozen men were working the freight. Some of them were operating forklifts as the others stacked the boxes onto pallets. One of the trucks was being unloaded as the other two were being loaded.

Two women and another man sat on metal folding chairs around a large metal desk when the two men entered the office. The air was thick with cigarette smoke from the two chain-smokers sitting at the desk. Two ashtrays filled with butts and ashes sat on opposite sides of the phone at the middle of the desk.

"Why are you two late?" the third man said. His voice was deep and raspy from age and years of smoking.

"We've got problems," Ortega said, and then spoke in a low whisper while looking at the younger of the two women and pointing at the phone. "Is the boss on the phone?"

"Man, you're so spineless, Ortega." The man that came into the room with Manny took a cheap verbal jab.

"Is that you, detective?" said the voice on the phone with a distinctive, Mexican accent.

"Yes, sir. We've got…"

"I will assume the two of you have explanations for your tardiness, but it will cost you ten grand a piece regardless," the voice said.

The rules were well known and not being late to a scheduled conference call was one of them.

"We've got more problems, Boss," the detective said. "He's killed another man."

"Who?" the older woman asked.

"Carlos." Detective Ortega said with a pained voice. "He's dead." Manny rubbed his head. "He blew him up. I had just gotten off the phone with him. He found Gene twice with the information you gave me, but he's smarter than we give him credit for."

The hurt in the detective's voice was obvious. All eyes were on him until the voice on the phone spoke.

"Is Gene still on the run?"

"He's trying to get back to El Paso, but that's not the biggest problem," Manny said. "He's convinced Detective Stanton he's innocent, at least of Eddie's murder at the cabin. So I'm certain Stanton believes he didn't kill Elliot Jones either, but I have another plan to fix that."

"That's just like him, as long as I've known Gene, he's always been a thinker," the voice on the phone said. "Put some more guys on him and make sure they know what the hell they're doing this time."

Manny was offended that the boss didn't think Carlos knew what he was doing. He wanted to defend his brother-in-law, docked in pay or not, but he let it go.

"I don't like any of this," said the man with the raspy voice as he turned and looked at the man that the detective confronted outside the warehouse. "This entire operation is in jeopardy because you can't keep your pants up and you sure can't control your women."

The man in question smiled. "You can kiss my ass, old man. At least I get mine."

"Shut up. Both of you." the voice on the phone cut in. "Detective, what's your plan in case we don't get him before the cops do?"

"Today, I got an anonymous tip that Mr. Martine was trafficking drugs out of his home and when we searched it, we found three kilos," Manny said.

"Did you have to find that much?" the younger woman asked.

"Quiet, young lady," the voice on the phone said in a fatherly tone. Continue, Detective."

"It was enough nose candy to put him in federal prison, but he's rich enough to get a good lawyer who'll get him off."

"Then what's the point, jerk?" the young woman said.

"That amount of coke makes him a suspected Free-Lander, which ties him back to Elliot's murder. All I have to do now is give him an accomplice and a motive. I'm working on that now."

Ortega spent the next several minutes discussing his plans. The group argued about its success.

"I'll agree to let you implement your plan," the boss said. "But I want everyone in the room to understand that I want Gene Martine eliminated before the police ever get a chance to arrest him. Now, my jet arrives in El Paso at Cutter Field at eleven tomorrow morning. Darling, please have the limo waiting. After the funeral, I'm headed straight back. Let's get this mess cleaned up."

The call disconnected with a loud click. Little was said after the call ended and everyone, except the detective and the older woman, left the warehouse without saying a word. The woman turned off the office lights and waited for the detective to follow her out, but he stayed.

The odd group of five people running the large cocaine operation in El Paso had been hand-selected by the boss himself. Over the past five years, each person had served his or her purpose, helping move cocaine from place to place. For the most part, they were a diverse group, connected only by the drug ring. Other than doing their part in the trafficking, they tried not to associate with the each other in their day-to-day lives, which is the way the boss liked it. But it wasn't perfect. The human element would inevitably creep into the group and cause problems. This time, the problem got out of hand and the boss's own daughter was the cause of it.

The detective was standing in the dark second floor office watching the workers through the large glass panes pondering his brother-in-law's untimely death. The woman approached him from his right and placed her hand on his shoulder.

"I'm sorry about Carlos and Eddie," she said.

"Thanks," Manny said.

The two of them watched the workers for several seconds. The light from the warehouse fell on their faces but stopped there. Behind them was only darkness.

"I don't care how much money we're all making," she said. "It's not worth it if the people we love are dying because of it."

"I knew the dangers when I signed on and so did Carlos and Eddie," Manny said.

"What about Elliot and Gene? What about the old man that died for nothing?"

"I don't know those people any more than I know the people that O.D. on the coke we bring in," Manny said.

"Well, I know Elliot and Gene. I knew Eddie and Carlos, too, and I care. It just makes me sick," she said as she stepped over to the desk and picked up one of three packs of cigarettes left on the desk and shook it only to feel its emptiness.

"I mean, the money's good and all, but it's not worth it."

She crumpled the wrapper tossing it aside, picked up the second pack, shook out the last two cigarettes and placed both between her sticky red lips. Without removing them, she stepped back to the detective.

"Tell me the truth, Manny. When was the last time you had a good night's sleep?"

The woman cupped her lighter and held it close to the end of the tobacco. Flicking it twice without success, she shook the lighter and forced the flame out on the third flick. She dragged the warm smoke of both cigarettes into her lungs and exhaled it through her nostrils.

"Here," she said offering a cigarette to the detective.

"I know what you're saying," Manny said, then took a half-hearted puff and blew the smoke against the glass. "Let me tell you what makes me sick. One night almost six years ago, a husband and father of a two-year-old boy decided he and his buddies from work would go out for some drinks before going home. He was a good man. He called his wife, got permission, and went out.

His wife worked, too, but she still found time to keep the house clean, cook their food and take care of their baby. But that night, the husband had too much to drink. He had convinced his buddies that he was okay to drive himself home. They all left and he stumbled out to his car. He unlocked it and sat in the seat, but then he got sick."

Without looking away from the window, the detective took another longer hit from the cigarette. During his long exhale, the smoke curled off the glass like a fast moving horizontal mushroom cloud.

"There was another man in the parking lot. He watched this guy, puking his guts out. The stranger told the man he was too drunk to drive and offered him a ride home, which he accepted. When they got to the house, the stranger practically carried the husband to the front door. When the wife opened the door, she was wearing a sexy negligee." Manny paused again for another drag. "I guess she thought she would surprise him when he got home. Anyway, she could see her husband was out of it so she let both men in. Hell, he seemed like a good guy. But the moment she closed the door behind them, the guy threw the helpless husband down on the living room floor. She screamed, but the stranger punched her with full force. It knocked her to the floor and broke her jaw. Blood poured from her lips as she looked in shock at her pathetic husband. He tried to get up, but their assailant kicked him and broke four of his ribs and told him,

'You're going to watch me rape your wife and there's nothing you can do about it. And every time you move, I'm going to punch her and kick the life out of you.'"

"I don't want to hear anymore."

The woman was standing with her left arm under her right elbow as if supporting the arm holding the cigarette. She vacuumed the smoke from her mouth into her nose. "I know you detectives see all kinds of sick crap. You shouldn't be one if it's going to mess you up."

"Manny said, "The husband could barely breathe and even if he could, he was too wasted to fight the guy. He watched and wept as the stranger brutally raped and beat his wife on the floor just four feet away. When he finished, he beat the husband until he was unconscious."

"Manny, stop already," she said. "I understand."

"No you don't," he said. "When the husband woke up, he couldn't move. The attacker was gone, but his two-year-old son was standing over his dead mother who lay naked, covered in blood. He told his son she was okay, but daddy needed him to call 911." Detective Ortega looked at the woman. "Can you believe I told my own son his mom was okay? I told him she was okay," he said in a loud whisper as he shook his head.

"I had no idea," she said rubbing his back with her hand.

Manny dropped his cigarette butt, and crushed it out with his boot.

"Since then, I could care less about anyone but myself and my son. I'm going to take what money I can get from the drugs until I have enough to put my son through college and I can move to some beach somewhere in Mexico. Screw everyone else. Three or four more major shipments and I'm done."

The woman said, "I guess we all have our reasons for doing what we're doing, but I just don't believe people have to die."

It was almost 10:00 on Monday night when Detective Stanton reached the line of cars waiting to get through the roadblock. Twenty-five miles south of Alamogordo, New Mexico, the U.S. Border Patrol station was on the east side of Highway 54. Most nights it was manned with seven to ten agents. Each took his turn under a well lit canopy stopping and checking northbound traffic for illegal aliens and drugs. But that night, there were dozens of uniformed officers from different agencies and just as many portable lights set up outside of the canopy on both sides of the highway.

A sign at the exit of the station boasted the amount of drugs seized, year to date, in street value. It read $30,560, a laughable figure to any Free-Lander. Train tracks ran north and south a hundred yards east of the border patrol station. A Santa Fe freight train with more than fifty cars sat idle, the engine pointed away from El Paso.

The highway traffic traveling in both directions was being stopped. The northbound drivers were told not to pick up any hitchhikers. In the middle of each of the two southbound lanes, four, black New Mexico State Police cars and three green and white border patrol units sat staggered and perpendicular to the road. Dozens of yellow, red, white and blue lights flashed in random patterns. One officer briefly interrogated each driver while another used a flashlight to search for Gene inside each vehicle. The line of cars was thirty to forty deep.

Detective Stanton turned on his flashing lights, pulled onto the left shoulder, and drove slowly past the traffic. He, too, visually searched vehicles at random as he passed. A petite old lady in a Volkswagen Beetle sat alone in her seat gripping the steering wheel tightly with both hands. Blankets and boxes filled the passenger seats. There was no place for anyone to hide. Further ahead, an old rusted pickup with the windows down sat idling. The driver, a large man wearing a cowboy hat, was yelling at his female passenger who was huddled against the passenger door, crying. Stanton stopped and quickly turned his siren on and off to get the cowboy's attention. When the man looked over, Detective Stanton rolled down his window, pointed at the man and shook his finger from side to side. Like a kid caught with his hand in the cookie jar, the large cowboy sheepishly acknowledged Stanton's signal. As he continued driving down the shoulder, Stanton watched the couple in his mirror.

He began to realize how much stress the roadblock was putting on so many innocent people. They had to sit in the long line for thirty minutes or more while the manhunt for Gene continued and they still had fifty more miles to travel to get to El Paso, if that was their final destination. When he reached the front of the line, Stanton turned off his flashing lights and parked in the median facing the southbound traffic. As he shifted the transmission to park, his cell phone rang. He looked at the display. It was the call he was dreading all day.

"Hi, Honey."

"I'm not feeling that sweet right now, detective," Mrs. Stanton said.

"I know and I'm sorry. How was your dinner?"

"Well, since you weren't here..."

"Your brother Rick burned the steaks," he interrupted.

"You got it."

"Unbelievable."

Mrs. Stanton was standing in her kitchen holding the phone to her ear. She watched her extended family through the window above the sink. They were sitting next to a grand fire pit that Stanton had built over the past summer specifically for her winter reunion. Her sister, three brothers and their spouses were laughing, drinking and playing cards while her five nieces and nephews chased two beef calves in the corral.

"No, detective, what's unbelievable is that my husband made me a promise that he would be here, but alas, he never showed up. I don't know what to do with him. I'm thinking about trading him in on a newer, more predictable model. What do you think?"

"Well, Mrs. Stanton, I don't think that would be necessary. I've dealt with that kind of husband before and I understand how you might feel. But, it's been my experience that if you will just kick him and scream at him a little, there's good chance he'll straighten right up," he said. "On the other hand, you could cut him a little slack."

"And just why would he deserve such grace?"

"Well, there's a good chance he's been chasing bad guys like murderers and drug runners in New Mexico all day and he's wanted to call you, but he's been so busy trying to save a life or two."

"I don't think so. My husband is a *Texas* detective."

She smiled as she leaned her hip against the counter and twirled the phone cord around her index finger.

"He's got no business being in New Mexico. Besides, he's too much of a wimp. He would run the other way the first sign of trouble. No, I think he's seeing another woman."

"In that case, tell me what the S.O.B. looks like and I'll shoot him for you." Mr. and Mrs. Stanton giggled. "Mrs. Stanton, mind if I ask you a personal question?"

"Why, detective, are we getting a little fresh?"

"I was just wondering. Do you love your husband?"

"Well, let me think. He is quite the animal in bed and he does seem to care about me a lot even if he does break promises every now and then. Yeah, I'd say I love him."

The detective didn't respond in kind. "I've got to go."

There was a disturbance around one of the cars in the line. He watched four border patrol agents running to the scene. He got out of his car and started running.

As he approached the scene, Stanton saw three German shepherds clawing savagely at the old woman's Volkswagen before their handlers could order them to stand down.

Stanton showed his badge. "I'm an El Paso Detective Stanton. What's the problem officers? Is Gene Martine in that car?"

One of the K-9 handlers said, "All of the dogs just went nuts over this car. They aren't trained to find people, just narcotics and explosives."

An officer opened the driver side door and helped the old woman out. She was at least seventy years old, weighed no more than ninety pounds, and stood just four and a half feet tall. Another officer opened the passenger door and began sifting through her blankets and boxes.

"Now, I've seen everything," said the officer with the boxes. "These boxes are loaded with bags of marijuana."

Chapter Fourteen

Gene was uncomfortable lying on the gravel and railroad ties under the fourth freight car from the engine. He had picked that spot because the light from the station fell just short of his position, yet he was close enough to see the approach of the landscape.

His amateur display of pyrotechnics back in Cloudcroft had proven to be a big enough distraction for his undetected escape from the small community. He had ridden the ATV through the back mountain roads until he reached the bottom of the southern slopes and by then the sun had long gone down. The temperature dropped to below forty degrees. From that point on, he rode through the desert until he reached the highway by the border patrol checkpoint. The ATV's single headlamp was all that illuminated the narrow trails making navigation between the sand dunes slow and difficult.

Gene could barely see the activity surrounding the Volkswagen. He couldn't make out faces and had no idea Stanton was on the scene. He

knew the roadblock was for him and he felt sorry
for all of the off-duty policemen who would be
spending the cold night away from their families
searching for him. They didn't know him, but he
knew they had distain for him.

He watched as officers gently handcuffed
the old woman and walked her to the check station.
Other officers directed the line of traffic around the
little yellow car while a flatbed tow truck winched it
aboard, only to take it two hundred yards and
unload it in the parking lot of the station.

Gene crawled backward over the train
tracks. Except for the light underneath the freight
cars, it was dark on the opposite side of the train.
He looked in both directions before breaking into a
full sprint toward the train's engine. The line of
southbound traffic had grown. He needed to
maneuver across the highway and behind the line
before another car arrived that might see him. He
ran back into the sand dunes, and then cut to his
left, sprinting another seventy-five yards before
stopping. There was no northbound traffic, but there
were headlights in the southbound lanes off in the
distance and they were approaching at highway
speeds.

The air was cold but beads of sweat trickled
from Gene's forehead and his lungs ached with
every breath he took. He adjusted the saddlebags on
his shoulder and re-gripped the duffel bag, then ran
in a semi-crouched position across the first two
lanes, stopping in the median for another look. Then
he ran across the southbound lanes just behind the
last pair of cars, a large Ford sedan towing a smaller
Honda Civic. The headlights of an oncoming car
were getting larger. Time was running out. In the

lowest position he could get in, he approached the passenger side of the Civic, lifted the handle of the rear door and the door cracked open.

As he climbed in, he heard the squeaking brakes of the approaching car. Gene locked the back doors and stayed crouched on the floor between the front and rear seats.

He took off his gloves, coat, shirt, boots, socks, and wrestled out of his pants. There was very little space between the seats, but he arranged himself as flat as he could. Then, he covered himself with his clothing, tossing them about in disarray, being sure to conceal his bags and leaving only a small hole to see light through. For thirty minutes, he laid waiting.

The sound of generators grew louder as the towed car approached the roadblock. Bright halogen lights filled the inside of the car as if it were under interrogation. Gene ached from the awkward position and his heart began to race again. He didn't dare move as he concentrated on his breathing, taking long slow breaths to keep the illusion of being a pile of dirty clothes. He heard at least two male voices coming from either side of the car, but the windows muffled the words. As he strained to listen, light from a flashlight hit the passenger rear window and showed directly on him.

"Bring the dogs over here," an officer yelled as he grabbed the handle of the door closest to Gene's head.

Gene heard the linkage inside the door move slightly, but it stayed secure. He lay thinking about a time when he toured the military K-9 training facilities at Fort Bliss military base, in El Paso where the border patrol dogs were trained. He remembered learning that the dogs were trained to smell drugs and explosives, even in the smallest amounts. He had the residue of one and plenty of the other.

"Look, the dogs are tired and thirsty, man," another officer said. "They need a break."

"This one's clean," the officer with the flashlight said. "Let them through."

After getting through the roadblock at the border patrol station, Gene remained lying on the rear floorboard of the Honda Civic in tow. The hump in the middle forced sharp pains up his spine when the car hit even the smallest bumps. His clothes lay on top of his naked body, but he was still chilled. Yet, it was the safest he had felt in the past forty-eight hours.

He stared at the soft steady red glow on the ceiling that illuminated from the taillights of the Ford sedan doing the pulling. When northbound traffic approached, the red glow was consumed with white from the headlights then dimmed back to red as they passed. He realized that if the approaching traffic had that affect on the ceiling, any headlights from the rear would certainly do the same. He watched for the change. There was none.

He maneuvered onto the back seat and looked through the back window. No one was following, but there would be as soon as others got through the roadblock and sped up to make up lost time. He quickly dressed himself.

He opened the duffel bag and pulled out one of his homemade explosives and some matches. Staying as low as he could, Gene rolled down the passenger side rear window. Certain there were no cars approaching from either direction, he lit a match. Just as the flame hit the fuse the Ford hit a bump that jostled the Honda and he dropped the explosive and watched it roll under the front seat.

The explosion temporarily deafened Gene and caused a ringing in his ears.

The muffled bang made the driver flinch and duck. The bright flash from inside the Honda reflected in his mirror. He pulled to the shoulder and looked back to see fire ripping in the passenger's seat.

The driver jumped out, ran to the hitch and struggled to release the tow bar. While the man was busy, Gene got out and crouched down on the driver's side of the burning car. After the man separated the two cars, he opened the passenger door of the burning car to do what he could to smother the flames. Gene moved his position to the truck, opened the door, got in and drove away. He noticed fast food containers and candy wrappers in the passenger floorboard and some dirty file folders along with the man's cell phone in the passenger seat. He suddenly felt a little shame for leaving the guy stranded but he knew someone would be by soon to help.

One hour later, Gene had succumbed to the nausea from the lack of sleep and food. He pulled over to the side of the road, opened the door and threw up yellow bile. Shortly thereafter and just five miles north of El Paso, his body started giving in to the abuse. Only a few other cars had passed him and he didn't realize he was only moving at thirty miles an hour on the highway. Both of his hands clung to the top of the steering wheel and his face only inches from his hands.

When Lisa and Marlene arrived at the Chapel, Lisa quickly opened her door and hurriedly walked inside, not waiting for Marlene. Lisa pretended to be completely focused on her intent to see Elliot.

A black sign with white removable letters listed three viewing chapels. The first two were occupied and the third was vacant. One read, 'Elliot Jones - chapel 101 – Burial Services Tuesday 2:00 p.m.' She ignored the second name of Roger Thatcher in chapel 102. With Marlene close by, Lisa walked down the hallway to chapel 101 where the aroma of fresh flowers filled her nostrils. She tried to clear her mind of any other thoughts as she focused on her memories of Elliot.

At least two-dozen people were dispersed among the twenty pews that lined both sides of the small chapel. She was full of pride at the sight of the many people still honoring Elliot after two days of viewing. Flowers filled the room around the open casket at the back wall where she and Marlene were standing.

Elliot was dressed in a black suit. The heavy starched white shirt modeled a solid blue silk tie and his favorite gold cufflinks. His pants sported a leather belt Gene had made for him.

The funeral home had done well capturing her husband's facial expression, but Elliot's eyes and cheeks were sinking. His smile looked fake and stretched around the stitches that held his lips together. His hands looked as if they were made of wax. The gold wedding band he and Lisa picked out when they were teenagers was loose around his finger as was the watch around his wrist.

"Excuse me. Mrs. Jones," a frail old woman said, taking Lisa's hand like a mother would of her daughter.

"Please call me Lisa. Did you know Elliot?"

"My husband knew him better. I'm sorry for your loss, Dear."

"Hi, I'm Marlene Martine, Mrs...?" Marlene said.

"Mrs. Thatcher. My husband is Roger Thatcher in the next chapel." The old woman looked down at the handkerchief twisted in her bony hand. The name didn't mean anything to Lisa at first. "Mrs. Jones, I was wondering if you and I could talk a while. You see, my husband..."

Then Lisa remembered, "Your husband is the security guard at my husband's office building."

"Was, I'm afraid." Mrs. Thatcher sighed.

"I'm sorry, Lisa, I need to get some air. I'll be back." Marlene excused herself then walked back down the aisle.

"Let's sit over here." Lisa guided the old widow to an empty pew facing Elliot's casket. "I'm so sorry for your loss as well, Mrs. Thatcher. Elliot spoke highly of Roger. Was he sick?"

Mrs. Thatcher looked up, scanning Lisa's face with a wondering expression. "I thought for sure you knew."

"Knew what, Mrs. Thatcher?"

"Roger was attacked and killed Saturday night."

"Oh, my God," Lisa said, pulling Mrs. Thatcher's hands up to her chest.

"They think Roger's murder is related to your husband's. I'm really sorry. I really thought you knew."

Lisa hugged Roger's wife. "Don't be sorry for anything."

It was at that moment Lisa knew she would do everything in her power to stop the madness, to stop the bloodshed and make the person or persons responsible accountable.

Marlene returned with her cell phone in her hand. She had a business-like demeanor when she spoke, "Lisa, I need to get back. Something's come up at the office. I'm sorry, but I need to take you home now."

"Oh, please don't go," Mrs. Thatcher said, "We have so much to talk about. I'll take you home."

Lisa agreed and she saw it as the perfect opportunity to get away from Marlene.

"Is that okay with you, Lisa?" Marlene looked at her watch. "I really do need to go."

"Yes," Lisa said almost too excitedly, "But, are you sure you want to go out of your way Mrs. Thatcher?"

"Most certainly, Dear."

"Okay then," Marlene said, as Lisa stood up to hug her good-bye. "I'll call you later tonight to check on you."

Mrs. Thatcher and Mrs. Jones talked about their husbands. They compared stories about what their husbands said about each other. When the subject came up about the time Elliot saved the Thatcher's Christmas, Lisa remembered how humble of a life the Thatcher's led.

"May I see your husband, Mrs. Thatcher?"

When Lisa entered chapel 102, she didn't know what she expected to see. There were only three older people paying their respects to Roger in the front pews. A handful of small flower arrangements sat in front of the plain wooden casket, which was closed.

"May I ask why you chose to close the casket?" Lisa said.

"It's closed because..." At that moment, Mrs. Thatcher's legs went numb, her breathing became erratic, and she began to collapse before Lisa caught her and guided her to the nearest pew.

"Are you okay?" Lisa said.

"It's just that the reason the casket's closed is because whoever did this to him crushed his skull and I don't want to remember him like that."

Lisa felt flush. "I'm so sorry. I didn't mean to be insensitive. I should have... Where are your children?"

Mrs. Thatcher wiped her eyes with her wrinkled handkerchief, "Our two sons will arrive tonight. Our daughter will arrive in the morning."

Lisa guided the conversation as Mrs. Thatcher boasted about her children's successes, marriages and her grandchildren.

Lisa was embarrassed about the spectacle in chapel 101 where her husband lay, but she was wise enough to know the two men led completely different lives and would be remembered in different ways.

Nonetheless, as the women were leaving and heading to Mrs. Thatcher's car, Lisa went back inside the funeral home, she said to use the restroom. She instructed the funeral director to find all of the flower arrangements in chapel 101 that came from media groups, remove their cards and place them in chapel 102.

The sound of a semi's brakes startled Gene's subconscious from sleep. His right hand fell from the steering wheel and tapped the horn. Gene sat up to see his headlights shining onto a cinderblock wall directly in front of him. He slammed the brake pedal and tried to turn the car to the left, but the keys were off. The steering wheel was locked and the car was already at a complete stop.

"What the…" Unsure of what was going on, he continued to apply pressure to the brakes. He shook his head and rubbed his dirty face. When he opened his eyes the scene had not changed. He looked at the passenger side of the car, back to the wall, then through all of the car windows, seeing nothing but a dark empty parking lot.

"Where am I?"

He realized where he was as the words trailed.

On the Texas – New Mexico border is a destination steakhouse called the Edge of Texas. Nothing but ranchland and Highway 54 surrounded it for miles in every direction. Gene had managed to drive to the restaurant, maneuver through the parking lot and park at the backside, completely hidden from late-night patrons and highway traffic.

At three in the morning, Lisa answered the phone after the first ring.

"Hello?" Lisa's voice was unexpectedly fresh and awake.

"Lisa?"

"Gene, are you okay? Where are you?" Lisa quickly sat up. "What's happened to you?"

"I'm fine except for some cuts and bruises. I'm at the Edge of..."

Gene stopped short of his disclosing his full location when the thought crossed his mind that Lisa's phone might be tapped.

"The cell phone shows fifteen missed calls. Are all of those from you?"

"Gene, it seems like the whole world is looking for you. Every news channel is reporting that you're the primary suspect of Elliot's murder and you're on the run from authorities. What are we going to do?"

"Right now Lisa, *we* aren't going to do anything. You need to go back to sleep. When you wake up, focus on Elliot and the funeral. I..."

Lisa's voice was surprisingly firm and steady. "We are in this together. I met Roger Thatcher's wife at the funeral home. Do you know why Mrs. Thatcher was there?"

Gene was so caught up in his own problems, he had all but forgotten about Roger Thatcher's murder.

Lisa said with anger, "Because her husband was beaten to death Saturday night and you knew it. Didn't you? You know the cops think it's related to Elliot's murder. Don't you?

"Price told me, but you've had enough on your plate. You're on edge. Just listen to yourself."

"I'm way past the edge, Gene. I don't know what Elliot got himself into, but I'm not going to sit idly by and let innocent people get killed over it. I want us to go to Stanton and tell him what we know."

"We can't right now. I think I killed a man yesterday."

"The guy at your cabin? But you said…"

"While I was trying to get out of the mountains the second guy was hunting me like an animal. This guy killed his own partner, the guy at the cabin. He took shots at me, killed one of my horses and murdered a border patrol agent." Gene walked the parking lot in the darkness. "I thought I lost him, but he just kept coming. I had to do something. I just wanted to hurt him, but I think I killed him and Stanton knows it."

"You had to defend yourself, right?"

"Stanton wouldn't buy it, and even if he did, I've already been convicted by the media and there is enough evidence to connect me to four deaths, drugs, assault and who knows what else."

"If I tell Stanton what Elliot told me, he can help."

"We need to stick to our plan. In fact, we may have to wait even longer now. I've got to get back and think this through. I have some ideas where to start, but we can't talk about it over your phone. It might be tapped. I've probably said too much already. Go buy one of those disposable cell phones and text me the number. I'll contact you that way."

"Disposable cell phone? What…" The line went dead and Lisa placed the receiver back in its cradle.

As Gene approached El Paso, he thought about continuing to go straight. He would be in Mexico in five minutes. He had enough money in the duffle bag to last a while and he could get his savings wired to a bank in the Bahamas before anyone could freeze his accounts.

His home had been torn apart by cops. It would be taped off and under surveillance. He needed to find a hotel room to hide and downtown El Paso had plenty of old, run-down, pay-by-the-hour rooms for rent.

A police cruiser was on the right shoulder waiting for speeders. Gene passed him and watched in his rearview mirror for movement from the officer behind the wheel. The cruiser stayed parked.

He took the downtown exit, turned left on Kansas Street, took a right on Main Street and pulled into a self-pay parking lot just before the next intersection at Santa Fe Street. He parked in the farthest corner of the lot.

Adjacent to the parking lot, the De Soto Hotel was one of downtown's oldest, and most run-down, but it was still in business and was just two blocks from the P & M office.

Gene went inside. The smell of mold, dust and rotting wood filled the air. No one was behind the dirty bulletproof glass mounted on top of the counter to his left, which divided a small space. In front of him was a tight wooden staircase leading up to the rooms. He barely had space to set the saddlebags and duffel bag on the floor. Gene could see light coming from a television in a room connected to the office.

"Hello?" he said. "Anyone there? He slapped the glass with his hand.

Footsteps came down the stairs.

"Shut up down there," a gruff voice said, "You're going to wake up the Mexicans."

The man was Anglo. He was unshaven and wearing only a pair of boxers and dirty T-shirt. "What do you want?"

"I need a room and I need the most private one you have."

Gene could tell by the look on his face the man had heard the same line thousands of times from other men that came in with prostitutes. They were usually drunk and really didn't care what room they got as long as it had a mattress, but Gene was alone and sober. He looked like he was running from something.

"What's privacy worth to you?"

"Two hundred a day." Gene tested.

"Three hundred."

"That's highway robbery.

"You need the room," the man said. "I don't. Tell you what, you make it three hundred a day and I'll make sure no one knows you're here."

The room was the last one on the fifth floor at the end of the hall on the right. Gene worked the old lock with the key and went inside. The room had an old chest of drawers, nightstand with lamp, clock, phone and a twin bed complete with a dirty bed spread and stained sheets. The bathroom had a small toilet with a broken seat, but it looked clean. There was a stall shower with a dirty curtain, but the showerhead was missing, as well as many of the tiles.

Gene shoved his bags under the bed and ripped the bed covers back. After shedding his coat and shoes and setting the clock for 8:00 a.m. He fell back on the mattress, turned the cell phone off and then fell fast asleep.

Chapter Fifteen

Tuesday morning at 10:15, Gene was wearing a black Italian suit with a white dress shirt, gray tie and a gray scarf. He wore the scarf tightly wrapped around his neck making sure to use it to cover his mouth and the scratch on his cheek. His hair was slicked straight back and his eyes were sufficiently covered with dark sunglasses. He stood in the crowd of mourners presiding over a funeral, but it wasn't Elliot's.

Two hours earlier, Gene had woken with a jump from his bed in the De Soto Hotel, not to his alarm clock, but to a cockroach crawling on his neck. He slapped his neck, killing the roach and let out a yell of disgust and wiped the insects innards on the mattress.

A child was crying and another was screaming, sounding as if they were in separate parts of the hotel. He heard a man and woman arguing in Spanish somewhere below him. And the sounds of the downtown traffic were no match for the room's single-pane window. He was sure that if his yell had been heard, nobody cared.

Gene turned on the cell phone and placed the phone back onto the nightstand. He walked into the bathroom, turned the handle marked 'hot' and watched the headless shower spout gurgle and spit air until water flowed freely in a straight stream.

The hot shower was therapeutic. The hard, steady stream of water massaged his muscles and the wounds sustained from two days of battling an unknown enemy for unknown reasons. After his shower, Gene picked up the phone and read the text from Lisa.

"The number is 655-3853. Careful."

"That a girl," he said then dialed the number.

"Gene?" Lisa answered.

"I'm glad you followed my instructions," Gene said. "I'm pretty sure they're listening to your conversations on your phone so be careful what you say when you use it. They don't know I have Elliot's so I think I'm safe."

"Did you get any sleep? I've been worried about you. Our families are here. Marlene and Roy are here and I just haven't had a second to myself. I'm in the bathroom pretending to touch-up my make-up before we leave to the funeral home."

"Lisa, are you okay?" Gene could hear distress in her voice.

Lisa didn't answer right away. "Yes. I'm fine," she said and sniffed back her tears. "The only person missing is you, Gene. If I ever needed you for a shoulder to cry on, now would be that time."

"It makes me feel good to hear you say that Lisa and I think I can make that happen."

"How?" she said.

Thirty minutes later, Gene was standing in a dark corner on the second floor of the parking garage across from a bank on Kansas Street where Lisa had parked her car. She got out of the car, looked around and then opened the trunk. That was her signal. Gene stepped from the shadows. Lisa was dressed in a conservative black dress. A string of pearls was around her neck. Her eyes widened at his appearance, but when he reached her, they embraced.

"Gene," she sighed as she nuzzled her nose to this neck.

"Did you have any trouble getting away from everyone?" he said.

"I just told Marlene I wanted to go to the funeral home before everyone else so I could spend some time alone with Elliot. I wrapped one of Elliot's suits in my long overcoat and carried it over my arm to the car." She pulled the clothes from the trunk. "Nobody noticed."

"Did you find a scarf?"

"The scarf and tie are in the pocket of the jacket and so are his car keys. I checked on it before I came here and it's still there." She reached inside the car, "Here's a Starbucks coffee and a muffin. I thought you might be hungry."

Gene was grateful as he had not eaten in more than a day.

Lisa hugged Gene, and then left the garage.

Gene took a cab to the cemetery. He wasn't sure how he was going to hide and he didn't want to draw any attention. He wasn't going to miss Elliot's funeral.

"Where do you want to get out?" the cabby said.

"I'm not sure where it is. Please just keep driving for a minute," Gene said.

He was lying. Gene could see the mound of dirt taken from the six-foot hole covered with a blanket of deep green artificial turf, starkly contrasting against the pale fall-green Bermuda grass covering the rest of the cemetery. Dozens of floral arrangements stood at the grave. A portable awning covered dozens of chairs. The driver slowed the cab down as he approached and passed a line of cars. In front of the line was the hearse. A coffin was lifted from the back of a hearse by the pallbearers, but something was off.

"Stop here."

"You going to get out?"

"That's not him." Gene talked to himself. "There aren't enough people here and I don't recognize any of them."

"Mister, the meter's still ticking."

Gene handed the driver a hundred dollar bill. "Please stay here. I'll need a ride back."

"Sure thing, Bud," the driver said.

The weather was clear but cold. When Gene got out of the cab he felt a pinch of the coldness on the scratch on his cheek, still raw and pink. He wrapped the scarf around his neck and face, adjusted his dark shades and then joined the mourners around another gravesite. From there he had a view of Elliot's ceremony only a hundred yards away. As the casket of a complete stranger in front of him was positioned over the grave, he watched the hearse carrying Elliot's casket enter the cemetery from the main gate. Unlike the funeral he was attending, two limousines and an endless line of cars followed close behind Elliot.

It took more than fifteen minutes for the multitude of cars to park and the people in them to find their way to the gravesite. Lisa, Elliot's mother, and her parents stepped out of the first limo. Marlene, her father, Roy Whitaker, and six pallbearers exited the second limo. Too far away to make out the details, Gene still recognized two of the pallbearers as Elliot's brothers and another was Elliot's father. Gene didn't know who the last three were. His chest ached knowing he missed that honor of carrying the casket.

"Ashes to ashes, dust to dust..." the preacher was saying when Gene spoke out loud.

"Would you like to add something, sir?" asked the preacher.

Gene focused first on the preacher then surveyed the rest of the small group. Everyone was looking at him with curiosity and he noticed none of them were visibly crying. "I'm sorry. We're all going to miss him."

"I'm sure *she* would be glad to know that," the preacher said. "Let us pray."

Gene bowed his head more in shame than prayer. He also knew his cover was about to disperse, but Elliot's funeral was only beginning. When the preacher finished, Gene stood back and let the real friends and family pay their last respects to the departed. He looked across the lawn to see that all of the chairs under an awning to shade them from the El Paso sun were taken and the rest of the people were standing around it. Lisa sat with his and her parents on either side. With the exception of Elliot's father, the pallbearers stood together. Gene recognized many of Elliot's friends and family, even some that he didn't expect to see.

William Price was in the third row. Joe Garcia's white teeth flashed in the crowd.

Before he knew it and much too early, the crowd had dispersed from around Gene. He knew he had to leave before someone from across the grass recognized him.

He looked over his shoulder to see some of Elliot's mourners looking in his direction. At first he was worried about being recognized. Two people stood out of the group more than anyone else. Detective Stanton was standing on the outside of the crowd and directly behind him was a blonde woman with a little boy. They too were looking in his direction. Gene studied them briefly then opened the cab door and got in. The cabby drove slowly around the cemetery until they reached the exit. Gene's thoughtful stare focused back and forth between Stanton and the blonde woman. Stanton stared back.

"Get me back downtown as fast as you can," Gene said.

It took less than ten minutes to get to downtown El Paso.

"Where do you want me to drop you off?" The cabby wanted to know.

"Take me to the El Paso Electric building on Texas Street."

When they arrived, Gene got out and gave the driver another hundred-dollar bill.

It was almost 10:45 in the morning when the elevator lumbered upward eight, nine and ten. The doors opened, Gene stepped out into the foyer and walked down the hall to the great glass doors. He walked in confident no one was there because the office was closed as most of the employees were at the funeral. Not surprisingly, the receptionist wasn't behind her desk and the offices were eerily quiet.

He looked at the clock on the receptionist's desk, 10:55. Gene needed to hurry. He ran to Elliot's office. There were no signs of cleaning of any kind. Fingerprint dust was everywhere but there was no longer crime scene tape blocking the entrance. He thought it strange that the cleaning crew had not cleaned, but was hopeful that he might find what he was looking for even though he had no idea what it was.

Gene rummaged through Elliot's papers, finding only meeting reports and project sheets for VoiceComm and yellow Post-It Notes with reminders. The police had gathered and stuck notes together in one pile. He opened all of the desk drawers and filing cabinets. He didn't have time to look through the dozens of files. Gene sat behind the desk thinking, staring at every item lying in front of him; the reports, the notes, pens and markers, a stapler and tape dispenser, the lamp and even the phone. Everything was covered in fingerprint dust.

Gene pulled the chair closer to the desk, looked the phone's display over and pushed the button marked 'log'. Choices appeared on the display asking Gene to choose between incoming or outgoing. Gene chose outgoing. The first six numbers were revealed and Joe Garcia's number was number one on the list, but it was also number two.

Joe Garcia? Why did you call him twice, Elliot? Gene thought.

He studied the phone numbers then wrote down the other four on a thin pad of Post-It Notes, when he heard a noise coming from somewhere in the agency. He placed the note pad inside his jacket pocket and was about to leave, but something made him look at the phone again. He hit another display button marked 'detail'. The last time Joe Garcia's number had been dialed from Elliot's phone was 9:00 Monday evening, two days after the murder. Gene took an even closer look. The black fingerprint dust on the keys was smeared. Another noise broke his concentration. He moved to the office door, listened and slowly looked out in every direction.

He started for the glass doors, but yet another sound came. This time he could tell it was coming in the direction of the accounting department..

At the cemetery, the funeral was over and people were still lined up all the way around the large awning, in a receiving line, waiting for their chance to give their condolences to Elliot's parents and Lisa and to say goodbye to Elliot. Gene arrived just in time. From across the cemetery he watched from the driver's seat of Elliot's BMW roadster. When he left the P&M office, he walked to the parking garage where it had been sitting since Saturday night.

"The police have his keys and wallet, but I have my set. I'll bring them to you with the suit.

Elliot's car wasn't anywhere near the murder scene and the police didn't ask me about it," Lisa said.

Gene said, "It must still be there."

Gene tried to identify people from the long distance as they filed passed Lisa. Marlene and Roy had already paid their respects. Marlene stood by the casket smoking her cigarettes. Roy paced back and forth with his head down and his hands in his pockets. Several corporate executives of P & M's clients had made it. Even Julio Rivera, CEO of VoiceComm, had come in from California. Gene surveyed each person until he saw Joe. He instantly became infuriated with Joe's arrogance then remembered the phone numbers in his pocket and pulled them out.

Joe was next in line to greet Lisa and to Gene's surprise, Lisa screamed something at Joe then slapped him across the face. Joe tripped on his own feet and fell, hitting his head on the casket and he almost falling into the grave. Gene couldn't hear what she was saying, but Lisa continued yelling and stepped toward him. Joe got up, dusted off his white suit and walked toward the parked cars.

"Get the hell out of here," Gene said with a grin, "before Lisa kicks your ass."

Joe stopped and started yelling back and making gestures with his arm as if he were calling Lisa over to fight but Stanton and her family held her back. When she obliged, Joe moved back toward the line, but he didn't go to Lisa. He walked up to the blonde woman Gene had seen standing next to Detective Stanton earlier. Joe grabbed her arm and forced her to follow him. The woman yelled back to the crowd, but they didn't seem to respond until a young boy ran to her. Joe yelled at her all the way to his car.

Gene remembered the morning at the hospital where he and Stanton had met for the first time. A woman with a young boy had come into the waiting room. Bingo. He never forgot that face. Although she looked somehow elegant now, her hair was fixed and she was formally dressed.

The morning of Elliot's murder at the hospital, she had looked poor and desperate, like someone from a homeless shelter. From Gene's point of view, the woman with Joe was beautiful and elegant, but the boy was about the same age as the one from the hospital waiting room.

Gene scanned the then-smaller crowd at the gravesite. Stanton was gone. Lisa was looking in Gene's direction and moved her head in a gesture toward Joe and the woman, confirming what Gene was thinking. The woman was Sam, Elliot's weakness that got him killed.

Gene put his sunglasses on and wrapped his scarf around his face again. When Joe passed on his way out of the cemetery, Gene could see the woman in the front seat crying and the boy cowering in the back seat. Gene put the car in gear and started following Joe.

Joe was headed downtown on Interstate 10 until he exited Cotton Street in central El Paso. By the time he reached the exit, Joe's car was gone. He knew Joe had turned off. Unless Joe did a U-turn under the freeway, he had to have turned right because the only thing to the left were the railroad tracks. If Joe turned right he would be in one of the poorest neighborhoods in El Paso. There it was. Joe's car was sitting at a traffic light two short blocks up the street with its left turn signal on. Gene raced up the street to the first traffic light that had turned red and cars were crossing the intersection. He drove through the intersection narrowly missing two cars coming from both directions, causing them to swerve but avoiding any collisions.

Joe's car made the left turn. Gene made the green light and followed from a distance. Joe took another right, then a left, before stopping in front of a dilapidated two-story brick house. Gene knew the BMW would stick out in the old neighborhood so he continued down the street to the next block, turned left and parked out of Joe's line of sight. Sunglasses and scarf in place, Gene got out of the car, ran up to the corner then walked toward the brick house. The landscaping was nonexistent, covered with dormant weeds. Instead of curtains or blinds, sheets were draped over the windows on the inside. Gene watched Joe come out through the front door and walk to his car.

"What the hell am I supposed to do?" the woman screamed.

"You stay right there until I get back, you stupid bitch," Joe yelled back.

"So just how long will you be gone this time, you idiot? I got a boy to feed, in case you haven't noticed."

Joe got in his car, put it in gear, squealed the tires and left.

Gene walked back to the BMW.

Detective Stanton was back in his office sitting behind his desk. Everything about the case was sitting in front of him; files, interviews, pictures and the medallion. He was deep in thought, slouched down in his chair with a glazed look on his face. His fingers were intertwined across his stomach and his elbows rested on the arms of the chair.

"No show?" Manny asked, referring to the funeral. "Because if he had shown up, I know you wouldn't be sitting here scratching your head, wondering how the hell he made it back to El Paso. You would be down at central booking…"

"What makes you think he's here?" Stanton asked. "If I were Gene, I would have crossed the border by now and never looked back. Hell, he has enough money."

Manny picked up the stack of pictures from Stanton's desk and shuffled through them.

"This is why I know he's here."

Manny showed Stanton the picture of Gene and Lisa together in front of Gene's house, taken the night after the murder.

"I think these two are a lot more than just friends. I think these two lovebirds are part of the Free-Landers, or at least he is and she knows it. I think Elliot Jones found out and they eliminated him. It's that simple.

Stanton felt the temperature in his face rise as the blood of anger rose to the top.

"Manny, that's the biggest load of B.S. I've ever heard," his voice grew louder as he spoke, drawing the attention of the other detectives and uniformed officers.

"Why is someone trying to kill him? Why would he work so hard to get back to the one place where he knows we will find him or worse, where they'll find him and kill him?" Stanton stood. "We know someone's trying to frame him and this picture proves it."

"How?"

"Who took the picture and made some punk kid deliver it to us, Manny? Do you know? I sure as hell don't."

"What about the coke we found under his bed?" Manny said.

"What about that, detective? Do you really think a dealer with that much coke under investigation for murder would just casually hide three kilos of coke under their bed then leave town? This guy is the president of a multimillion-dollar advertising agency. He's not stupid."

"Are you still pissed because I tore apart the guy's house without telling you?"

"You're damn right I am, and if you as much as think about this case without telling me again, I'll hang your ass." Stanton said pointing his finger at Manny. "But that's not the point. The fact that you're not looking at the whole picture, all of the evidence and the fact that you're so quick to convict without hard evidence really pisses me off."

Other officers looked on.

"What do you want from me, Stanton? I've only tried to help your case while you were chasing ghosts in New Mexico, out of jurisdiction, I might add."

Stanton suddenly grabbed Manny's lapels with both hands, forced him against the wall, holding Manny several inches off the ground. Some of the spectators ran over to try to calm things down, but Stanton was in control.

Stanton's tone was calm and matter-of-fact. "I want you to start playing detective and stop walking around here like you own the place. Work the case like you were trained, rookie. If you can't handle it, and work it the way I want to work it, get the hell off of it and get out of my way. Now you know what I want. Is it clear to you now?" He let Manny go and sat back down at his desk.

Manny looked at the crowd of official spectators as he straightened his shirt. His face was dark red but he kept his composure. He walked behind Stanton, leaned over and whispered in his ear.

"If you ever touch me like that again, I will break your legs. Second, I AM working the case. I don't know what it is with you and this guy, but you better stop," Manny spoke through clinched teeth and spit a little with the T, "thinking about how to exonerate him and start figuring out how to bust his ass."

"Detective Stanton, there's a call for you on line one," a clerk said from across the room.

"This is Detective Stanton," he said, then picked up a pencil and wrote as he listened. "Are you certain?" He looked at Manny. "So the fingerprints on the medallion belonged to Elliot Jones, the victim? Thank you." Stanton hung up the phone then turned to face Manny, "I guess that didn't help us."

It was noon by the time Gene arrived downtown back at the De Soto Hotel. He walked up the narrow flight of stairs and hallway to his room. Before he put his key in the lock he saw splintered wood protruding from the door jam next to the doorknob. He stood with his back against the wall to the hinge side of the door, prepared to run. Then he hit the door with his fist. The door pushed through the splinters and slowly swung open, creaking the entire way. He looked inside to see his room had been ransacked, the furniture broken and thrown about. His bed was turned upside down, the mattress shredded by a dozen knife cuts. He was relieved to know the duffel bag and saddlebags were in the trunk of the BMW.

He raced out of the room, down the hall, then down the stairs to the man's room that rented it to him. He banged on the door several times.

Footsteps scooted across the floor behind the door and the lock turned. When the door opened, Gene saw the man had been severally beaten. His face was bruised and his lips were swollen. Blood was on his dirty t-shirt. The man turned and limped back toward an old sofa then fell back on it without a word.

"Who did this to you?" Gene asked, taking a seat on the man's coffee table to examine the wounds.

"I'm not giving back your three hundred dollars," the man mumbled.

"What are you talking about?

"It was three spics. They wanted to know what room you were in. I didn't tell them nothing."

Gene got up and went to the man's tiny kitchen, opened an avocado-green freezer, pulled out an ice tray and folded a few cubes into a dingy towel lying on the counter.

"I didn't tell 'em nothin'," the man repeated, "until they decided to beat the shit out of me. Sorry, I had to, or they would have killed me."

Gene gave the man the ice pack. "Did you call the cops?"

"I almost did, but I knew you'd be back. The way I figure it, if they are what you're runnin' from, then you'll pay a hell of a lot more than three hundred. You owe me."

"I owe you more than money."

"I'll take the money," the man said.

Gene cleaned the man up and told him about the last several days, making sure to leave out details that would make him look guilty of anything.

"What I can't figure out is how they found me," Gene said. "It's absolutely impossible for anybody to know where I am. The only person that knows is Lisa and now you. Can I use your phone?"

Chapter Sixteen

The clock on the wall of the smoke-filled room read 1:30.

"What's wrong with you people?" the boss said. He was still dressed in his Armani suit. His stature gave him a strong presence but his pock-marked face re-enforced his bad attitude. It was unusual for him to be anywhere close to the group, much less in the same room.

The group had come straight from the cemetery.

"I told you to fix this mess, not make it worse. So what the hell were you doing at the funeral?" he said. "I saw you and you and you." The boss pointed at each person. "And what about you, detective?"

"I was at the station."

The boss walked over and stood face-to-face with the detective, "I'm sure they pay you pretty good to be a detective, don't they?" His voice was firm and he looked extremely anxious as he moved his hips from side to side, opening and closing his hands repeatedly. He looked like he was about to punch the detective.

"I was working on…"

"You bet I do," The boss said and threw his arms up from his sides trying to make the detective flinch and then walked away.

The detective did not flinch.

"I've given you the only tool you need to find this guy, but you can't find your ass with both of your hands."

The tension in the room was unbearable. Everyone else was just as anxious and full of worry and fear. None of them were experienced drug runners and had never been in a situation like the one they were facing. Other than the Boss, only one of them had been around the drug scene all of their life. The rest were just pawns, brought together through a series of circumstances all masterminded by the Boss. They all knew that every one of them was expendable. Getting out was not an option unless they wanted to go out like Elliot.

"I think I know how we can get him," one of the two women said. "He respects William Price. Maybe I can get Price to either tell me where Gene is or get Gene to meet Price somewhere," she said as she walked slowly toward the detective. She traced her long fingernail down his cheek to his chin. "Then the good detective here can come get him."

The boss walked to the big window in deep thought and watched the workers down below.

"How is it that all of you are professionals at what you do, yet you can't think?" he said. After a few moments of silence he said, "I like it, honey. Make it happen tonight. That way we can keep all of this as quiet as possible."

"The shipment is happening tonight," the detective said. "I've got to make sure the truck gets across the border and I'm the only one that can do it. My people won't do anything unless I tell them to."

"Then we have no choice. Make it happen right now, Love."

"Okay, I'll call Price right..."

"That won't work, either," the detective said. "If I arrest him, and I would love to nothing more, then I'll be stuck at the station forever, filling out paperwork, dealing with Stanton and answering to my bosses."

The detective spoke arrogantly, "If I have to mess around with Gene, the drugs don't make it across the border."

"Then make it happen tonight, Honey," the boss said then pointed at another man, "You get Gene. Take him to one of the empty stash houses blindfolded and when the shipment arrives, take a few kilos over and make him choke one down until he's dead."

"But Gene knows me."

"Then I guess you better wear a mask and make sure you kill him this time. I don't want to hear another word about it."

Gene and Lisa's cars would bring too much attention to them in that particular neighborhood. He decided to drive the stolen Honda Civic. He met Lisa in a grocery store parking lot where she got into the passenger side of his car.

"I saw you at the funeral," she said.

"That's not a good thing, Lisa."

"I'm sure no one recognized you. You looked great and not at all like your real self," Lisa said. "Do you really think we can do this?"

"Look, I know we agreed to go straight to Stanton when the funeral was over, but now, this is the only way I know that might give us some answers to why Elliot was killed and why so many people want me dead," he said. "I think we can do it. I've seen the house. There's not much traffic and there doesn't seem to be many people outside of their homes, kind of deserted."

"I can't believe you and I are planning a kidnapping. It freaks me out."

"Believe me, if you've been through the crap I've been through the last few days, nothing would freak you out."

Gene drove down the Interstate and took the Cotton Street exit. He followed the same route Joe Garcia used earlier in the day until he reached the house where Joe had abandoned the blonde woman and her child. He parked directly in front of it.

Since Gene followed Joe and there wasn't time to change clothes after the funeral. They didn't have time to plan and were making it up as they went. He straightened his tie and put on his dark sunglasses. Lisa smoothed her black and dress then they got out of the car.

When they reached the door, Gene tried ringing the doorbell, but they didn't hear a chime. He tried the doorknob and opened the door. The hinges squeaked and the floor creaked as they crept inside.

The house had a moldy smell and was dark except for the outline of the windows silhouetted through the sheets that were nailed to the walls.

"This house was a fine home eighty years ago," Lisa said as she flipped light switches, but nothing happened. None of the fixtures had bulbs.

"You stay down here. I'll look upstairs."

Lisa searched the living room, dining room and study. When she reached the kitchen, a rank smell caused her to gag. The sink was filled with dirty dishes. Rotten food sat molding on the counter and maggots were consuming a piece of raw meat.

"Lisa," Gene yelled in a hoarse whisper. "Come up here quick."

She ran up the stairs.

At the top, she saw Gene crouched down. The woman Joe left behind was unconscious on her back in the corner of the room. The boy was sitting next to her playing with a syringe and a rubber tourniquet. A bent spoon and lighter were on the floor next to the woman. Hundreds of packages of cocaine were stacked like bricks against each wall from the floor half way to the ceiling.

"All of the other rooms up here are just like this one. The bathrooms and closets are packed," he whispered.

"What do we do?" she said barely audible.

"Hey, little boy, can I have that?" Gene said softly referring to the syringe with the needle exposed.

The boy didn't answer.

"That's dangerous, son. Why don't you give me that?"

Gene walked toward the boy, but the boy raised the needle as if threatening to stab him if he came any closer.

"Come on, son. I need to check on your mommy to see if she's all right. She looks real sick."

The boy ran out of the room.

"Keep an eye on him, Lisa."

When Lisa left the room, Gene checked the woman's pulse again, and then lifted her up off the floor and onto his shoulder in a fireman's carrying position.

"Let's get out of here," Gene said passing Lisa in the hallway where the boy was stabbing packages of cocaine with the syringe, one after the other.

"What are you doing?"

"It's called kidnapping. Let's go now."

"What about the boy?" Lisa said following Gene down the stairs.

"He's not going anywhere. We'll lock him in and call child protective services. They'll come get him right away and he'll be better off."

When they reached the front door, Gene struggled to make the woman stand. He placed one of her arms around his neck and Lisa took the other. They walked the woman to the car and poured her into the back seat. Gene ran back to the front door, locked it from the inside and closed it. He looked around for something to hold the door closed from the outside, but couldn't find anything except a rusty nail in the door frame. He took off his tie and knotted one end to the doorknob and the other to the nail.

When they returned to the grocery store, Gene and Lisa transferred the woman to the back seat of Lisa's car, making certain no one was watching.

"I'll wait here," Gene said. "You use that payphone and call child protective services. I will be able to see you from here. We don't want them capturing our cell phone numbers on their caller IDs."

While Lisa had gone, Gene checked the woman's pulse again. She looked bad, but she had a pulse. Lisa returned five minutes later.

"Did you get a hold of anyone?"

"They wanted to ask me a bunch of questions, but I only gave them the address and told them there was a boy by himself in the house and that it was full of drugs. I told them about the drugs so they would hurry."

"That should do it."

"Gene, I'm scared."

"This chick is Sam and she is going to help us, but you gotta get her cleaned up so you can talk to her. I wish I could help, but these people seem to be right on my tail where ever I go. Plus, I need to check on something I found at the agency."

It was almost 4:30 in the afternoon when Lisa pulled into her garage. The woman had begun moaning. Lisa closed the garage door then opened the rear passenger door of the car. She wrestled the half-conscious woman into a standing position. The two women stumbled into the house, down the hallway and into the guest bathroom. Lisa sat the woman on the toilet then undressed her and placed her in a sitting position on the floor of the shower.

Lisa turned on the cold water and moved the showerhead to spray the woman.

The woman moaned raising her arms in defense of the water.

"Come on, Sam. You need to sober up. We need to talk."

"Please stop it." the woman said.

"You are Sam, right? Come on, talk to me and I'll turn it off. Your name is Sam, right?"

"Sammmmanntha," Sam said.

Lisa was relieved to know it was Sam. She turned off the water. Another part of Lisa was beginning to feel angry, but she helped Sam out of the shower and back down on the toilet. Lisa took a towel and started to gently dry her off when Sam passed out again, her head resting against Lisa's hip.

"You need to sleep it off."

Lisa's rigorous work-outs at the gym gave her the strength to be able to dress Sam in a nightgown that clung to her wet body and put her to bed in the guest bedroom.

With nowhere else to go, Gene sat in the stolen car, parked next to the BMW now on the top floor of the parking garage where he had met with Lisa before the funeral. He was waiting for Lisa to call him with any information she could get from Sam.

He pulled the pad of Post-It notes from his coat pocket. His mind was focused on the two times Joe Garcia's office number was dialed from Elliot's office. The first call on the list to Joe was made on Monday. Who would be calling Joe yesterday and why from Elliot's desk?

The second on the list was the call Elliot made the night of his murder, just before 1:00 in the morning.

Gene started guessing. At least now I think I know why Elliot called him, Gene thought. Elliot meets Sam and tries to clean her up. Sam is Joe's junky lover. Elliot finds out about their relationship and she probably told Elliot that Joe was a coke dealer. Elliot must have thought he could reason with Joe to stop giving Sam the drugs or maybe he thought he could clear up her debt by talking directly to Joe. Joe can't trust Elliot not to turn him in, so he kills Elliot.

He couldn't do anything until he knew what Sam knew and confirmed his suspicions.

A car drove up the ramp and parked several spaces away. A man, took a briefcase from the back seat, and walked to the elevators. After the man disappeared behind the elevator doors, Gene focused his eyes again on the Post-It note, but this time he noticed something new. There was a faint black smudge at the bottom of the paper. He realized who ever had used Elliot's phone last, must have transferred fingerprint powder to their finger, written something down on the note pad, then used the same finger to hold the pad down while they peeled off the top note. At closer examination, Gene could see the imprint of the writing. He folded the top sheet back and saw that what was written had left the same impressions on the next page.

Gene scoured the car looking for a pencil, in the glove box and under the seats. Frustrated, he sat up and looked through the passenger window at Elliot's car.

At 3:30 that same afternoon, Stanton was filling out the day's reports at his desk when his cell phone rang.

"We need to talk."

"Gene?" he answered with surprise in his voice. He regretted saying Gene's name loud enough for Manny to hear from across the room.

Stanton and Manny's eyes met.

"We need to meet, detective," Gene said.

"We've got cops looking everywhere for you," Stanton said also loud enough for Manny's benefit.

"I've got information that will help my case and give you a lead on Elliot's murder. We have to meet. Be at Album Park in thirty minutes by yourself. If I see anyone else, I'm gone."

"Alright, Gene, but you know we're going to find you in that stolen car of yours. It's just a matter of time." The detective hung up.

"What did he say?" Manny asked.

Detective Stanton raised his eyebrows, "I don't know. He sounded out of his mind, yelling stuff like *'I'm innocent'* and *'why don't you stop chasing me'*. Just a bunch of nonsense, then hung up. He's losing it."

"Why did you tell him we know about the stolen car?" Manny asked.

"If he is losing it, then he'll try to find a place to hide it. With any luck, he'll drive right by one of our cars."

Stanton knew it was a stupid reason and he thought Manny was about to attack Stanton's judgment when Manny's cell phone rang. Stanton watched Manny answer it and walk to a more private corner of the office. Stanton slid out of the office.

Gene wanted to stay inconspicuous and thought about driving the stolen car but he remembered Stanton's words, *'we're going to find you in that stolen car'*. Stanton had given him advice. Gene drove Elliot's.

When Gene reached the park, he picked Stanton's car out, parked close to the east entrance in front of the recreational center. It wasn't because Gene knew which car to look for. It was because everyone knew an unmarked cop car when they saw one. Anyone near it moved to the opposite side of the parking lot. Gene entered from the south side along with three other cars and dialed Stanton on his cell phone.

"I see you, detective. Thanks for the tip on the car," Gene said.

"You've got thirty seconds to give me something to go on before I radio in and have this place surrounded with cops."

"Do you remember when you asked me if I knew why Elliot would have called Joe Garcia the night he was killed? I was at the P & M offices today while you and everyone else were at the funeral. I was looking for a clue how to get out of this mess."

"We've already searched Elliot's office from top to bottom. There's nothing there, Gene."

"I couldn't find anything either until I looked at the list of calls on his phone."

"We already know he called Joe last."

"Elliot made his call on Friday night. Someone else called Joe yesterday from the same phone. Check it out for yourself," Gene said.

"It doesn't matter if someone called the President from that phone. We've taken all the evidence we could out of there, which wasn't much. Because of Elliot's history with Joe and the close industry connection, it's not so crazy to think someone from your office called Joe from Elliot's line to taunt him or console him. In either case, it doesn't come close to getting you off the hook."

"I don't believe whoever called Joe was calling for personal reasons. They were calling him for information. I think they were in his office looking for something. They called Joe and then they wrote a phone number down on the Post-It note pad that I was able to read by shading it with a pencil. Tell me if you recognize it; 535-4734."

"That's the main line to my…"

"I know. I called it. Why would someone from my office call Joe, and then write down your phone number?" Gene said.

Stanton got out of his car and started looking closer at individual cars.

"Any ideas?"

Gene watched Stanton and waited for any sudden moves.

"I did get a fingerprint. I mean they left one on the pad of paper. I have it with me."

"That won't do us any good. We can't prove where or how you go it," Stanton said.

"It's made from the fingerprint dust your guys left on the phone."

"The office hasn't been cleaned?"

"They dialed the phone then touched the paper. You could run it and find out who it was that called Joe. Did I tell you Joe is into the cocaine scene?"

"How do you know?" Stanton asked.

"That's something else I did today. I found an entire house filled with…"

Gunshots rang out from several cars coming into the parking lot from both entrances at high rates of speed. Men, women and children screamed and ran, taking cover behind trashcans and trees or falling to the ground covering their heads with their hands. The shooters raced passed Stanton firing into the air.

The detective drew his gun, but held his fire because there were too many people running around in the background. Then he jumped into his car and called for backup as he squealed his tires quickly maneuvering from his parking spot.

Gene threw the cell phone into the passenger seat without ending the call, started the BMW, floored it and popped the clutch, scrapping several cars before breaking free and jumping the curb to cut across the grass with the shooters and Stanton in fast pursuit. He shifted to second then third, barely lifting his foot from the gas between gears. He ducked at the sounds of gunshots. Stanton's siren blared in the distance behind him.

He topped eighty miles per hour before he reached Montana Avenue, a main artery that eventually turned into a highway leading east out of town. Gene slammed on the brakes, made a hard right turn, and then floored the BMW again, racing through gears, down the street. Even as he reached one hundred miles per hour, the cars behind him seemed to be keeping up.

"The suspects are now headed east at the twelve thousand block of Montana," Stanton said. "There are four cars chasing and shooting at a blue BMW roadster."

Stanton was in the rear but keeping up with the four cars. He stuck his gun out of the driver's side and shot four rounds, hitting the back of a red Chevy Nova. He tried to move up to the side of the car, but it swerved back and forth keeping him behind.

By the time they had gone five miles three more police cruisers joined the chase.

"Cars 344 and 672 are with you," came over the Stanton's radio. Those two were behind Stanton then another one came in from a side street.

"Car 410 joining pursuit."

That police car was able to get between the four cars, leaving two behind Gene and two in front of Stanton. The detective rammed the Chevy, making the driver lose control briefly. On the second ramming, the driver lost control again. Stanton floored his car and rammed the Chevy a third time. The car spun sideways and flipped over several times off to the side of the road into a vacant lot.

The traffic was lighter than usual on Montana Avenue for a weekday rush hour. Gene was able to change lanes. The shooters couldn't be accurate as long as he kept the car swerving from lane to lane.

Gene pushed the accelerator harder: one hundred ten, then one fifteen. When he hit one hundred twenty, the shooting stopped. The other cars fell behind.

Stanton's adrenaline peaked giving him the controlled anger he needed to stay focused on the Euro racer in front of him. It could easily outrun the detective's car, but car 410 was in front of it, blocking it. Stanton drove steadily pointed his gun through the window again, but before he could get off a shot, a gunman in the Euro car climbed out of its passenger window and sprayed rounds from an AK-47, riddling the hood and shattering Stanton's windshield. Driving ninety miles an hour, Stanton swerved wildly to the left into the dirt median then back to the right, fish-tailing before he regained control. The gunmen targeted the police cars behind Stanton. The detective looked over his shoulder when car 672 burst into flames.

"Did you see that?" said the officer over the radio from car 410 in front of the gunmen who was still sitting on the passenger door taking shots. "Everyone back off."

Stanton and the officer in car 344 knew what would happen next and slowed to eighty miles an hour. Stanton drove on the left shoulder. Car 344 took the right shoulder.

"I got this bastard," said the officer in car 410 as he positioned his vehicle in front of the Euro racer then he quickly tapped his brakes just hard enough to force the racer to slam into the rear end of the police car. The gunmen lost his weapon and his grip as he was thrown from the car. His arms and legs snapped as he tumbled down the asphalt.

"Now's your chance, 344. Get behind him and let's pin him to a stop."

The police car 344 quickly pulled up behind the racer while Stanton drove along side of it, pointing his gun at the driver who gave the detective a wave of surrender with a free hand.

"I'm going after the others." Stanton raced passed the scene.

"This is Officer Duncan calling Detective Stanton. Your blue roadster just passed me doing one-twenty-five just outside the city limits. I'm in pursuit, over."

"Let him go, turn around and help us get these idiots with the guns," Stanton said.

Gene had lost the gunmen two miles back when they had turned onto a dirt road. Then he saw Officer Duncan start to chase him and suddenly turn around. Gene slowed the BMW to the speed limit. He drove ten more miles until he was sure he was safe and he was afraid to go too far in case the police called ahead to the next town. Just in front of him were a small community and his last chance for gas, which he was low on. He stopped in the parking lot next to the only gas pump and waited in the car for five minutes before getting out and filling it up.

When he finished pumping, he went inside to pay. When he returned, Stanton was waiting for him, sitting on his hood that had steam pouring out of the bullet holes. Gene was surprised, but not intimidated.

"What took you so long?" Gene said, keeping his distance from the detective.

"Well, it seems I'm having a bit of car trouble," Stanton said. "You mind giving me a ride back to town?"

"I don't know. What's in it for me?"

"How about I make you a promise?" Stanton said.

"Sounds weak. What kind of promise can you make me that won't end with me in jail?"

"First I promise not to kick your ass for almost getting me killed."

"That's a start," Gene said feeling a little less apprehensive about the situation.

"Second, I'll listen to all of your crazy stories and hare-brained theories, but you have to tell me what happened in New Mexico and how you made it back here."

"How do I know I won't be incriminating myself?" Gene asked. "I don't stand a chance against you, if you change your mind about me. And, how do I know you don't have cops waiting for me at the city limits?"

"You'll just have to trust me for once."

Chapter Seventeen

Price sat behind his desk, a tight knot still in his tie and barely a wrinkle in his ten-hour-old starched white shirt. He had just finished reviewing a forty-five million dollar request for a proposal for a nationwide furniture retailer. With Elliot gone, he would have to manage the entire process.

At 5:00 in the afternoon, the flat-screen across the room came to life. "This is KTSM News at Five," the female news anchor said. "In today's top stories, an hour-and-a-half ago… The reporter told of the high-speed chase and shooting in East El Paso.

Price watched the amateur video from an innocent bystander in the park. The gunshots were audible, people were screaming and chaos broke out when the cars drove through the grass. Then the reporter made it personal to Price's company.

The reporter said, "Now, El Paso Police are having trouble sorting out this story. It has all the

markings of a gang-related incident, but a source from the police department says he believes the driver of the BMW was Gene Martine, president of P&M Advertising located in downtown El Paso."
Price walked closer to the TV.

"Apparently, this whole thing could be related to the Elliot Jones' murder this past Saturday morning. If our viewers recall, when we reported on the murder, we showed you Mr. Martine standing just a few feet from where the body was found."

Price's mouth sagged open, as the news anchor and reporter continued discussing the story. He counted nine times P & M was mentioned. He didn't hear his desk phone ringing until the fifth ring. He hit the speaker button.

"Price, this is Julio Rivera."

Price snapped to his senses. "Hey, Julio. It was good to see you today. I'm sorry it took a funeral to bring you to town. I wish your schedule would have allowed you to join my wife and I for dinner, or is that why you're calling? Did you change your mind?"

"You're rambling, Price. You just saw the same news I did, didn't you Price?"

"It's a case of mistaken identity. It couldn't have been Gene. He's in Ruidoso. I can't wait to tell him. We'll sue the El Paso Police Department, the media and anyone else spreading rumors like that about Gene."

Julio said, "I don't like what's happening at your firm."

"We're business-as-usual here. It means nothing." Price was nervous.

"Who's going to handle my account? Elliot's dead, and who's going to make sure the creative is on target? Gene's under investigation for killing Elliot and now he's shooting at cops."

"He wasn't doing the shooting. Hell, he wasn't even there. Be fair about this. VoiceComm is important to us. I'll manage your account personally or I'll put Madeline on it with my supervision. You like Madeline and Gene will be back in a couple of days. Better than that, I'll call him as soon as I hang up with you and get him back here tomorrow. Business as usual, right?"

"Price, VoiceComm can't handle bad press right now. We're your biggest client, but your company is falling apart and VoiceComm needs the best, needs to get what they pay for and that can't happen like this. VoiceComm has stock holders to think about."

"I will have Gene in the office by mid-week and all of this will go away by the end of the week."

"I'll give you until the end of the week," Julio said. "But if VoiceComm is mentioned one time in the press associated with anything negative related to your agency, I will have to move our business. I'll have no choice."

Two fillets of breaded trout were simmering in a frying pan, vegetables were in a steamer and potatoes were baking in the oven. The aroma of the home-cooked meal filled the air and made its way to the guest bedroom where Sam was sleeping off the drugs.

Her eyes were bloodshot-red and dark, heavy bags circled under her eyelids. She put her bare feet onto the tile floor, finding solid ground and stood up, noticing the nightgown she was wearing. It was almost 7:30 in the evening and the

winter sun had long gone. The only light in the
room came from the doorway. Her feet scooted one
after the other until she reached the door. The light
was too bright as her pupils adjusted bringing into
focus the hallway wall that was covered with art
and family pictures. An expensive Persian rug ran
the length of the floor in either direction.

She walked down the hall until she found
the bathroom. Without the light, she turned on the
cold water then drank from the spout before
splashing the coolness on her face. She felt terrible,
but her strength was returning.

"God, where am I?" she said in the darkness.

"Feeling better, I see."

Sam turned to see Lisa standing in the
doorway of the bathroom, but said nothing.

"You must be starving. I've made dinner.
Follow me."

Lisa walked ahead of Sam then disappeared
into another room. Sam turned the same corner and
stopped as she looked around in awe at the nice
furniture, the lit fireplace and more paintings and
pictures. The smell of the trout was stronger now
and she followed it to the source in the kitchen. Lisa
had set the table and was placing the meal onto the
plates.

"Where am I?" Sam said.

"Sit down and eat," Lisa said. "What would
you like to drink, water or tea?"

"Water."

Sam devoured her food, but with
exaggerated manners. She sat up straight, held her
silverware appropriately and kept her napkin in her
lap.

"It's been a very long time since I've eaten such a wonderful meal. Thank you," Sam said.

"Would you like more?"

"Yes, please," Sam said in an embarrassed tone, turning her eyes to her lap.

They finished their meal without speaking.

Sam asked, "You're Lisa, aren't you? And this is Elliot's home. I mean, your home, right? How did I get here?"

"I brought you here," Lisa said.

"Where's my son?" Sam said in a panic and stood from the table just realizing his absence.

Lisa hesitated for moment, "He's fine. He's with friends."

Sam turned and walked back toward Lisa, "I want to be with my son. He needs me. He has special needs. He doesn't know how to communicate with anyone but me."

"I'm trying to help you, Sam, just like Elliot was trying to help you, so you're going to have to trust me. Your son is fine. Please sit down so we can talk." Lisa got up from the dining room table, walked into the living room and sat down on the sofa, signaling to Sam to do the same.

Sam walked to the sofa and sat down at the opposite end.

"Do you know Gene Martine?" Lisa said.

"I think Elliot mentioned him. He's Elliot's boss right?"

"Gene's in trouble with the same people who killed Elliot. The police think Gene killed Elliot and you're the only person we know that can tell us who these people are and what really happened to Elliot. You need to help us."

"I told you, I don't know anything. I can't say anything. You can't protect me and my son," Sam said, then stood. "Is that what this is all about? You're holding my son hostage somewhere until I tell you what you want to know, aren't you?"

Lisa spoke with authority, "I told you, your son is fine. I'm sure he's getting a hot meal and some rest in a real bed, not that hard floor in the house we found you in." Lisa stood up.

"How did you know where I was? What did you see in that house? Shit, Joe's going to kill me."

"He doesn't even know where you are."

"Lady, he knows everything. He'll hunt me down and kill both of us. You're as dead as I am."

Lisa considered those words. "Sam, you can't freak out on me. We'll call the police, explain it all to them and you'll be a free woman."

"I've got to get out of here," Sam started talking to herself. "I've got to get my baby and go to Joe. He'll forgive me. He'll beat the shit out of me, but he'll forgive me. He always does."

Lisa took her arm to calm her down. Sam grabbed Lisa's wrist and twisted it behind Lisa's back.

"Don't ever touch me again, bitch!" She pushed Lisa away from her and screamed, "Where's my son? He's here isn't he?" Sam turned away to walk frantically around the entire house, looking from room to room calling 'Honey' at every turn.

"I told you, he's not here," Lisa yelled.

Sam returned to the living room, "Then you better tell me where he is before I beat it out of you," she said with angry tears.

"Not until you tell me what I need to know and we go to the police so you can tell it to them."

"The police are just as dirty as the rest of them. They'll kill me and you, too."

Sam walked straight at her and slapped her. Lisa slapped her back. Sam grabbed Lisa and threw her down onto the floor and dragged Lisa through the living room by her hair.

"Where is he? Tell me!"

Lisa turned over onto her stomach, grabbed Sam's leg and tripped her to the floor. Lisa climbed on top of Sam as they fought and pulled at one another. Lisa punched Sam squarely on the nose. The punch seemed to only infuriate Sam. Lisa was strong from her regular workout routine but Sam had been abused and taken many beatings. With blood running out of Sam's nose, she grabbed Lisa's wrist again and twisted it. Lisa screamed in pain as Sam maneuvered behind Lisa, pulling the arm around Lisa's back again, shoving it between her shoulder blades, forcing Lisa's face to the hard tile.

"Where is my son? Tell me or I break it."

Lisa kicked Sam in the back, forcing Sam to gasp for air and release the pressure on Lisa's arm. Lisa lifted herself up to her knees, throwing Sam off of her back.

Lisa broke free and ran down the hallway toward the garage. Sam caught her from behind as she reached the laundry room. Sam grabbed Lisa by the hair again and slammed Lisa's head against the wall three times before Lisa hit Sam in the ribs with her elbow. Sam fell to the floor in the laundry room. Lisa was leaning over the washing machine when Sam's teeth sank into her leg. Lisa screamed and struggled to get free, but the more she moved the worse the pain got. Lisa pulled an iron from the cabinet above the washer and hammered Sam's head, knocking her out.

When Sam came to, she found herself on her knees and struggling to breath. Blood from her nose was all over the nightgown and wads of hair were lying here and there. Her legs were duct-taped together in a bent position. Her torso was pulled tight against the sink. Her arms and hands were wet and duct-taped over the sink directly underneath the waterspout, but Lisa wasn't there. Sam struggled to move, but to no avail.

"Where are you?" she said as her eyes squeezed tight.

"You killed my husband, didn't you?" Lisa said returning to the doorway.

Lisa walked into the room, reached for the knob marked 'hot' and turned it. Sam screamed as the scalding hot water hit her arms. Then Lisa turned it off.

"I didn't kill him. He was my friend."

"Then who did?" Lisa said.

"I don't know."

Lisa turned the water on again followed by another scream from Sam, then off again.

"No more games, Sam." Lisa had lost the ability to think rationally. "You are nothing to me you skanky drug addict. Your son is going to be motherless."

Sam yelled at the mention of her son, "Where is he? Please tell me where my son is. I'll tell you what you want to know. Just tell me where my son is," she said, then took a breath and cried even harder. "Please, don't hurt me again, Joe. Please don't hurt me again, Joe."

When Stanton got into the car with Gene earlier in the day, the detective had wasted no time before asking questions. Although Gene was shaken and apprehensive, he had no one else to turn to. He felt like he was on a witness stand as he rushed through the explanation of everything that had happened to him, from the time the two cholos gave him a hard time on the highway to Ruidoso, to his escape back to El Paso. He left out details that would somehow incriminate him, such as blowing up the motorcycle in Cloudcroft. Because of the car chase, it wasn't hard for Gene to build his case around the fact more than one person was hunting him.

"Who do you think is trying to kill you?"

"They must be the Free-Landers," Gene said. "They must think I know what Elliot knew."

"Do you know something or have something they want?" Stanton said. "Maybe you do and you just don't know it. What about the kilos of coke they found under your bed? Was that theirs?"

"I have never seen a kilo of coke, much less have it in my house. Besides, I've thought of nothing else for the last three days. I don't know or have anything they could possibly want, except..."

"Except what?" Stanton said.

"Do you remember when you saw Lisa in my guest bathroom? That night she told me some things about Elliot that she should have told you, but was afraid the information would leak to the press and tarnish his reputation. Looking back, I should have at least said something to you that morning."

"I'm listening."

Gene drove the rest of the way into town explaining Elliot's relationship to Sam, how Elliot was trying to help her with her drug problems and the arguments that ensued between Lisa and Elliot. He told him that his room at the De Soto Hotel was trashed and about the beating the manager took. Then he explained how he followed Joe and Sam to a stash house and where it was. What Gene didn't tell Detective Stanton was that he and Lisa had kidnapped Sam and left her son alone in that house for Child Protective Services to take care of. When they were three blocks from the crime lab, Stanton told Gene to pull over.

Stanton said, "I've never seen a gang go after someone with so many resources. I mean, these people have stopped at nothing to get to you. You've got to be one of the luckiest people I've ever met." Stanton was talking to Gene, but at the same time he was talking to himself. "I mean, how does a big city advertising executive evade ruthless killers over and over? You seem to be ahead of them every time they try." Stanton opened the passenger door and put his right boot down on the pavement.

Stanton looked at his watch. "I am on your side. Call it a gut feeling."

"Where can I go?" Gene said.

"I could put you in jail. At least there you would be safe."

"No, I'll take my chances as a free man. I'm confident you'll figure this all out."

"You're not out of trouble by a long shot. Even if I do clear you, the great state of New Mexico wants a piece of your hide and I'm going to make sure you give it to them. Hide this car. It's full of bullet holes and sticks out like a sore thumb. Stay out of sight and the hell away from anyone you love. You seem to attract Free-Landers everywhere you go. One more thing, Gene."

"What's that?"

"If you screw me," Stanton paused in thought. "If I find out you're playing me, I will hunt you down myself and kill you." Stanton closed the car door, and walked away.

Gene was parked in the parking garage, waiting for a call from Lisa. Elliot's cell phone broke the monotonous silence of the garage. The time on the phone said it was 7:30 in the evening. The number on the screen was from someone he hadn't thought about since he was in Cloudcroft, New Mexico.

"Marlene?"

"Gene? Are you ok?" Marlene was yelling over the background noise. She was calling from inside the River Rock Boot warehouse where the sound of forklifts, trucks and workers polluted the air. "Where are you?"

As far as Gene knew, Marlene had no idea he was back in the city. "I'm on my way back from Ruidoso. I'm passing through Alamogordo as we speak."

"Don't bullshit me. I saw you on the news today," Marlene said.

"What are you talking about?"

"Someone said they thought it was you, but I know for sure it was. I would recognize Elliot's Beemer anywhere, and since he's dead…"

"Can you get to somewhere you can talk without all that noise?" Gene asked.

"Price called me. He's really shaken up about something," Marlene said.

"Why would he call you?"

"Because I'm the only person he could think of who might know where to reach you," she yelled. "What the heck is going on with you, Gene? Why were…" Marlene gave orders to a forklift operator, "Put those crates over there and be careful. Why were you being chased? Does it have to do with the coke they found in your house?"

"Marlene, I can't have a conversation with you like this. I'll come over then we can talk."

"Come to the warehouse. I've got a big shipment coming in tonight. I need to stay here." She ended the call.

Until then, Gene and Lisa were alone in their troubles. He felt he needed another ally, someone he trusted, but he hadn't trusted her in years. If nothing else, he would try to warn her about Joe Garcia.

Gene traded the BMW and drove the Honda again. When he arrived at the warehouse it was close to 8:00 in the evening. He noted the large number of cars parked in the parking lot. Gene had not been to River Rock Boots in years. He was surprised to see them busy that late at night. He had to park a hundred yards away from the entrance.

As he walked between the cars, he noticed most of the license plates were from Mexico. She employed a small number of illegal aliens from time to time when she needed extra help. But there were many more than usual that night.

Inside the warehouse, he learned why Marlene was yelling on the phone. The open building amplified the sound of the forklifts and semi trucks at the loading docks. He was standing by the wooden staircase below her office, watching and looking out for Marlene when she appeared at the top. She waved him up. He was happy to see her and grateful she was worried about him. He ran up the staircase, skipping every other step, until he reached the top where the two of them hugged.

Marlene said, "What's gotten into you?"

"It's just been a long time," Gene said.

"Let's go into the office, Sugar."

Gene grabbed a metal folding chair, placed it in front of the desk and sat down.

"Tell me what's going on," she said.

"Did you love me when we were married?"

"What?"

"You heard me. Did you love me?"

"Gene, I've always loved you. I will always love you."

"Then, what happened to us? Where did we go wrong?"

"Come on, Gene. It was a little bit of you, a little bit of me. That was a long time ago. We're past all of that, Sugar."

"It's just that I've thought about us a lot recently. You know, re-evaluating my life now that I'm officially an old man. It was my birthday yesterday."

"Oh, my God, that's right."

Marlene got out of her chair, went around the desk and kissed him, leaving red lipstick around his mouth. He tasted the nicotine that he had learned to hate by the end of their marriage.

"What in the world is going on, Gene? I know you, or at least I think I do. You don't know the first thing about drugs, so why in Sam Hill would you have it in your house?"

"Someone is trying to frame me for Elliot's murder."

"From what I saw on the news, it didn't look like they were trying to frame you. It looked more like someone was trying to kill you."

"Detective Stanton is helping me out. I found something in Elliot's office that might help him figure out who killed Elliot and maybe who's trying to get to me. He thinks Elliot somehow stumbled into a bad situation with a group called the Free-Landers."

Marlene put out her freshly lit cigarette. "Sounds like a rock group. Who are they?"

"Apparently they are the nation's number one drug smuggling ring and Joe Garcia is involved with them."

She reached for another cigarette. "He's too stupid to get into that crap."

"Don't ask me how I know. You need to fire his agency tomorrow so River Rock isn't associated with him. Give your business to another agency as soon as you can."

"I suppose you want it now that VoiceComm is about to leave you."

"What do you know about VoiceComm? Is Joe spreading rumors?"

"Honey, you still haven't talked to Price? With Elliot's death and your great press today, the CEO feels like your agency has some serious problems that he can't afford to be part of so, he's threatening to move the VoiceComm account if you and Price don't get things under control by the end of the week."

Elliot's cell phone rang. The display read 'Home'. It was Lisa. "Well speak of the devil," Gene said to Marlene. "It's Price. Let me take the call."

Marlene left the office, closing the door so Gene could hear his call.

"Gene, where are you?"

"I'm in Marlene's office at the River Rock warehouse. Did Sam tell you anything?"

"Marlene's?"

"Why are you calling me from your house phone? Did she tell you anything?"

"Yes, she talked. Is there anyone around you?"

"Marlene walked back into the office with Joe Garcia behind her. The noise from the warehouse drowned out Lisa's voice.

Stunned at Joe's presence Gene said, "Price, I'll have to call you back. We'll discuss it in a little while."

Marlene looked at Gene with concern, "Gene, look who's here."

Joe shook Gene's hand.

"It's been a long time, Joe. How are you doing?" Gene said.

"I guess your drug buddies didn't catch you after all."

Marlene said, "Gene, I'm busy and I need to get back to work." Then she hugged him.

Gene walked out of the office then turned and said, "I'll be in Mexico for the next couple of weeks. I'll call you when I get back and if you ever decide to get a real ad agency, we'll work for half of what he's ripping you off for." Gene walked down the staircase and out through the front door. He hoped Joe bought his lie about Mexico.

"You won't touch him while he's on my property," Marlene said, shaking her finger at Joe.

"The boss doesn't want him anywhere near here. What did he know?" Joe asked.

She lied. "He has no idea who's after him or why. He knows he's being framed, that's it. I wish your guys would just leave him alone."

"You know that's not possible, especially now. Either he goes down or the rest of us will," Joe said as he dialed his cell phone to call Detective Ortega.

"If he keeps running, they're going to kill him," Marlene said.

Joe hung up the phone. "Fine, I'll give him a head start before I call Manny."

Marlene had never felt more ashamed. She couldn't think of any way to warn Gene that wouldn't get her killed or thrown into jail. She thought she would be willing to take any punishment for Gene's sake, but her Dad would certainly serve the same sentence because of her stupidity. It was a game of self-preservation now, and there was no turning back.

Chapter Eighteen

Gene knew he was under surveillance as he walked to his car. He knew there was something wrong the second he laid eyes on Joe. How did Marlene know to call Elliot's phone, he wondered.

He got into the car and then drove out of the parking lot, watching his mirrors for any sign of being followed. He made several unplanned turns down dark streets. Then he turned his lights off and pulled into a dark vacant parking lot and killed the motor. Gene needed to think.

With the motor off, the temperature in the car dropped to the outside temperature of forty-two degrees. Gene was still dressed in his funeral clothes, less the tie, and he was hot with anger. Why would Joe be at the warehouse late at night? He wondered and he couldn't figure out how she knew he had Elliot's phone. Then he had a thought. It was a suspicion that made him start the car and tear out of the parking lot back toward the warehouse. He parked a block away, took his saddlebags from the trunk, and abandoned the car on foot. Elliot's dark suit helped Gene blend into the darkness, but did little to keep the cold from stinging his legs. He scaled a short chain link fence surrounding a pipe yard next door to the River Rock Boots warehouse. From rack to rack, Gene ran and hid until he reached the fence closest to the rear of the warehouse.

Two long-nose, sleeper-style, semi-trucks were backed up to the loading docks. Fifteen of Marlene's Mexican laborers were visibly working hard unpacking, moving pallets and throwing the leftover plastic wrap into an industrial trashcan on Gene's side of the docks. There were two forklift operators. Each raced into the truck trailers with empty forks, returning with two pallets each of River Rock Boots wrapped in plastic. Each load took less than a minute to drop off in the warehouse between the endless rows of racks, where other workers unpacked and sorted the boxes of boots.

The men were talking, but the noise of the forklifts made it difficult to make out any words. He hopped the fence in the darkness and ran to the side of the building. He worked his way toward the docks, thinking how much Marlene really knew and hid next to the large trashcan. The men were complaining about the speed at which they were forced to work.

Orders were barked from just inside the building. It was Marlene's voice. She came outside onto the docks. She was standing above the trashcan only a few feet from Gene.

"This trailer's empty. Take it and pick up the last shipment and hurry up. We're on a tight schedule on this one, guys. If you want to get paid on time, the boots better be delivered on time. Now, vamonos."

One of the men said, "Enrique is in the restroom and he's the driver tonight."

"Then you pick up the load."

"I don't have my credentials with me. Enrique is the driver tonight. I'll go get him." He walked inside the warehouse with Marlene on his tail, yelling at him about his incompetence.

When the man left, Gene had a clear path to the cab of the truck and it gave him an idea. He moved quickly and quietly.

Enrique opened the truck's door, stepped up and sat inside behind the big steering wheel. He pushed in the clutch, shifted to neutral and turned the key half way. When a bright yellow light illuminated on the instrument panel, he turned the key the rest of the way, starting the diesel engine. Gene could feel the power of the roaring motor through the dirty mattress he was huddled on directly behind Enrique. He camouflaged himself with some wadded up sheets and a crumpled sleeping bag. He had pulled the privacy curtains closed part way, enough to cover his feet and saddlebags.

From under the covers, Gene had a good view of the cabin's interior and the darkness beyond the windshield. He watched Enrique jam the shifter in gear and check his mirrors. When he lifted his foot from the clutch, the cab of the truck lifted and heaved forward. Gene wasn't expecting the sudden motion and rolled onto his back, barely making a sound. Enrique turned his head, looked over his right shoulder directly at Gene, and then returned his attention back to driving. The truck drove west on Interstate 10 to the Juarez exit. If they were stopped and searched, Gene would be caught with no way back.

The darkness of the night turned to light as Enrique approached the border where bright lights illuminated everything, including the inside of the truck's cab. Crossing into Mexico was easy. Enrique drove the truck over the long bridge and approached Mexico. The cargo holds of all trucks of that size were checked on both sides of the border. If the trailer were full of goods, the chances of having it inspected were high, but this rig was empty when he stopped at the point of entry.

A Mexican agent dressed in a green uniform approached and spoke in Spanish. "Que tienes, Senor?" *What do you have?* the agent said.

"Nada." *Nothing,* Enrique said.

"Abre lo." *Open it.*

Enrique left the motor running, got out of the truck and left the door open. Another Mexican agent approached. The agent took his flashlight from his utility belt, climbed up the side of the cab and looked it over. He noticed the unkempt cab and grungy sheets in the sleeper.

"He's good," the agent with the light heard the other agent say and as he climbed down from the cab and closed the door.

Gene adjusted his view so he could see the mirror on the door. He could see both agents laughing and shaking hands with Enrique as he climbed back into the cab.

The truck leaped forward once again. Gene steadied himself on the mattress. It took thirty minutes for them to reach the plant where the trailer backed up to the loading dock. The River Rock Boot Mexico manufacturing facility was a one hundred thousand square foot metal building where mostly Mexican women did the leather cutting, sewing and boot construction. Hot in the summers and cold in the winters, the working conditions were bad compared to most U.S. standards. It was where Gene found his love for working leather and making his belts when he and Marlene were married.

As Gene watched the reflection in the mirror again, he surmised there was no way Joe could get his drugs into the boxes at the plant. The boots were built in an assembly line fashion and at the end of the line the boots were boxed and stacked on pallets. When a pallet was full, black plastic straps were wrapped around it and secured with metal clips.

If Joe's not using Marlene's shipments, where did he get that coke I saw in the stash house? He sat up on the mattress and monitored both door mirrors, watching the workers, the forklift operator and Enrique. The only activity he couldn't see took place behind the trailer, but everything seemed to be in order.

According to the clock on the radio in the cab, it was 10:00 at night when Enrique climbed back into the cab. It had taken thirty minutes to load twenty-five pallets. Gene lay on his back underneath the pile of bedding not watching where they were going as they drove away. The U.S. was strict about what the country. Of the three thousand trucks that crossed the border daily, only five percent were checked, but those that were selected were checked thoroughly. The trailer's cargo would be unloaded and inspected.

The truck started to shake. Enrique shifted down, then up and down again. Gene maneuvered his line of sight again to see through the windshield. They headed south down a dirt road for several miles into total darkness. The lights of the city of Juarez in the mirror were disappearing into the distance.

The truck made a wide left turn until the truck was pointing north again and stopped. Enrique shut the motor down, climbed out and closed the door, leaving the headlights on.

Gene could see headlights coming directly toward the truck. It was an old 1970s Volkswagen van. The van passed the truck, turned around and parked about thirty yards behind the trailer. Five Mexican men exited and met Enrique at the back driver's side of the trailer. One of the men barked orders in Spanish. They all put their hands in their pockets and pulled out a silver medallion. He was sure they were just like the two he was carrying inside his saddlebags. One man opened the doors to the trailer and latched them open.

Enrique ran back to the cab and opened the door, climbed up, reached behind the passenger seat and pulled out a large knife. He climbed out and ran back to join the other men. All of the men were either inside the trailer or standing behind it, out of Gene's view.

Gene climbed out of the sleeper into the passenger seat. He unlatched the door and climbed out and ran across the dirt road. He dove behind a sand dune, but his knee landed on a cactus with large thorns. He let out a short screech and swallowed the rest of his expression of pain. The sound was heard by two of the men who pulled handguns from their belts and started walking in his direction. Gene sat down grinding his teeth and breathing through the discomfort. He couldn't see the thorns in the darkness. He slid his fingers across his pant leg to feel them and pulled them out with his fingers.

"Hey, get back to work," the apparent leader said.

"But we heard something," one man said.

"It's just an animal. Get back here. We've got to be ready for the drop."

Gene pulled the last thorn from his kneecap then moved from dune to dune until he could see the back of the truck where the men were working. Four of the men were dragging the pallets to the ground and unloading them. Enrique used his knife to cut the black bands holding the boxes and pallets together.

"Here it comes. Be ready," one of them said.

Gene heard the sound of a small airplane flying in from the south without lights and very low. The plane throttled back as it approached. The sound stayed steady for only a few moments and then throttled back up. He could tell by the sound it banked left and headed south again.

"Mira," one man yelped pointing and running toward a parachute attached to a large bundle.

"There's another one. I'll get it," said another man, also pointing and running.

A large canvas bag hit about ten feet away from Gene. He turned in the direction of the sound just as the parachute landed on his head. Enrique was chasing that particular drop. When he reached it, Gene was gone. From behind the next sand dune, he watched Enrique unhook the ropes from the parachute, roll it up and stuff it into the bag. Enrique grabbed a handle on the canvas and dragged it back to the truck.

One of the men took Enrique's knife and cut plastic zip ties that were holding the four corners of the canvas together. When the canvas was opened, Gene saw hundreds of small bags of cocaine. Four of the men worked with the boxes, two opened each box and two stuffed each River Rock boot with one bag of cocaine. The two other men resealed the boxed and stacked them onto an empty pallet.

It took the men more than an hour to finish packing the boxes. Gene knew the only way out of the desert was in the truck and he needed to get back in it before they finished. He crawled between the dunes, careful not to find another cactus, until he was parallel with the passenger door. The men were struggling to lift the heavy pallets back into the trailer. When one of the pallets started to fall just as it was being loaded, Gene ran to the truck, opened the door and slipped back into the sleeper. His breathing was erratic, but by the time the men were done he had it back under control and waited for Enrique to climb back in.

The door opened and Enrique got in with his knife in hand. He reached to put the knife behind the seat when he noticed Gene's saddlebags behind the privacy curtain. Twisted, with his back to the windshield, Enrique reached for the saddlebags when Gene kneed him in the face, breaking his nose.

Enrique fell against the dashboard and slid low between the seats. He wheeled his knife in the air as Gene hurled himself into the cab, cutting a deep gash in Gene's left thigh. Gene could immediately feel warm blood from the wound soaking through his slacks. He stood hunched over in the cab and stomped on Enrique, kicking his chest and arm until Enrique let go of the knife. Both men wrestled in the tight space trying to find the knife in the dark. Enrique grabbed Gene's leg and pressed his thumb deep into the wound. Gene yelled loud enough for the other men to hear from outside of the van behind the trailer, but Gene found the knife first. He grabbed Enrique's hair with one hand and stabbed his chest with the other repeatedly.

Gene couldn't drive the truck with Enrique in his way, so he pushed and heaved his body to the passenger side. When he sat down behind the steering wheel, he saw the men in the mirror walking along side of the truck yelling Enrique's name. Gene locked the doors then turned the key to start the truck, but nothing happened.

"Wait for the light Gene," he said. He turned the key half way. "Come on. Come on."

Just as the motor fired up, one of the men jumped onto the side, holding on to the mirror.

"I'm going to kill you," he said sadistically.

Gene pushed the clutch halfway down, but the pressure shot pain from the knife wound up his leg. He couldn't get the shifter into gear. Another man jumped onto the passenger door. Both men were hitting the windows with their fists, trying to break the glass. Gene fought through the pain and almost stood on the clutch allowing the shifter to fall into gear. His right foot pushed the accelerator to the floor, he let go of the clutch and the truck broke forward. The van moved in alongside. Gene avoided shifting as long as he could. When his RPMs hit five thousand, he stood, yelled and shifted. The two men continued their assault on the truck windows.

"Get off the truck! Get off the truck! Let go of the truck!" he yelled.

Gene shifted again and again. The truck reached forty-five miles an hour down the dirt road, shaking and jerking over the bumps. The men struggled to hold on so Gene drove to the right side of the road, hitting small sand dunes. The van dropped back behind then He drove the truck to the left, hitting more dunes and jarring off the man hanging on to the driver's door before Gene straightened the truck back onto the road. The dunes slowed him down so he down shifted and then shifted up again. When his speed hit fifty-five miles an hour, Gene looked for the second man, but he too, was gone.

The van tried to drive beside the trailer. He swerved from side to side forcing the van to stay behind. Gene saw the paved road that would take him back to Juarez, but he was going too fast to make a safe turn. He grabbed the steering wheel with both hands, slammed the clutch and brakes and turned the wheel to the left. The sounds of rubber from all eighteen wheels screeched across the asphalt, ripping through the dusty air. The front tires wanted to straighten out, but Gene held firm until he noticed the left side of the trailer was off the ground and beginning to roll. He let go of the steering wheel, letting it spin as the front wheels found a straight path. When the truck and trailer straightened out, the trailer fell back to the ground and Gene worked through the gears again and navigated onto the road.

The van was gaining on his right side. As Gene started to swerve to the right to block it, the second man he thought he had lost on the dirt road, jumped from the top of the cab onto the hood blocking Gene's view. The man held onto the windshield wipers and caught Gene off guard when he smiled, exposing multiple gold caps.

He was fighting for his life and this cholo was smiling? The man rolled onto his back and cracked the windshield with his boot. As the man was about to strike again, Gene swerved to the right making the man fall from the truck. The van didn't slow down as it ran over the man's body.

When the van approached the passenger door, the driver was pointing a gun at the truck's front tire. As the gun fired, Gene jerked the truck's steering wheel towards the van. The collision sent the van off the road, causing it to shoot into the air and flip several times before bursting into flames and moments later exploding.

Straight ahead were the sea of lights of Juarez and El Paso. Gene looked around the cab for his cell phone. He remembered it falling from his pocket when he fought with Enrique. Just when he figured that it probably fell out of the truck, he kicked something on the floorboard as he plunged the clutch.

He dialed the detective's number, but the display read 'No Service'.

"Now what?" he said. "Think, Gene. You need to get this truck back across the border."

It was midnight and cigarette smoke filled the room. Joe, Roy Whitaker and another woman sat in metal folding chairs near the speakerphone waiting for it to ring. Marlene was sitting behind her desk, chain smoking. Her mind was on Gene and how ashamed she would be if he ever knew what she was doing. She looked over at Roy, her father and felt overwhelmed with guilt.

Marlene had taken control of the business over a year ago and Roy was enjoying his retirement, playing golf most days when he was in town, traveling with friends when he wasn't. His retirement and relationship with Marlene were put on hold when he came into the warehouse one day for a new pair of boots for himself. It was his company and he didn't need to ask permission to grab a pair of boots from his own warehouse. Marlene saw Roy pull up that day from her upstairs office window. She waited for him in the office, but he never made it up the staircase. Marlene went down into the warehouse, yelling *'Dad,'* as she walked past the aisles. She found him down an aisle with a box on the floor, a boot in his right hand and a bag of cocaine in his left.

Roy coaxed Marlene into telling him who was behind the drug smuggling operation. That was his biggest mistake. When he threatened to go to the police, someone paid him a visit at his home the same night and threatened his life. Since then, he'd been required to show up at the monthly meetings.

"Where's Manny?" the woman said.

She was dressed in a tight-fitted black halter dress revealing the absence of a bra. A wide red belt around her slight waist matched her red shoes, fingernails and the lipstick on her cigarette butt.

"He's ensuring that our last shipment gets across okay," Marlene said.

"You two have a date tonight?" Joe said.

The woman replied, "He's a lot more of a man than you are."

"You would sleep with anyone who looks your way," Joe said.

"You can look all you want Joe," she said, "You ain't ever touching these goods again."

"Don't worry," Joe said, "When I wear out my cars, I give 'em away and don't care how many people ride in them."

"Cut it out, both of you," Marlene said, "Haven't you caused us enough trouble already?" She put out one cigarette and grabbed for another. The phone rang.

Marlene hit the speaker button, "Hello?"

"Is everyone present?" the voice said.

"Everyone but the good detective," Joe said, shooting a scowling look at the woman.

"He's at the border making sure everything goes well," the woman said in Manny's defense.

"Roy, you there?" the voice said.

"Kiss my ass," Roy said.

"Still pissed I see. Marlene, how are we on time?" the voice said.

"We're ahead of schedule as long as the next shipment gets here on time. The cleaning crew will be here at 2:00 in the morning and we'll be done before daylight."

"Is there anything to cause a delay?" the voice said referring to the shipment.

"I sent Enrique out in plenty of time."

"Joe, do you know the whereabouts of Mr. Martine?" Joe gave Marlene a glance. He didn't call Manny like he said he would but looked as if he wished he did.

"We will before the sun rises, I promise," he said.

"Careful what you promise, Joe. The last person that did that... Well, let's just say they aren't making promises anymore. Where's your real problem?"

The word 'problem' was the voice's way he referred to Sam. Sam was Marlene's administrative assistant for just a couple of months and a part of the smuggling team until Joe had wooed her into his bed. He had given her coke on their first date and from that day on, she could never get enough of it. She started borrowing money from Joe to pay for it. It was easy to control her and it was going fine for him until he found out she was pregnant.

"I have her locked up in a stash house. She's drugged out of her mind by now."

"I want this mess cleaned up," came over the phone. "I want it cleaned up permanently and I want it done tonight. Make her go away. After today, I don't want to hear her or Gene's name ever again."

Sam was still tied up in the laundry room. She was in the kneeling position and her arms were still taped together under the faucet, bright red from the scalding water. She was also suffering from withdrawals. She felt as if the life was slipping out of her body. Sam was at the lowest point in her life, ready to die.

"Why me, God?" she said, "What did I do to deserve this?"

As bad as things were for her, she was done crying. Sam had nothing left to give. Tied up and unable to move, she began to pray.

"God, please, hear my cry for help. I've messed up my life and I have no one to turn to." she said over and over, "Forgive me. Please, God. I'm asking, please."

Lisa knew what happened to Elliot. Every ten minutes, she dialed Gene's number, but the calls went straight to voicemail. She had spent the past two hours walking around the house holding the disposable cell phone in her hand. Every fifteen minutes, she dialed Stanton's number, but never hit the 'send' button.

The cries from the laundry room stopped and Lisa pulled herself together. She walked down the hallway to the laundry room and she found Sam semi-conscious. Lisa checked for a pulse. Sam was alive. She cut the tape binding Sam to the sink and gently eased her down to the floor. She sat on the floor, leaned her back to the wall and pulled her knees to her chest. She stared at Sam's swollen face, feeling sorry for her and wondered what type of life she must have been leading.

"Where's my son?" Sam mumbled. "Please, tell me."

"He's with Child Protective Services." Lisa sat down next to Sam on the floor and stroked her hair from her face.

"I don't have anything left to fight for. I love him so much. How do I know you're telling the truth?"

"What's his name?" Lisa whispered.

"Johnny. He just turned five."

"Sam, you need your rest." She said encouraging Sam. I'm going to help you. I promise I called Child Protective Services. Let's clean you up. It's really late."

Lisa wet a washcloth, sat Sam up and cleaned the blood from her face. Sam put her arm around Lisa's neck, grabbed the utility sink with her other hand and stood up. Lisa helped Sam to the guest bedroom, sat her on the bed and left the room. She returned with another nightgown and a glass of water. She helped Sam change into the nightgown again.

"Elliot was a good man," Sam said. "You need to know that. He was really trying to help me. I'm sorry. I just couldn't…"

"That's why I loved him," Lisa said and left Sam alone.

Lisa went to the kitchen and made a pot of coffee. When the machine finished brewing, she retired to the living room, a strong cup of coffee in one hand, and the disposable cell phone in the other. It had been almost four hours since the last time she talked with Gene. The wood in the fireplace was all but consumed.

She set her cup down on the coffee table, walked over to her woodpile and picked up a thick stick to stoke the fire. From the corner of her eye, something caught her attention. Joe was standing next to her. She swung the stick, hitting him in the forehead. He didn't flinch. He grabbed the stick from her hand, slapped her to the ground and without saying a word, dragged her by the arm to the front door.

Lisa did all she could to break his grip, but the more she struggled the tighter his grip became. When they got outside of the house, Joe closed the door, holding her at arm's length. His thumb crushed her arm as he dragged her to his car, opened the rear door and threw her inside. He pulled a gun from out of nowhere and pointed it at her head.

"Stay inside or I'll kill you right here," he said, then closed the door and got into the driver's seat.

Joe backed out of the driveway and took off down the street.

"Where are you taking me?" she said.

"Tell me where Gene is. He's got something of mine and I want it back."

Joe was driving fast and running neighborhood stop signs.

"He's supposed to be in Ruidoso. Now stop the car. I'm getting out before you wreck and kill us both."

"Shut up."

"Slow down," she screamed as Joe took a corner too sharp, losing traction on the rear tires and drifting sideways.

"You know what?" He grinned a stupid-looking bright-white toothy grin. Blood trickled from his forehead. "Where does he have her? You better tell me or I'll kill both of you."

"You're talking like a madman."

"Where's the boy, Lisa?"

Lisa sat back in the seat with tears rolling down her cheeks.

"You know where they are. I know it." His grin was getting bigger and it was making Lisa angrier. "You want to know how I figured it out?" he said.

She stared through the window.

"I went to get her. Imagine my surprise when I pulled up to the house and saw all of that crime scene tape. So, I know she's gone, right, but I've got to check anyway. When I got to the front door, guess what I found? A tie, an expensive red tie. It was cut in half. Now, I'm thinking. What idiot would use an expensive tie like that to hold the door closed? Then it hit me."

"Then why don't you go to Gene's house and ask him where this woman is?" Lisa said.

"You damn well know why. He can't go home and I know he's been talking to you, so stop playing stupid."

"I'm not, Joe."

"Listen to me closely, Lisa. I like you. Your husband was an idiot, but I've always liked you. You got class, but you're in something so deep right now that I don't know if I can keep you alive. So, here's the deal. I need Sam back. You can keep the boy. He's a retard anyway. But I do need Sam. If I don't get her, Gene dies and you die. It's that simple. But, if you cooperate, I'll see what I can do to save your life."

"Why do you think there was crime scene tape on the house?"

Lisa looked into his rear view mirror. His grin was gone and he was sweating.

"We called the cops when we found the drugs," she said calmly. "It was an anonymous call, but can you guess whose name we gave them?"

"Bull."

"When was the last time you talked to your wife, Joe? I'm sure she has lots of questions for you."

Joe slammed the brakes, skidding to a stop and then he turned around in his seat. Lisa leaned forward and slapped Joe on the side of his head. She tried the handle but the door was locked. Joe grabbed her hair with one hand and punched her face with the other, knocking her unconscious.

Chapter Nineteen

Just south of Juarez, Gene pulled to the side
of the highway and found some oily rags behind the
passenger seat. The suit pants he wore to Elliot's
funeral were damp with his blood. He tied three of
the rags end to end and wrapped them around his
leg above the wound. He laced the ends together,
breathed deeply and pulled as hard as he could,
wincing in pain as the cloth cinched tight. He used
another oily cloth to wipe the blood from his hands
then took off his ripped suit coat and tossed it onto
the sleeper. He drove the rest of the way to the
border.

The clock on the radio said 1:45 in the
morning. The border traffic was light, as he
expected. As he approached the line at the border,
there were ten semi-trucks between him, U.S.
Customs, Border Patrol and D.E.A. agents. He
assumed Enrique had the right documents
somewhere, if he planned to get across with a

truckload of coke. He turned on the cab light and looked around. Blood was splattered all over the cab and on some of the paper work from several files that were scattered on the floorboard on the passenger side.

While waiting in line, he applied the emergency brake, crawled over to the other seat and picked up the cleanest papers he could reach. He started to sort out the mess, but the truck behind him honked.

The line in front of him had shortened by four trucks. That was four trucks that had made it through without an inspection. His odds of not being inspected were not in his favor. He released the emergency brake, moved the truck up to close the gap and sorted through the papers again. Some looked familiar and others made no sense. Two more trucks went through minor inspections when customs agents walked around the entire rig, giving only insignificant looks underneath the trailers. Each one was waved through.

He placed some of the important looking papers into a file folder and rolled down his window. Another driver was getting the walk-around inspection like the others had before him. A young Hispanic DEA agent in a leather coat yelled at another customs agent seeming in charge of the booth and walked across the wide driveway toward the man.

"Hey, I need to talk to you," the man in the coat said to the agent.

Gene thought someone had already picked him out. They might have recognized him on one of the security cameras. The two men talked inside the booth for almost two minutes. Gene thought both men looked in his direction several times during their conversation.

The truck in front of him was ordered to drive across the large tarmac to an inspection station where agents would unload all of the cargo from the trailer and inspect every piece. He felt relief, thinking that his odds of inspection were less but then he heard the barking. Three agents were struggling to hold onto the leashes of three German Shepherds. The dogs were trained to find drugs, even in the smallest amounts and they were headed toward Gene's truck, ripping at their leads. The trainers fought and pulled until all three dogs were forced toward the truck pulling forward on the tarmac. The man in the leather coat followed the dogs and ordered Gene to pull forward.

"Where are you from?" the agent said, looking up at Gene.

"The U.S.," Gene said.

"What happened to your windshield?"

"Punk kids got it when I stopped for a piss in Juarez," Gene said.

"What's your cargo?"

"Boots. River Rock Boots. Do you want a pair?" Gene tried to play to the agent's sense of humor, but the agent wasn't smiling.

"Paperwork?"

Gene handed over the file folder. "This is my first time driving across the border. I wasn't sure what you needed, so I just put it all in there."

The agent rifled through the papers. "You're missing some paperwork," he said handing the file back to Gene.

"I don't understand. I'm sure it's all here,"

The agent said, "I'm going into my booth to run your plates. When I come back out, you're going to hand me that file again. If the right paper work isn't in there..." The agent looked him in the eye as he continued and exaggerated, "I mean ten really clean sheets of paper, I'm pulling you over."

The man turned around and entered the booth. Gene knew the ride was over. He had no idea what the agent was looking for. Then the agent stuck his head outside of the booth and looked Gene in the eye.

"It better shine, too."

He frantically searched the cab for a clue. He looked under the seats and tossed around the blankets and mattress in the sleeper. "I know you didn't come over without a way to get back." He opened the glove box where he found a white envelope and looked inside.

"I'm back. Shall we try this again? Paperwork."

Gene handed him the file. The agent flipped through the papers just as he had done before, but this time found the envelope. The agent flipped it open with his thumb to reveal ten one-hundred-dollar bills and a medallion. The agent went back into the booth for a moment then came back and handed Gene the folder, less the envelope.

"He's clear," the agent said to other agents walking around the trailer, and waved his arm without looking at Gene.

Gene had enough evidence to uncover the smuggling ring but he still didn't have what he needed to clear his own name. He had to take more risks.

He could see the River Rock Boots warehouse from the end of the block where he had stopped to think about his next steps. Once he had crossed the border he couldn't wait to call Stanton and tell him about the real meaning behind the medallion.

He put the truck in gear and drove down the street. There were fewer cars in the parking lot than hours before. He drove slow, watching for anything that looked like they had been tipped off. Once in the parking lot, he could see the silhouettes of at least three people standing in Marlene's office and he knew they could hear and see the truck pulling in, but it was too dark and they were too far away to see who was driving it.

Eight workers were in the break room drinking coffee and playing dominoes. The warehouse was silent when Marlene stepped out of her office.

"The truck's coming in," she said loud and clear. "Let's get it unloaded before the cleaning crew gets here."

The eight men swallowed the last of the coffee from their cups, put on their work gloves and walked to the loading docks. By the time they reached the bay doors, the truck was already there, but it was parked parallel, the driver door was open and the engine was still running.

"Enrique?" one man said. "Where's Enrique?"

"Why didn't he back it up?" another man said.

"He must still have the runs," the first man said and they all laughed. "I bet he ran to the bathroom. I'll back it in."

The man climbed into the cab, without noticing the blood splatters and began maneuvering the rig.

Gene was behind the large trashcan next to the docks. His leg was throbbing and he knew he needed to get it stitched up.

Four of the men disappeared into the warehouse, taking their positions among the aisles ready to unload the boxes from the pallets. Two men jumped onto the forklifts and waited for the doors of the trailer to open. Once the trailer was in position, the driver ran back and helped open the doors. The first forklift went in and returned with his forks loaded and as soon as he was clear, the second forklift did the same. The other men cut the plastic wrap off and then tossed it into the trashcan.

Marlene called, "Where's Enrique?"

"He had a bad stomach. He had to run to the bathroom."

Gene looked up and over the trashcan. He could see the backs of Marlene, Joe and a man wearing a leather coat. It was the same man he'd seen at the border talking to the customs agent. When the man turned around, Gene saw his badge. He was wearing it on his belt just as Detective Stanton wore his.

"Let the pallet down and turn off the lift," Manny said.

The operator complied.

"There was something wrong at the border," Manny said. "Marlene, my guy told me your driver had no idea what he was doing. He said he practically had to spell out the procedure to him."

Marlene said, "Enrique has made that run dozens of times. He knows what he's doing."

Joe opened one of the boot boxes and took out a bag of coke. He opened a pocketknife, stabbed the bag and then licked the dull side of the blade.

"It's pure," Joe said. "Get these guys back to work, Marlene."

The forklift operator started the lift and went back to work.

Gene wanted to kill Joe. He was filled with disappointment in Marlene and confused about the detective. That's why Stanton knows so much about the Free-Landers. He works with them. And if that's true, it would explain why he let me go instead of arresting me when he had the chance. You don't let someone who's wanted for murder, drug dealing and evading arrest go free when you're sitting right next to him. Any detective would be a hero to catch someone like me. He doesn't want to catch me. He wants me dead. Gene thought.

Another sound interrupted his thoughts. It was the sound of several vehicles. He peeked around the trashcan to see four cargo trucks and three vans backing up to the loading docks. Each one of them had large *Clean Sweep* logos painted on the sides. All of the drivers exited their trucks and opened their cargo doors. Then each man removed a trash bag from inside the vehicle. Marlene, Joe, Manny and Roy ran to the edge of the docks like the building was on fire and took the trash bags from the men.

The contents of each bag were checked and confirmed. Marlene looked out into the darkness then turned and waved to her workers inside the warehouse. The forklift operators were removing the last two pallets from the semi, but the rest of Marlene's workers started bringing different black trash bags to the Clean Sweep drivers, and then loaded the bags into the vehicles.

"The last load isn't ready yet," Marlene told one of the Clean Sweep drivers.

The driver pulled a nine-millimeter gun equipped with a silencer and pointed it at her. It was at that very second Gene knew for sure the bags given were full of money. The bags taken were full of cocaine.

Everyone stopped what they were doing. Joe hid behind one of the forklifts. Gene was surprised by his sudden feelings for her safety as he almost blew his cover to warn her, but Manny pulled his gun and pointed it at the man. Marlene stayed steady and calm, as if she had been at the wrong end of the gun before.

"She said it wasn't ready yet," Manny said. "She didn't say you couldn't have it."

"Our orders were to not leave without all of it," the man said.

"Then stay, but put your gun away, right now or you die," Manny said, but then the other six men pulled out their guns and pointed them at him.

"I guess you'll die, too," the man said.

"Not before I kill you. I won't miss."

The man lowered his gun and signaled the rest to do the same. Manny reciprocated by putting his back into his holster.

"When?"

"We need two hours. The truck was late."

"You get one."

The men continued loading the bags.

When the forklifts started backing up and made sufficient noise, Gene hobbled with his saddlebags and climbed over the pipe yard fence, ducking and running until he made it to the stolen car. He had a clear view of the docks. He needed to see where the Clean Sweep trucks were going.

When the trailer was empty and the doors closed, one of Marlene's workers got in the cab to leave, but then he got back out and walked toward Manny carrying the suit jacket that Gene left behind.

"Manny, this isn't Enrique's jacket and the cab is covered in blood."

"He's here," Manny said.

"Who?"

"Never mind. Get out of here."

Gene's body was tight, making it hard to breathe. His teeth chattered and his legs shook, but the pain from the knife wound was mostly numb. He didn't dare start the car. The windows were fogging and that concealed him. He decided to try Lisa but she didn't answer after several attempts. He worried for her and what might have happened with Sam, but he couldn't leave.

He saw Enrique's semi-truck pass by, but he waited twenty more minutes before the blurry headlights of the seven Clean Sweep trucks were visible at the end of the street.

Gene crouched as low as he could to still see over the dash. All seven trucks turned right, passing Gene, then took the next left. When the last one was out of sight, he started the car, wiped the windshield and did a U-turn. He drove without headlights and approached the street where they had turned left. He arrived just in time to see the last set of taillights turn north.

He turned the headlights on and raced to catch them. He turned left at the next intersection and immediately caught up with the convoy under the freeway overpass, where they waited for at a traffic light. They were no longer single-file. Three of the trucks were ready to turn left onto I-10 West, two were in the center lane to continue going north and two were in the right lane, ready to drive down I-10 East. Gene chose to stay behind the three turning left, keeping as much distance from the others as he could.

At 2:30 in the morning, there was no oncoming traffic. When the light turned green, Gene gave all of the Clean Sweep trucks enough time to put space between them. He drove onto the freeway and moved to the center lane as the trucks stayed in the far right lane.

When all three blinkers flickered, Gene realized they were headed downtown. He slowed, turned his signal on, followed until the trucks turned south onto Kansas Street and moved to the far right lane of the one-way street.

Gene stayed in the left lane and raced past them. He didn't want them to see him turn into the parking garage across from the P & M office building. He adjusted his speed to catch the red light at the intersection just beyond the building. Using his mirror, he watched all three trucks turn into the underground freight entrance of the P & M building. He drove around the block as fast as he could, turned into the parking garage and raced to the top floor, parking near Elliot's BMW. He reached into his saddlebags and grabbed three homemade battery bombs and shoved them along with a book of matches into his pocket. As he jumped out of the car and started toward the stairs, he noticed the BMW. All of its windows were bashed in. The tires were slashed and the entire body was almost unrecognizable, completely demolished. Gene knew who did it, but he didn't know how they almost found him again.

With the Clean Sweep bag-men in the garage below, he knew he couldn't slip in the same way he did earlier in the day. He stood in the shadows, away from the street lamps. He was twenty-five yards away from where Elliot's body was found. He looked at the planter where Elliot had taken his last breath.

Gene hobbled across the street, down the walking path next to the building and stopped short of the entrance to the lobby. The security guard behind the desk was Al Gonzales, the same guard Elliot had talked to before he got into the elevators for the last time. There was no way of getting past him. Gene was growing frustrated. He was running out of ideas. But then he saw Al answer his phone, place the receiver back into its cradle, step from behind the desk, and walk toward the elevators.

"What do you guys want? Over." Al spoke into his two-way radio.

Gene used the opportunity to sneak in through the open door and take cover next to a wall behind the security desk.

"Send all of the elevators to the basement. Over," a voice replied.

"Ten-four. Alex, did you copy that?" Al said.

"Yes, Sir. They're on their way."

Al said, "The elevators should be there. Over."

The voice said, "They're here. Is anyone in the building that we should be concerned about? Over."

"None you need to worry about. We've got a lawyer on seven working his ass off. He won't be leaving any time soon and we've got the CEO of P & M on ten, but he won't be a problem because she's here, over."

"Okay, keep watch. We'll work fast. Over and out."

Al placed his radio back onto his belt, walked back to his desk and started watching the monitors. Gene approached him from behind and hit him in the head with the bottom of a fire extinguisher, knocking him out cold.

He pulled the security guard's body behind the large desk, out of sight under the security monitors. Gene surveyed all of the screens and witnessed the activity. It was then that Gene grasped what the cleaning crew *really* did at night and why his office shelves were so dusty as Stanton pointed out.

Al was more than a security guard for the building. He was the security guard over the cocaine as were the rest of the guards. One guard was standing with gun in hand at the edge of every monitor. Including inside the elevators, eight armed guards and six men handled the trash bags. The only area of the building he couldn't see was inside the Clean Sweep offices.

The three drivers unloaded the trash bags from the trucks and loaded them into the elevators. The guards escorted the bags to the eleventh floor. Three more men took the bags inside the Clean Sweep offices.

He watched the monitors. He knew he had all of the answers he needed to bring them all down, but he would have to find someone other than Detective Stanton to tell what he knew. He felt betrayed by Stanton.

He leaned over and looked closer, studying the monitors. The screens that changed views every thirty seconds confirmed his suspicions. All of the building security guards were accounted for, busy guarding the trash bags. He stretched his leg, feeling the skin around the cut pull apart. He blew out a deep breath, then hobbled across the lobby and passed the elevators to the entrance of the building's stairwell where a heavy metal door with a small window was closed. He wrapped his hand around the doorknob, but just before he turned it, he heard voices from a two-way radio coming from inside the stairwell. Gene peeked through the window and saw another guard standing next to the elevator control panel.

He turned the knob, releasing the door, but without opening it. He tapped the glass to get Alex's attention. The guard flinched at the sound and looked through the glass. Gene slammed the door open against the guard, striking his forehead. The guard fell back onto the stairs. Gene pulled the gun from the guard's holster and used the butt of it to knock him out. Then he handcuffed him to the stairwell using the guard's handcuffs and tucked the gun inside the back of his pants.

He studied the elevator control panel as Alex lay unconscious. Each elevator had a master power switch and lights indicating where they were: all on the eleventh floor. He waited until all six lights marked with the number eleven turned off almost simultaneously. Two seconds later, the lights marked with the number ten illuminated. He timed the lights until the elevators were on the fourth floor. As soon as each light turned off, he flipped off the master switch, stopping the elevators between the third and fourth floors. Alex's two-way radio was distorted with voices trying to tell him they were stuck.

Another detective brought Stanton home around midnight. He paid little attention to Evelyn. His face was hardened. His eyes fixed. She went to the kitchen and heated up a plate of fried chicken, mashed potatoes and corn. Both of them sat at the kitchen table. He ate and she watched. He wanted to tell her what was on his mind but he didn't want to talk about the car chase. He cleaned his plate and complimented her on her cooking, then kissed her on her forehead as they walked to their bedroom. She took off her robe, crawled into bed and watched him undress.

"This one's getting to you, isn't it?" Evelyn said. "All you need is a little rest. Things will be clearer in the morning."

He turned off the light, pulled the covers up to his chest, folded his arms behind his head and stared at the ceiling. The moonlight from the window fell across the deep crow's-feet at the corners of his eyes, the gray curl of his mustache and the gray stubble around the edges of his square jaw. He knew she was ready for him to retire, but she wanted him to be ready.

Later, Evelyn rolled over and tried to put her arm on Stanton's chest, but he wasn't there. She sat up, rubbed her eyes and focused on the clock on her nightstand, 2:10. She got out of bed, put her robe on and went to him.

She found him sitting behind his roll-top desk. He was wearing a plaid robe, worn threadbare over time. His eyes were scanning the pictures hanging on the bulletin board and others strewn across the desk mixed with his printed notes and police reports. She walked behind him and started rubbing his shoulders.

"What's got you so uptight, Detective Stanton?" she said. "I rolled over and found an empty spot where my husband was supposed to be."

"I can't sleep."

"I don't blame you. Who could sleep after having an exciting day like you had? I have to admit, I was ready call your butt home for good when you told me what happened."

The detective took his eyes off the pictures and looked up at Evelyn. "When I called you today, to let you know I was okay, I didn't tell you the whole story. I didn't want to worry you. I didn't want you to call my butt home."

Evelyn turned Stanton's chair to face her, then she sat on his lap and put her arm around his neck. "Now you're home and you're safe. As long as we're under this roof, you're under my protection. I won't let any bad guys get you, so you can tell me everything."

Stanton hugged her tightly then he told her why he was at the park and the details of the car chase. Knowing all of the facts as Stanton presented them gave her an uneasy feeling, but she didn't let on to him.

"If all of that wasn't enough, I caught up to Gene at a gas station at the edge of town."

"Did you arrest him?" Evelyn's voice rose and she stood up.

"Well, this is where you're going to think I've lost my mind. Gene gave me a ride back to town."

"What?"

"Well, my car was shot to hell. It wouldn't have made it another mile."

"So you just promised not to arrest him if he would give you a lift?" She smiled disbelievingly.

Stanton stood up. "You see? That's why I don't tell you stuff. I know you'll make a joke out of it."

Evelyn put her hand on his chest, "Come on. Tell me the rest."

Stanton folded his arms and leaned back on the desk. Evelyn leaned back against the wall across from him.

"I think the only thing Gene Martine is really guilty of is stupidity. I think he and Lisa Jones are having some kind of an affair, maybe not a major one, but something's going on between them, but I don't think it has anything to do with Elliot Jones' death. No, unfortunately Elliot somehow pissed off some Free-Landers and the Free-Landers wanted Elliot dead. Why? I don't know, except that…" Stanton paused and sighed. "On the ride back into town, Gene told me Elliot was involved with another woman."

She said, "So Gene is messing around with Elliot's wife and Elliot was messing around with another woman? They both deserved to get shot."

"That's almost right, except that Elliot wasn't having an affair. He was trying to save this woman from herself. She was a drug addict and he was trying to get her cleaned up. That's where their troubles started."

"The woman you're talking about was connected to the Free-Landers? So, where is she?"

"My guess is, she told Elliot information about the Free-Landers, they found out and that's why he's dead. Now I think they were trying to frame Gene so we would think he did it, but something went wrong in Ruidoso and now they want him dead."

The Detective motioned her to join him at the desk. "Someone had these pictures delivered directly to me Sunday morning, the morning after Elliot Jones was killed," he said, then showed her three (8X10) glossies of the Gene and Lisa embracing in front of Gene's house.

"That doesn't prove anything. Even I know that."

"The fact that someone was spying on them to take these pictures negates their legitimacy, but the next morning, I interviewed Gene at his house. I found her in his restroom, wearing only one of his shirts. So, then, fast forward twenty-four hours."

"When Gene was in Ruidoso?"

"Two goons pay him a visit late at night. One of them ends up dead. That's what went wrong. I don't think that was supposed to happen." Stanton showed her more pictures of the cabin and the dead man, "Gene wakes up finding himself hand cuffed to a chair in his cabin, a bag full of money and cocaine sitting on his coffee table and some stupid sheriff's deputy standing over him. Now, Gene is a clean-cut businessman, without so much as a parking ticket for the last twenty-plus years. He doesn't fit the profile of a drug-crazed murderer. He said he only beat the guy up in self-defense and that someone else killed him. He also said when the cops came and he realized how much trouble he was in, he panicked, knocked out the deputy and escaped."

"This is crazy."

"We had over one hundred law enforcement officials looking for him that couldn't find him, but the second goon apparently found him everywhere he went. The Free-Landers seem to know where he is all of the time. That's why we got into the car chase. Someone is feeding them information, but Gene's been lucky enough to stay one step ahead of them and me."

"If he's innocent... that poor man," she said.

"Don't feel too sorry for Mr. Martine. He blew the goon up, killing him, not to mention the manhunt. Someone's got to go down for that. He might be innocent of killing Mr. Jones, but past that, I'm not convinced yet. Manny found three kilos of coke in Gene's house. Maybe he stole it from the Free-Landers, so they killed Elliot to scare him into giving it back."

"Maybe that's part of setting him up," Evelyn said.

Stanton pulled out more photos to show Evelyn. He rubbed at his mustache as if the gears in his mind started turning faster. "The night after the Elliot Jones murder, this guy was found beaten to death with a shovel."

Evelyn took the pictures from his

hand, "I remember seeing this picture. He was the security guard on duty the night Elliot was killed. You think Gene could have had something to do with this?"

Stanton didn't answer.

She picked up the pictures and studied them briefly and said, "The footprints at the scene were made by a women's tennis shoe."

"I've got to go." He walked to their bedroom, with Evelyn right behind him.

"Where do you think you're going at 3:30 in the morning?"

"There's a chance Lisa's been playing everyone this whole time. We think Roger Thatcher's killer was a woman. The footprints suggest that. What if she killed Elliot or had him killed so she could be with Gene? She's the one who told Gene the story about Elliot and the other woman and the Free-Landers. She could have made the whole thing up."

Evelyn watched Stanton rush to get dressed.

"Maybe she and Elliot were both somehow connected with the Free-Landers and they didn't like what she was doing," Stanton said. "This whole case is one big mess. Lisa's involvement doesn't make sense. I'm going to get some answers and I'm not waiting another minute." Stanton put on his shoulder holster and checked his gun for bullets.

"What if you're wrong?" Evelyn asked. "What if she's in as much danger as Gene?"

"Good point," Stanton said and then he opened the secret compartments in his desk, pulled out two more guns and loaded each with their respective bullets.

"You're scaring me."

<u>Chapter Twenty</u>

Gene limped up the cement stairs in the stairwell of his office building. His leg was bleeding again and the wound was sending a burning sensation up his thigh. With all six elevators and six of the armed security guards locked down for the time being, he only had limited time before the guard on the eleventh floor would meet him coming down, or one of the men from the basement would discover what was wrong. At the seventh floor, a door slammed in the hollow chambers of the stairwell above him, followed by the sounds of footsteps and jangling keys.

Gene tried to open the door to escape the stairwell on the seventh floor, but it was locked. He could hear the footsteps gaining speed and the sound of the guard's keys getting louder.

"What the hell is going on up there?" a voice said over the guard's two-way radio.

The guard huffed as he spoke. "I'm on my way down to check it out. Alex, can you hear me? Alex, talk to me, man."

Gene was hanging by his fingers with his legs bent from the edge of the seventh floor landing. As the guard started down to the sixth floor, Gene fell on top of him. Both men tumbled hard, down to the sixth floor landing. The guard cushioned Gene's fall, but the guard's head hit the wall at an awkward angle. Combined with the weight of Gene's body, the force was too great, breaking the guard's neck.

Gene had to fight through the excruciating pain in his leg and struggled to get up. Dazed and nauseous, he stood over the man's body. His chest was heaving as he tried to catch his breath and his heart was racing. He removed the keys from the guard's utility belt and stuffed them into his pocket. The rest of the way up to the eleventh floor, he could hear echoed voices from the two-way radios below, more than one at a time, yelling back and forth.

At the eleventh floor, Gene knew there were still at least three men on the other side of the door. He put his ear to the door and listened, but didn't hear anything. He tried four of the guard's keys before he noticed one was marked 'Stairs'. He inserted it into the lock, turned the knob then opened the door. He was alone. The men were with the cocaine in an office. He limped across the entryway until he could put his back against the wall and look around the corner. The Clean Sweep office door was propped open with a doorstop and mumbled voices came from a room further inside.

Gene crept against the wall until he was inside and was able to tell where the voices were coming from. He got down on his good knee, leaving his bad leg stretched out and crawled to the doorway where could look inside without being seen. Dozens of plain cardboard boxes were stacked five-high along two of the walls. Each one was pre-labeled with a shipping address. Next to them, stood stacks of pallets supporting twenty-four empty, one-gallon jugs each.

The men were wearing surgical masks and standing around a long table working in an assembly line fashion. The first man was taking the cocaine from the trash bags, unwrapping the individual packets and then sliding them across the table. The second man ground the solid pieces into powder and poured it through a funnel into one of the jugs until it was full and then slid the jug down to the third man, who placed a label on the front of it that read "Clean Sweep Industrial Strength Scrubbing Compound." The jugs were put into the boxes. The inconspicuous boxes were then sealed and stacked again against the wall.

Gene stood up, and pulled out a battery-bomb. He pushed the fuse deep into the welding oxide powder until he had only one-quarter-inch of fuse. The sound of his match striking against the book got the first man's attention, but the fuse lit quickly. Gene threw the explosive into the room and closed the door before they could react and then he stumbled toward the stairwell again. The explosion was louder than he thought it would be. One of the men screamed in pain. Another threw open the door, ran to the stairwell and started after Gene, but Gene was already unlocking the door on the tenth floor. He opened it and closed it out of view just as the man rambled down the flight of stairs.

Behind him was his P & M office, but he didn't have time to figure out which of the guard's keys worked. His hoped that Price was still there, remembering what he heard Al say into his two-way radio earlier. His leg throbbed when he limped to the glass doors where the etched "P" and "M" were. A few lights were on inside and the 'M' door was unlocked. When he was inside, he heard Price laughing followed by a muffled female voice coming from Price's office. He limped down the hallway until he reached it. Price was sitting in his chair and a woman in a sexy black dress was sitting on his lap nuzzling his neck.

"Price!" Gene yelled.

Price looked at Gene with a shocked expression.

"Oh, my God!" Madeline said. She stood, grabbed her stiletto heels from the floor and ran out of Price's office, past Gene.

"What the hell are you doing, Price?" Gene said and was so distracted by what he saw that he almost forgot why he was there.

"Call 9-1-1," Gene said.

Price was reaching for the phone when Madeline came back.

"Look out Gene."

Madeline hit Gene in the head with the butt of her gun, knocking him unconscious and then pointed the barrel at Price.

"Hang up the phone, Hot Lips," she said.

"Put that thing away," Price said. "You don't know who you're dealing with."

Madeline pointed her gun at Price's flat screen TV, shot it and then turned her sight back onto Price. He hung up the phone.

Seconds later, the building fire alarm began sounding because the battery bomb started the carpet on fire that quickly reached the pallets of jugs. The sprinklers in the Clean Sweep office released, soaking the boxes and all of the open packets of cocaine on the table.

Detective Stanton raced west on Interstate 10, in his Ford F-350 diesel truck. It was his cattle ranching truck, but it was equipped with a police radio. The pieces of the puzzle were there, but no matter how hard he tried, he couldn't make them fit. Lisa was now his prime suspect.

Lisa had the motive. Stanton's mind raced as he talked to himself. "She had to get rid of Elliot to have Gene. It was a stupid love triangle but I was focused on the wrong person. I fell for it, too, when she was at the hospital. She was way too dramatic. She overacted and I didn't see it. She also had access to Gene's house. She could have planted the coke under his bed when she slept over."

The more Stanton thought about it, the angrier he got and the faster he drove, seventy, then eighty miles an hour.

"What about the Free-Landers? Elliot, Gene and Lisa don't fit the profile, but then, who does and why would a cartel try to pin it on Gene? Unless, they wanted to get the attention away from one of their own — Lisa — but then there's Joe. So he's a cokehead and a first-class jerk. That doesn't make him a Free-Lander. Did Lisa make that part up, too? Did Gene use it to convince me?"

The radio broke into his thoughts when he was just east of the downtown exit. He listened to the woman dispatcher report a building fire alarm downtown at the El Paso Energy building.

He picked up the radio handset, "Dispatch, this is Detective Stanton. Did you say the twenty on that fire was at El Paso Energy building?"

"Ten-four," she said, "but it seems to be contained on the eleventh floor and just smoke."

Stanton was less than a half-mile away. He raced to the exit and straight to the building. He parked his truck in the middle of Kansas Street, got out and ran to the fire chief, who was trying to organize the efforts of his men. The firemen were unrolling their hoses when he arrived.

"Is there anyone inside?" Stanton showed his badge to the chief.

"We don't know yet. We just got here."

"Chief, it's real important that I know the answer to that question as soon as you know anything.

"I'll do what I can, but right now I have a situation of my own. Please back away from the scene."

Stanton got back into his truck and drove for Lisa's house. He parked in the driveway. Her car wasn't outside of the garage and except for the soft glow of the kitchen lights, it was dark. He thought Lisa would be in bed. Detective Stanton walked to the front door and rang the doorbell as he noticed all of the flowers on the stoop. He gave Lisa enough time to get up, put a robe on and answer the door, but she didn't. He rang it again and knocked on the door. Looking through a big bay window at the front of the house, he had a direct line of sight to the fireplace, which was smoldering with embers. He rang the doorbell and knocked hard once more.

Everything looked to be in order through the window, except for the thin log Lisa used to hit Joe. It was lying on the floor, behind the sofa.

A shadow moved across the back wall and fireplace. Someone was in the kitchen. Stanton pulled his gun from his shoulder holster, cocked it and started surveying the area. There was enough light from the moon that night for him to notice divots and long dragging marks in the fall grass, stretching from the porch to the driveway. He thought about backup, but there wasn't time. He put his back to the wall next to the door, knocked three more hard times and yelled, "This is the police," he said. "Come to the front door now or we're coming in."

Stanton turned the doorknob. He knew something was wrong when it turned a full rotation and opened.

Sam was still in the guest bedroom. She was lying awake on her side, staring into the darkness and praying. She heard the diesel engine of Stanton's truck when it pulled into the driveway. She looked at the clock on the nightstand and saw how early it was. She got out of bed and felt her way to the bedroom door. She was afraid to turn on any lights. She opened the door slowly and stepped into the dark hallway.

"Lisa?" she whispered loudly.

She walked halfway down the hallway toward the front door when the doorbell rang. She waited to see if Lisa would appear to answer it. Then the doorbell rang again and someone pounded on the door. She scooted against the wall until she could see through the bay window, but making sure to stay in the darkest part of the hallway. The silhouette of a large man was looking through the glass. When his figure moved away, she ran past the window through the living room, almost tripping on the piece of wood, then into the kitchen. The bell rang again, followed by more pounding.

Sam looked frantically for a knife to defend herself. She pulled open drawers and clawed at cabinets in the dim light until she found Lisa's butcher block on the kitchen counter. She grabbed the biggest knife and then hid behind the island in the middle of the kitchen holding the knife with both hands, ready to attack. She heard the man pounding on the door louder than before.

"This is the police. Come to the front door now or we're coming in."

She was shaking with fear.

Stanton pushed the door open, letting it swing wide. He pointed his gun in all directions. He walked into the living room where he knelt down and inspected the log. Blood was on the floor and on the end of the piece of wood.

He walked to the kitchen, where he spotted all of the open drawers and cabinets. He had no doubt that a major struggle had taken place in Lisa's home.

He walked back toward the front door and turned down the hallway. He flipped on the light. At each bedroom, he kept his back to the wall, reached inside the doorway, turn on the light and swung in, pointing his gun in all directions.

The guest bed had been slept in, but not the master bed. When he reached the laundry room, he followed the same procedure, turned on the lights and pointed his gun. A moment of terror flushed through his body when he saw the waded duct tape and blood smears on the floor. He holstered his weapon and walked out into the hallway to get to his truck and call for back up. With his guard down, Sam came down with the knife.

When Gene regained consciousness, his vision was blurred and his hearing was dulled. The smell of cigarette smoke made him nauseous. He could see several figures standing in front of him and there were undecipherable sounds.

"Gene? Can you hear me?"

"I think you hit him too hard."

One of the figures got closer, leaned in and looked into Gene's eyes. When the image came into focus, he saw Joe Garcia's bright white grin just inches from his face.

"He's coming around," Joe said.

Gene tried to jump from his chair, but his hands and legs didn't cooperate. Clear packing tape bound his wrists behind his back and his ankles were taped to the legs of a folding chair he was sitting in.

"Get me out of this, now," he said.

He tried to break free of the tape. He recognized Marlene's office and the people standing in front of him. There was Joe, Marlene, Roy and Madeline and the detective he saw on the River Rock loading docks and at the border. Gene focused on Marlene. His stare was burning holes through her. She saw his anger and his hurt.

"You need to calm down, Sugar, or they'll hurt you even more," Marlene said.

He struggled even more, making his chair hop up and down, "Screw you Marlene! Cut me free, right now!"

"Gene, stop. She's serious."

Gene stopped moving and whipped his head around. It was Lisa, and Price was sitting next to her, both strapped to their chairs. Unlike Gene and Lisa, Price had been gagged. His chin was bruised and fresh blood trickled from the corner of his mouth, dripping onto his starched white shirt. Lisa's face was black and blue on both sides. Blood filled the white in her right eye. Her lips were swollen and crusted with blood and her clothes were disheveled and bloody.

"Lisa put up a pretty good fight," Joe said, stroking the cut on his forehead. "But I slapped her into shape."

Gene looked at Marlene. "How did you get messed up in this, Marlene? Are you screwing Joe? How about it Roy, is your daughter screwing this piece of crap?"

Roy turned his back and stared out the window overlooking the warehouse. Tears of mascara started falling from Marlene's eyes.

"That's it, isn't it? You're doing him, aren't you?" Gene said.

Marlene sat down in her chair and lit a cigarette. "I didn't have a choice and I still don't."

"I watched you tonight and you seemed to have everything under control. You didn't even flinch when that guy pointed his gun at you. You've turned into a cold-hearted b..."

"Gene, you're just a screw-up," Joe interrupted. "You've always been a screw-up, just like Elliot. What a piece of work he was."

"Did you kill Elliot, Joe? Please tell me it was you, then the rest of these son-of-a-bitches can go home, because all I want is you."

"It was me," Madeline said.

"What? You?" Gene said. He thought she was joking. "When I saw you with Price tonight, I wasn't a bit surprised."

Price tried to say something through his gag in his defense, but no one seemed listen.

"You've been trying to screw your way up the corporate ladder since the day you interviewed at my agency," Gene said. "I bet you were just another one of Joe's whores. You don't have what it takes to kill someone."

"You don't believe me?" Madeline said defensively. "I stuck my knife in his chest and I didn't even blink. It almost didn't go in…" She walked across the room to Lisa, bent down and looked Lisa in the eye, "…but Elliot thought he could push it away and that's all I needed. He never saw it coming, just like you never saw this coming." She smiled and walked back in front of Gene. "I not only killed Elliot, I killed that old security guard, too. Don't ask me why. I really just wanted to scare him into telling me what we needed to know. It just felt so good swinging that shovel. The more he begged and cried for his life, the more pathetic he was. So, I bashed his skull."

Everyone in the room stared with shock on their faces as they listened to Madeline's murderess confessions, not because she did them, but that she found pleasure in doing it.

"You, bitch," Lisa's eyes dried up, her face twisted with pain and anger, and then she struggled briefly to free herself.

"If Elliot would have just left Sam in the streets with her retarded, bastard son where they belonged, you wouldn't be sitting here," Joe said.

"You're wrong there," Manny said. "If you hadn't had to have sex with everything that moved, nobody would be here. But you had to start banging Marlene's drug addict secretary and feeding her full of coke."

"To hell with you, Manny," Joe stood at attention, pointing at Manny.

"Gene, you want to know why Elliot was killed?" Manny walked around the room. "Joe is so coked up half of the time, he can't keep his mouth shut."

Gene listened closely. It was the first time he started to understand why Elliot was murdered.

"Manny, you don't know what you're talking about," Joe said.

"He told Sam all about our little organization," Manny continued. "He used to beat the crap out of her and her son, you see. He kept her drugged up and treated her worse than a dog. But one day, he beat her when she was halfway sober, after she tells him she's pregnant with his baby. She threatened to go to the police and bury us all. Isn't that right, Joe?"

Joe didn't respond.

"She thought it was her way out, but Joe here took a handful of coke and shoved it in her mouth. He thought for sure she would overdose and she should have. She went into a seizure and collapsed and then Joe took her body and dumped it behind some buildings downtown. You told us she was dead, didn't you Joe?"

"We've already been through all of this and now you're saying too much," Marlene said.

"Don't you think your ex-husband and Elliot's wife should know the truth before they die?" Manny said. "Somehow Sam survived, but she lost the baby. She was sick and in bad need of a fix so she went to the only place she knew she could get it, Joe's office," Manny pointed at Joe. "I wish I could have seen the look on your face when she showed up at your office. Instead of telling us she was still alive so we could figure out what to do with her, he promised her that he would keep her on drugs as long as she stayed quiet, and he threatened to kill her and her boy if she didn't. She agreed, but she and her boy had no place to go and she needed to eat. That's when Elliot met her, when she was begging for money. I guess he tried to help her several times until she felt compelled to tell him about Joe. Elliot thought he was going to Joe's office to settle the matter for Sam's benefit on the night he was killed, but that's…"

Madeline said, "That's when I stabbed him. I told you."

Manny walked over to Joe and stood toe-to-toe, and said, "You were right about one thing, though. Madeline is nothing but one of Joe's whores. As soon as Sam was supposedly out of his life, they wasted no time climbing into bed."

"When you think you're man enough to take me, come and get it," Joe said.

"Right here, right now," Manny said, then he punched Joe in the face, knocking him into Marlene's desk.

Joe spit out one of his front teeth and then scrambled back to his feet, but with Marlene's desk phone in his hand, ripping the cord from the wall.

"Cut it out, or take it outside!" Marlene screamed. "You're acting like a couple of kids."

"Leave him alone!" Madeline yelled at Manny.

"It's about time I kicked your ass," Joe said and then threw the phone at Manny.

Manny ducked as the phone flew by and hit the wall. He grabbed Joe's arm and twisted so that Joe flipped over, landing on his back. Manny placed his right knee on Joe's throat, crushing his windpipe. Madeline approached to pull Manny off, but he backhanded her to the floor.

"I suggest you shut the hell up, before one of us kills your sorry...," Manny was saying, but then the cold steel of the barrel of a gun was place behind his right ear. He put his hands in the air with his back to the gunman, but kept the pressure on Joe's throat. "Okay, okay, which one of you thinks they have the balls to pull on gun on me?"

"Get up."

"Julio Rivera?" Gene said. Gene was shocked to see him and relieved at the same time. "Thank God you're here. Cut me loose."

Manny released Joe and stood up.

Madeline picked herself up off the floor and stood in front of Manny.

"You better think twice the next time you want to hit your boss's daughter," she said then kneed Manny hard in the crotch.

Manny dropped helpless to his knees.

"Stand up and turn around," Julio said.

Manny groaned and gasped for air then stood up to face Julio.

"What you do you mean daughter?" Gene pulled at the tape. He felt it start to give, but Julio pointed the gun at him.

"Shut up, Gene," Julio said. "You've caused me enough problems already."

Without any warning, Julio pistol-whipped Manny's face with the gun. "If you so-much-as look at my baby wrong again, I'll kill you and mail your body in pieces to your son. Am I clear?"

Manny had the skills to overtake Julio, but Julio's two bodyguards were standing in the doorway and they both had guns.

Julio said, "I don't know why I don't shoot all of you right now, damn it. You're the biggest bunch of idiots I've ever assembled."

"You're behind all of this?" Gene asked.

"I AM all of this. I'm the king of the Free-Landers. You got that? I have operations like this all along the border. Being the CEO of VoiceComm is a good cover for me. It took me a year to set this one up. Joe was first on the team and he recruited Marlene and poor 'Ol Roy just got caught up in the middle. He doesn't want to end up like you, do you, Old Roy?"

Roy looked out into the warehouse.

"Now, Detective Ortega over there is dumb as a stick, as you just witnessed, but he's greedy and he's got connections with the border. He was investigating Joe's cocaine trafficking when I met him and got him to sign on. The whole operation was clicking until Elliot got in the way."

"So, you had him killed? I didn't know anything, so why were you trying to kill me?"

"It wasn't an easy decision on my part to have Elliot killed, but he gave me no choice. I liked Elliot. Marlene did try to convince me otherwise, but my decisions are final." Julio sat on Marlene's desk. "It seems my lovely daughter lost her medallion when she tried to clean up Joe's mess. Unfortunately, your great Detective Stanton found it. We knew if they thought someone like you killed Elliot, we could help them convict you by giving them all the evidence they needed. We even thought about killing Lisa and pinning that one on you, too, because Elliot might have given her information. But when she told everything she knew to Marlene and that she was more concerned about protecting Elliot's reputation than catching the killer, I was satisfied she didn't know enough to hurt us."

"But your guys have been trying to kill me, not get me arrested," Gene said.

"We weren't trying to kill you. Manny sent his men to Ruidoso to frame you, but you killed one of them at your cabin. That was your biggest mistake because now you're wanted for that murder too."

"I didn't kill him," Gene said.

"That's a lie," Manny said.

Julio said, "That man was Manny's cousin. The other man was his brother-in-law. That was your second biggest mistake."

Gene knew his luck had run out and he had nothing to lose. "Did anyone tell you I blew your brother-in-law into little pieces?"

Manny rushed across the room and punched Gene in the face and started strangling him while shouting in Spanish. Everyone in the room but Julio and Roy was yelling for him to stop. Gene toppled to the floor. He was lying on his right side with his back facing Lisa. Manny was about to kick Gene in the head, but Julio fired his gun into the air causing chips of ceiling to fall.

"Cut it out," Julio said. "It doesn't matter anymore. Like I said, Manny's not the smartest guy. He's the one who gave the order to have you killed. When I first learned of Manny's instructions, I was pissed off, but then I realized it didn't matter anymore. You convicted yourself in both cases."

While Julio was talking, Gene had freed his right hand. Lisa watched him slowly slide his hand into his right pocket, open the cell phone and feel for the "send" button. Stanton was the last number he dialed when he was driving the semi-truck back from Mexico.

Come on, Stanton, wake up. I'm only going to get one shot at this, Gene thought and then moaned in pain to cover up the beeping sound when he pushed the button.

"The fact you're still alive concerns me," Julio said. "Our guys missed you at every turn."

"Tell me how you knew where I was," Gene said. "Is Detective Stanton on your payroll, too? I mean, finding me at the park was pretty coincidental."

"He's too good of a cop. He would never sell his soul to the devil. As far as tracking you is concerned, that was easy. I'm the CEO of VoiceComm, remember? We just tracked your cell phone. But when you had it taken from you in Ruidoso we thought we'd never find you. Lucky for me, my people noticed Elliot's phone was still in use. Tracking you was simple."

"Now what do we do?" Joe said.

"I'll tell you what we're going to do. The top story for the five o'clock news tonight will be about the tragic fire that destroyed the River Rock Boot Company. The headline in the newspaper tomorrow will read Tragic Boot Company Fire Kills 3."

"No it won't, not today, not tomorrow, not ever," Roy turned around. "Mr. Rivera, I started this boot company by working the leather with my own two hands."

"Don't, Dad." Marlene walked over to her father. "He will kill you."

Roy kissed Marlene's hand. "I've been quiet for too long," he said and gently pushed her aside. "It took me over fifty years to build River Rock Boots into what it is today, through good times and bad. Over three hundred people have jobs because this boot company exists, here and in Juarez. It's made me rich, bankrupt and rich again and now it belongs to my daughter whom I love with all of my heart despite her mistakes. I love her as much as you love Madeline. I would die for her and I will fight you if I have to, in order to keep River Rock Boots alive. You already have plans to move your operations to another facility. As a gentleman, I implore you to leave this place and let us go back to our normal lives. You have all of your shipments. None of these people want anything to do with you and we have no reason to go to the police. What's done is done. We know you hold all of the cards," he finished.

Julio clapped his hands. "That was a heartfelt speech, Roy, and I can appreciate where you're coming from, but the thing is, I don't believe you. I can't afford to believe you, but let me think it over. No, it burns and they die. That's my final decision. Now, everyone..."

Roy lunged at Julio, but Julio was quick with his gun, shooting Roy in the stomach. Roy fell to the floor, face down.

"Then you die," Julio said.

"Dad." Marlene screamed and dropped to his side. "No, Dad, no. Please get up. You didn't have to shoot him. He's just an old man. He's my father." Marlene cried hard over her father's body.

All the talk about who was going to die suddenly became reality.

"Tie her up with the rest of them," Julio said.

"Come on, Julio..." Manny said, but Julio turned the gun on him again.

"You got a problem with the way I handle things, Detective?"

"No."

"Then you and Joe tie her ass to a chair, now."

Both men grabbed Marlene by her arms to pick her up off the floor, but she went kicking and screaming.

"Gag her, too."

Marlene was taped-tied like the others and gagged. Price and Lisa were whimpering, afraid of their imminent death. Gene lay on his side. He now knew Julio was serious about carrying out his threats. He prayed Stanton was listening to their conversation and heard the words River Rock Boots. If he did, the cops would be coming in at any moment, but if he didn't, he needed a plan B.

"This is perfect," Julio said. "Except for Price, all of these guys are intimately related to

Elliot. It will be a triple homicide and suicide. Madeline, you'll write some kind of suicide note that talks about how Gene admits to killing Elliot over his love affair with Lisa, and how Gene's life as a drug dealer was crashing down on him. He just couldn't take it any more so he decided to kill everyone closest to him and then himself. Put it on his desk."

"Yes, Daddy."

"Everyone downstairs and get this place ready to burn," Julio said. "How many workers are left?"

"Three, boss," Joe said.

"Get them to help and tell them they have ten minutes to get it ready.

Julio, Manny, Joe, Madeline and the bodyguards walked out of Marlene's office and down the stairs. Gene wasted no time undoing the tape on his left wrist and legs.

"Hurry, Gene," Lisa said.

Gene limped over to Marlene's desk where he found a pair of scissors, and freed Lisa and Price, but he stopped when he got to Marlene. He looked into her pitiful eyes. Mascara was streaked from her eyelids to beyond the gag. He laid the scissors in her lap then turned his back to her.

Gene got down on his hands and good knee and then signaled Lisa and Price to do the same and then he crawled to the window. Gene looked out over the warehouse. There was no one close to the office stairs that he could see from his point of view, but there were too many rows of shelves in his way to see anyone among them.

"There's nobody close," Gene said.

"What about your phone?" Lisa asked. "I saw you open it in your pocket. Who did you try to call?"

"I tried to call Stanton." Gene pulled out his cell phone, only to see a blank screen. He pushed buttons. "The battery is dead."

The three of them crawled to the door, Gene lead the way. He looked out then down, over the railing. The area was still clear.

He said, "Stand up and move as fast you can, but as quietly as you can."

To get to the front entrance, they needed to get to the bottom of the stairs, turn left through the plastic draperies, another left down the short hallway to the reception area. When they reached the bottom, Lisa and Price followed Gene to the plastic draperies, where he stopped. One of the bodyguards was standing on the opposite side of the plastic. Gene signaled to Lisa and Price to move back to the base of the stairs.

"The guards are posted out front," Gene whispered. "We'll have to make our way to the loading docks."

The warehouse was two hundred thousand square feet. Thirteen rows of shelving and fifteen aisles were in front of them. Each aisle was twenty feet wide, enough to drive the two large forklifts through, but more than four hundred feet long. Each of the four sections of shelves stretched seventy feet long and twenty feet high with crossover aisles between them. Once they were in one of the aisles, they would have to hurry to the loading docks or they would be trapped with no place to run.

Gene led Lisa and Price, looking down each aisle before moving to the next.

"Listen," Gene said.

Two forklifts were starting.

Do you smell that?" Lisa whispered. "Gasoline."

Gene moved several boxes until he could see through the shelving to the next aisle, but his line of sight was too narrow. "Lisa, I can't climb because of my leg. If we lift you, can you climb up to get a better view?"

Gene and Price cupped their hands for Lisa's feet. They lifted her until she was able to grab onto the second to the top shelf. She pulled herself up and tried to get her footing on the shelf below, but slipped. Both men held out their arms to break her fall, but her fingers were strong enough to cling to the metal framing. She pulled herself back up and regained her footing. She could see farther down the next aisle and Joe, raised high above the shelves on a forklift, standing on a pallet.

"I'm coming down," she mouthed, then lowered herself to the next shelf.

Lisa released her grip, falling backwards several feet when the men caught her.

She said, "Joe is standing on a forklift. He's pouring gasoline all over the boot boxes."

They moved toward the loading docks as fast as Gene could go. As they reached the first crossover, Julio yelled from the top of the stairway to Marlene's office and they stopped. The forklifts shut down.

"What's up boss?" Joe yelled back.

"They're gone. They got away. All of the exits are blocked so they're in here somewhere. Find them."

Gene, Lisa and Price headed toward the loading docks. Price started running as fast as he could, leaving Gene and Lisa behind.

"Price, come back," Gene said in a loud whisper, but Price turned left at the next crossover then disappeared.

Gene and Lisa were further behind. Before they were halfway down the next set of shelves, Joe appeared from the right side of the crossover, carrying a crowbar from the forklift.

"There you are," Joe said and walked toward them.

Gene and Lisa ran back up the aisle, but Gene knew he was slowing her down and couldn't outrun Joe.

"Go, Lisa," Gene said.

Lisa turned and ran, stopping at a crossover, looked and then disappeared to the left.

Gene limped to the middle of the isle and faced his enemy.

"I'm going to enjoy this," Joe said.

Stanton exited the interstate, raced to the intersection and around the first two blocks before slowing down at the top of River Rock Drive. He was parked across the street from where Gene sat in his stolen car earlier that night. The detective turned off the truck and headlights. He could see the warehouse just past the pipe yard, lights brightly shining from its loading docks.

His cell phone rang.

"Detective Stanton? This is Fire Chief Cordova."

"Go, Chief."

"We found one dead guard. Apparently, he fell down the stairwell and broke his neck. There was no one else in the building. The fire was small and contained by the sprinkler system on the eleventh floor, but there's more."

"I'm listening."

"The room where the fire started is filled with boxes, jugs, and bags of cocaine."

"Can you repeat that, chief?"

"It looks like someone was packing cocaine into jugs marked 'Industrial Strength Cleaner'. We're not sure how the fire started yet, but the flashpoint was inside one of the boxes that blew up. We've already sealed off the room for your guys to do their part."

"That's all I needed to know." Stanton ended the call.

When Sam had attacked him in the hallway at Lisa's house, her knife cut through Stanton's leather coat, but missed his flesh. He easily over took her, removed the knife from her hands and stopped just short of hitting her when she screamed. It wasn't the scream. It was what she said.

"Don't hit me, Joe. Don't hit me again. I promise I won't tell. I promise."

Those words were repeating themselves in Stanton's head, feeding his anger. Those words would haunt him.

Stanton looked around just to be sure there were no other vehicles coming or going, then he got out of the truck and raced across the street. He hopped over the pipe yard fence just as Gene did, pulled his gun from his holster and ran from pipe stand to pipe stand. When he reached the side closest to the warehouse, he jumped the fence again, and then ran to the large trashcan. He looked over the docks into the warehouse, but saw nothing. Voices came from all over the warehouse, but he couldn't make out what they were saying.

He climbed up onto the cement platform outside of the oversized garage doors and stood in the shadows with his back against a wall. Then he saw the left arm of one of the body guards, holding a hand gun, standing inside the large doorway.

From outside on the loading docks, Stanton looked into the warehouse, and could see the vast rows of shelves and aisles.

Price ran down the nearest aisle toward the guard when the guard pointed his gun at him.

"Hold it right there," the man said.

Price ran back up the aisle.

The guard yelled, "Stop."

Stanton stuck the barrel of his gun in the guard's ribs. "I wouldn't do that if I were you."

The guard dropped his gun. Stanton grabbed the guard's shirt, pulled him outside, pushed him up against the wall, chest first and then hit him in the head with his gun as hard as he could, knocking the guard out cold. Then he rolled him off of the dock into the dumpster and jammed it closed with a piece of scrap metal.

"There she is. Get her."

Julio pointed Lisa out from the top of the stairs outside of Marlene's office. She ran to another aisle and started running toward the loading docks in a full sprint. When she reached the next crossway, Madeline tackled her to the ground. The two women struggled and wrestled for several seconds before they broke free of each other, stood up and squared off. Madeline's face was bleeding from Lisa's fingernail scratches. Madeline wiped blood with the back of her hand, looked at it then licked it off.

"I'm going to kill you," Madeline said.

"You killed my husband, you bitch."

Joe swung at Gene with the crowbar, but Gene was able to dodge it.

"Come on, Gene. Stand still for me."

They moved in a circle. Gene grabbed a box of boots from a shelf, pulled out an ostrich-skin size eleven and held it with the heel side out. Joe lunged at Gene, taking another swing with the crowbar, but the bar glanced off a shelf, before hitting Gene in his thigh above the knife wound. Gene grabbed the bar and pulled, forcing Joe to stumble to his knees. Gene whipped Joe with heel of the boot. He hit Joe in the ribs, his back and finally his face, tearing skin from Joe's cheek. Joe collapsed to the floor, but held onto the crowbar with both hands. Gene seized the opportunity to run, leaving the crowbar with Joe.

Price was lost. He stood at a crossroads of aisles, not knowing which direction to run. To his left were the loading docks. To his right, he could run to the staircase, but with the guard at the front entrance, he would only be at another dead end. In front of him, he could only see several rows of shelving and a cinder-block wall. He turned around, only to see that Julio was standing directly behind him. Julio was holding his gun at his side.

"Hey, Price. Fun little party we're having, don't you think?"

"Julio, you're a sick Bastard," Price said.

"That's a little harsh, don't you think? You and I are just alike Price. It's always all about the money. You exploit people's strengths to get what you want. I exploit people for the same reason. Why don't you consider changing careers? I could use a good business-savvy person like you."

"I knew there was something wrong the day you gave us your business. Now that I know Madeline is your daughter, it all makes sense."

"Well, I had to make sure she always had a job with P & M. That way, my most trusted person was always close to the drugs. They've been right above your head all this time."

"You and I are nothing alike. I might be an ass, but I have values and provide honest livings. I don't kill people."

"That's too bad, Price, because I do." Julio raised his gun.

Price punched Julio in the stomach as hard as he could. Julio doubled over, stepped back and pulled the trigger, shooting Price in the shin as Price was coming at him. Price yelled and fell in front of Julio. He grabbed Julio's leg, causing the drug lord to lose his balance and fall. Julio fired again as he fell, missing the target. Price crawled on top of him. He hit Julio several times in the face with his fist, but Julio forced the men to roll, putting Price on the bottom. The hands of both men were on the gun as they wrestled, but Price lost the battle when Julio was able to squeeze off another round that entered Price's chest and shattered his shoulder blade.

Detective Stanton's bullet entered Julio's brain above his forehead. Price and Julio lay side-by-side pouring blood onto the cement.

Three workers were standing five aisles away.

"I don't care what they pay us," one of them said. "I didn't sign up for this."

"Let's go," another said.

All three took off toward the loading docks.

Stanton was standing more than fifteen feet away when he shot Julio and then rushed over to Price's body and checked for a pulse.

Price opened his eyes. Stanton's face was over his, and then Price closed his eyes as he mumbled something Stanton didn't understand.

"What did you say?" Stanton said and placed his ear close to Price's mouth.

Price mouthed the words just above a whisper, "Look out."

Stanton look behind him just as Manny's fist hit his face.

Lisa and Madeline faced each other once again, exhausted. They had fought their way between two rows of shelves. When Madeline decided to attack again, she charged at Lisa with fury in her eyes. Lisa grabbed a fist full of Madeline's hair and slammed her head into the metal shelving, crushing her nose and both cheekbones. Madeline collapsed to the floor motionless.

Lisa kicked Madeline's ribs repeatedly until they broke. Lisa fell to her knees and cried, but not because of the fight. She cried for Elliot.

When Joe regained his composure, he went on the hunt for Gene, crowbar in hand. He heard boxes moving several aisles over, so he ran to the nearest crossway and looked up and down every aisle. He stopped when he saw Price's body at the opposite end of an aisle. Joe walked toward Price until midway down the aisle. Julio's body was visible.

"Where are you, Gene?" he yelled. "Let's get this over with."

A box of boots dropped from a shelf just above Joe's head and hit the floor.

"There you are," he said and grinned, showing his broken bright white teeth as he looked up.

Gene rolled off the shelf, landing on top of Joe and both men fell to the floor. They struggled, and Joe hit Gene in the back with the end of the crowbar. Gene rolled off in pain, lying with his back arched. Joe got to his knees, and swung the crowbar. Gene rolled toward Joe and the bar hit the cement. He grabbed the crowbar from Joe's hands and Joe sat up on his knees, trying to scramble, but not before Gene whirled the bar and struck Joe across his mouth, ripping his lips, shattering his teeth and breaking his jaw. Joe fell backwards with his legs bent underneath him. Gene struggled to sit up and saw that Joe was stunned, but he was alive and breathing and trying to get up.

"You aren't going anywhere, but to jail," Gene said, then he broke Joe's knee with the steel rod.

He tried to take a step but dropped to the ground but the tourniquet on Gene's leg was taking its toll. His leg had starved for blood for too long and rendered it almost useless. He knew if anyone else found him, he wouldn't survive.

Manny held his gun to Detective Stanton's head as the two men headed for the front entrance of the warehouse. When they passed through the plastic curtain, Julio's bodyguard started to draw his gun. Manny shot the guard in the chest, killing him.

"I knew you were dirty, Manny."

"Screw you, Stanton. You don't know the first thing about me."

Red, yellow and white lights were shining on the walls and receptionist's desk as they walked down the hallway to the reception area. Manny turned off the lights. He could see at least eight police cars and at least a dozen police officers pointing their guns at the door. Manny was surrounded. He had been on the other side many times before. He also knew it was over and that it was up to him to live or die.

"Manny, it's over," Detective Stanton said.

Manny cocked his gun in Stanton's ear.

"It's time to start thinking about your son."

"Shut up, Stanton." Manny was becoming unstable and Stanton knew it.

"You know how this works, Manny. If you get anywhere near that door, a sharpshooter is going to take you out. You don't want your son to live with that the rest of his life. Don't you think he's been through enough watching his mother die?"

"That's it. You die." Manny was about to pull the trigger.

Stanton yelled, "Think, Rookie. Look at your chest."

Numerous laser lights circled his heart. If the sharpshooters heard his gunfire he would die.

Stanton said, "Let's do this right, Manny. Give us all of the evidence and you'll get a deal. You can start over. You still have your son."

Manny pushed Stanton away, lowered his gun and shot the floor.

Twenty-One

The keys jangled, and the main cell door opened and at least two sets of footsteps headed Gene's way. He was in the holding tank inside the courthouse. He had spent eight months in a state penitentiary as his lawyers tried to get him acquitted on more than a dozen charges. It was the last day of his trial. Detective Stanton, Lisa and Marlene were his key witnesses.

By the time the sun had gone down on the day after the warehouse shootings, he had been arrested and charged with everything from three first-degree murders in two states, assault on a New Mexico Police officer, assault on a border patrol agent, grand theft auto across state lines, possession of cocaine with intent to sell, all the way down to resisting arrest and speeding.

Price survived his gunshot wounds and wasted no expense hiring a leading defense law firm. William Price went back to work six weeks after he was wounded.

Even though Marlene had missed her dad's funeral, she was present at every one of Gene's trials where she told her story over and over again. In most cases, that was all the courts needed to hear before dismissing Gene's charges. He was grateful, but he had lost any positive feelings he had for her. She was convicted on federal drug smuggling charges and sentenced to twenty years in a minimum-security prison. She plea bargained and because the information she gave to authorities was instrumental in the arrest and conviction of fifteen other Free-Landers, which included DEA agents and border patrol agents, the judge in her case was lenient. She would be out in two or three years.

Eight months had gone by, but Joe and Madeline were still recovering from their injuries. Both had undergone major plastic surgery to rebuild their faces, but they were far from being handsome or beautiful. Joe was sentenced to life in a maximum-security prison with the possibility of parole for drug smuggling, attempted murder, tax evasion and abuse. His wife filed for divorce the day after his trials were over.

Madeline was sentenced to two life terms in a maximum-security prison. She melded well with the other female inmates because she had ways of supplying them with cocaine in trade for her guaranteed safety.

Instead of retiring, Detective Stanton was promoted to lieutenant. Evelyn wasn't happy about it when he told her the news, but she was proud of his accomplishments. She was relieved to find out he would be sitting behind a desk for the next several years.

Lisa was arrested with Gene that night. She was charged with withholding evidence and obstruction of justice. Price made sure his lawyers got her off and he made sure she received ten years of severance pay he said he owed to Elliot. She also received two million dollars from Elliot's life insurance policy of which she donated three hundred thousand dollars to the Center for Family Violence. She and Sam became close friends, as Lisa helped her enter into a drug rehab program, where Sam attended chapel and read her Bible daily. The courts granted Lisa temporary custody of Sam's son, Johnnie, who got to visit his mother every weekend.

"They have your verdict," Stanton said.

"Can you believe it's finally going to be over?" Gene said.

The bailiff opened his cell. Gene shook Stanton's hand, and then he shook his lawyer's.

"I can't believe we even had to go through this trial," the lawyer said. "Where did Joe get off thinking you would be convicted on attempted murder for hitting him with the crowbar?"

The door to the courtroom opened, Gene, Stanton and the lawyer sat down at the defense table. After all of the preliminary questions were asked by the judge to the jury, the defense team and Gene stood.

"We, the jury, find the defendant not guilty."